# Macarons Can Be Murder

## Hadley Wilds series
*Dead Girl's Guide to Style*

## Haunted Vintage mysteries
*Fashions Fade, Haunted Is Eternal*
*A Passion for Haunted Fashion*
*If the Haunting Fits, Wear It*
*Haunted Is Always in Fashion*
*Haunt Couture and Ghosts Galore*
*All Dressed Up and No Place to Haunt*
*If You've Got It, Haunt It*

## Bayou series
*Lost on the Bayou*

## Haunted Tour Guide mysteries
*Haunting in a Winter Wonderland*
*Haunt Around the Clock*
*Haunt Like Nobody's Watching*
*Haunt With Me*
*Haunting in a Winter Wonderland*
*A Haunted Walk to Remember*
*Walk in My Haunted Shoes*
*Haunted Girl Walking*
*The Walk That Haunts Me*
*You'll Never Haunt Alone*
*I Want to Haunt You Home*
*Keep on Haunting*
*Hauntin' After Midnight*
*Take a Haunted Walk With Me*
*Walk This Way, Haunt This Way*
*Haunt the Haunt, Walk the Walk*
*A Walk on the Haunted Side*
*These Haunts Are Made for Walking*

## Chase Charley mysteries
*Seems Like Old Crimes*
*For Old Crime's Sake*

## Paranormal P.I. mysteries
*The Hext With It*
*What the Hex?*

## Sweet Shoppe mysteries
*Goody Goody Gunshots*

## Haunted Craft Fair mysteries
*Murder Can Frost Your Doughnut*
*Murder Can Haunt Your Handiwork*
*Murder Can Confuse Your Chihuahua*
*Murder Can Mess Up Your Masterpiece*

## Cupcake Whisperer Culinary Cozy mysteries
*Death by Strawberry Cupcake*
*Death by Chocolate Cupcake*

## Paradise Spa and Retreat series
*Good Witchy Vibes Only*
*Two Faced*
*You Made Me Kill You*
*The Flower Girls*
*The Witch Is In*
*My Haunted Family*

# Macarons Can Be Murder

## A PARIS KENTUCKY BAKERY MYSTERY

### Rose Betancourt

CROOKED LANE

NEW YORK

Copyright © 2023 by Rose Betancourt

Published in the United States by Crooked Lane Books, an imprint of The Quick Brown Fox & Company LLC.

Crooked Lane Books and its logo are trademarks of The Quick Brown Fox & Company LLC.

Library of Congress Catalog-in-Publication data available upon request.

ISBN (hardcover): 978-1-64385-976-7
ISBN (ebook): 978-1-64385-980-4

Cover design by Mary Ann Lasher

Printed in the United States.

www.crookedlanebooks.com

Crooked Lane Books
34 West 27th St., 10th Floor
New York, NY 10001

First Edition: July 2023

10 9 8 7 6 5 4 3 2 1

To my parents. I love you. My mother showed me how to be kind, courageous, and grateful. My father taught me that I can overcome any challenge with hard work and perseverance.
I was blessed to have you both.

# Chapter One

"I need to ask you something," the woman said.

After glancing around at the other customers in the bakery, the blonde focused her attention on me again, leaning closer to the counter.

Was she about to pass along top-secret information? She surely acted like that was her intent. I had no access to top-secret anything. Well, other than when my sweet Grandma Maude gave me her chocolate gravy recipe and made me swear on my life that I'd never share it with another living soul. Somehow I'd managed to keep it a secret, but it hadn't been easy.

I had news for this customer: I was just Marci Beaucoup from Paris, Kentucky.

Marci Beaucoup? Yes, that was my real name. My mother thought it was the best play on words ever, considering where I'd been born and raised. I'd learned to love it over the years. Admittedly, I received looks when I told people my name. How could a woman with a moniker like that not love all things French, right?

"What can I do for you?" I asked as I wiped my hands on my pink apron.

At this point, I was almost afraid to find out what she wanted. Not that I didn't enjoy chatting with customers, but I needed to get back to making more croissants.

"The heat in this kitchen is getting to my hair, Marci," Aunt Barb yelled from the kitchen. "And you know what they say—the higher the hair, the closer to God. Right now the top of my head looks like an old, deflated tractor tire."

I pictured the dark hair on top of her head slowly losing its height like a collapsing cake just taken out of the oven. Typically the raven locks piled on top of her head were swirled upward toward the sky like a giant licorice-flavored ice cream cone.

Aunt Barb's words were my cue that she wanted me back in the kitchen to help her with the pastry. She'd insisted on assisting me with the bakery, but French cooking wasn't her thing. Aunt Barb preferred traditional southern fare. My aunt couldn't be left alone in the kitchen for too long because she might go rogue and start making up a batch of biscuits instead of pastries. She'd spend twenty years cooking in the mess halls at Fort Knox, which was quite different from a pâtisserie.

"Um, I want a half dozen croissants, please." She glanced over her shoulder as if checking to see if anyone was listening. "That's not all, though. I need to know more . . . I have a question."

I packaged up her croissants but kept my eye on her as I handed them over.

Why was she acting strangely? Not that I was all that surprised by her demeanor. I'd had my share of odd customers since the first day I opened the doors of my shop.

La Belle Patisserie had been a dream come true for me. Small white iron tables and matching chairs where patrons could enjoy their confections dotted the space at the front of my shop. A beautiful crystal chandelier hung from the ceiling in the middle of the sitting area, and the sparkly glass added glitz and glam—*très français*. Pastel shades of pink and teal mixed with soft white completed the decor. The aroma of sugar and melted butter floated through the air as if on a heavenly breeze. Hints of cinnamon and chocolate mingled in the scent, surely making everyone's mouth water.

"About my question," the woman said, snapping me back to attention.

Maybe the young woman in front of me just wanted to know about the expired coupon in today's newspaper. I'd told the *Paris Gazette* not to run it again, but the editor, Mitchell Sampson, had a tendency to make mistakes. Most recently he'd accidentally printed a recipe that called for four cups of cement instead of celery. I sure hoped no one had actually tried out that salad.

Pastries filled the tall glass cases that lined the counter area, too many varieties to mention—glazed, sugared, powdered, garnished with nuts, drizzled with icing, filled with pastry cream. I also offered paper-wrapped muffins and a wide selection of cookies. Fresh-baked loaves of bread in baskets or wrapped in bags filled the area around the counter. Tarts, éclairs, and macarons added color to the display cases. Above the case I had a fun sign that read: Macarons are marvelous. My mother had gotten the sign made for me for Christmas. It added a whimsical touch, I thought. Needless to say, it was hard to resist sampling the goodies every day.

"I heard you can help me." The woman's voice barely reached above a whisper.

"Help you with what?" I pressed.

"You know . . ." She glanced down at the pretty pink box containing her order.

"I'm not sure I follow what you mean," I added.

"Well, it's just that I've heard that you can create love with your food. And I'd like to try some of that magic. The love." She gestured widely with a sweep of her arm toward the glass case. "So if you could just recommend which pastry would enable me to meet the man of my dreams, I'd appreciate it very much."

I chuckled. "I'm sorry, but that's just a rumor. I have no magic. There's no magic here. It's just delicious pastries and breads. It's a bakery, not a magic shop."

Magic was make-believe. Part of fairy tales and promises of happily ever after. I didn't believe in happily ever after.

With eyes the color of the Mediterranean Sea, she stared at me. "Then how do you explain people finding love everywhere around town after eating your baked goods?"

"I don't know." I rearranged the puff pastries in the glass case. "Maybe the ingredients cause a natural glow. Or maybe it's just a coincidence. I have no special magical powers."

Disappointment flashed in her eyes. "I understand."

I hated seeing anyone sad. Especially in my bakery.

"You know what? I do have some advice for you." I closed the glass door.

"What's that?" she asked, perking up.

"I think you'll find the man of your dreams when you love yourself." I squeezed her hand. "When you love yourself and you stop looking, that's when he'll show up out of nowhere."

She studied my face. "Is that what you've done?"

"Stopped looking?" I asked with a chuckle. "Yes, I suppose that's what I've done."

"But he hasn't shown up yet?" She handed me a few crumpled dollars for the pastry.

"No, he hasn't appeared yet, but we can't rush these things, you know? Someday Mr. Right will step right through that door." I pointed.

The words had barely slipped from my lips when a strange feeling settled in the air. Something loomed in the distance. I felt it in my bones and coursing through my veins. The bell above the front glass door jingled, capturing our attention. Wind whipped against the windows, whistling and hissing through the cracks in the jambs. A storm brewed outside even though moments earlier it had been a sunny and bright day.

Now dark clouds had formed, rolling in quickly from the south. Rain surged in through the open door, bringing with it the stranger. He closed his black umbrella and scanned his surroundings before finally turning his attention to the counter. His gaze remained intent on me as he strolled across the bakery floor. My posture stiffened immediately. The tall, dark-haired man, wearing a tailored black suit, white button-down shirt, and burgundy striped tie, walked toward us. Denying his magnetism would have been impossible.

# Chapter Two

When he made eye contact with me, he flashed a dazzling bright smile. I stared at him without speaking. His deep-brown eyes matched the shade of the dark chocolate I used in the pastries.

"Bonjour," he said when he stepped up to the counter.

The greeting rolled off his tongue with a thick, buttery accent. A French accent, of all things. He was what dreams were made of. Well, my dreams at least. The drawn-out flair in his tone would make any woman swoon.

Where had he come from? He'd strolled into my bakery almost as if by magic. Again, I gaped at him without uttering a single word. Not as much as a hello or even a grunt. What must he think of me? My brown eyes probably looked bigger than the ramekins used for the chocolate soufflés.

I couldn't get over the fact that a Frenchman stood in my bakery. It was almost as if he'd gotten the two cities confused. But Paris, Kentucky, was over four thousand miles from Paris, France. He couldn't have taken a wrong turn or gotten the two mixed up.

Given my fascination with all things French, one would have thought I'd have learned the language better by now. I supposed, with no one in town to practice with, I'd been lax in my studying. Yes, I knew some words, but not nearly enough to feel comfortable speaking with this gorgeous man in his native tongue.

A crash rang out from the kitchen. I envisioned all the pots and pans that had surely tumbled to the floor. The sound echoed and bounced off the walls. It seemed as if the whole kitchen might be under attack.

Aunt Barb screeched before yelling out, "Get out of here. I thought I told you we were through."

Uncle Gene? They'd divorced years ago. Surely he wouldn't dare show his wrinkled old face around here after what he'd done to her.

Another screech pierced the air, followed by barking. A flash of black and white streaked by, followed by poofy white fur. The tinging sound of bread pans hitting the floor reverberated off the walls.

I grimaced as I realized what was taking place in my bakery. I turned my attention to the dreamy visitor. Based on his expression, I assumed he wondered what kind of disaster he'd walked into. This was completely unprofessional. I shouldn't be surprised, though. After all, this was my life. It was always this chaotic—drama followed me every step I took. My mama said I had an aptitude for pandemonium.

Just as another customer opened the front door, the cat zoomed out of the bakery, the dog giving chase close behind.

Aunt Barb ran up to the front of the counter. "Land sakes alive, that dog will be the end of me one of these days. I told him I was done with him."

"I hardly think he's going to pay attention to you, Aunt Barb," I said with a nervous chuckle.

I avoided the gorgeous man's stare. Fifi was my canine companion, a large white poodle who loved to chase my fluffy black cat, Pepé Le Pew. I'd thought about making sure Pepé Le Pew stayed home to avoid chaos, but she just loved the bakery so much. And Fifi adored Pepé Le Pew. Yes, I had a cat and a dog in my bakery, but this was Paris, Kentucky, so it came with the territory. Aunt Barb paused and eyed Mr. Right up and down. Next, she attempted to spruce up her appearance by fluffing her hair.

"Well, well, what have we here? He's finer than frog's hair split four ways." She wiggled her penciled-on eyebrows.

Did she have to say that so loud? As a matter of fact, did she have to say that at all? I moved so that I'd potentially block Aunt Barb's view of the handsome customer. Or maybe I was just trying to block him from hearing something else decidedly southern. Like that would really work. Her booming voice would just float right over my short frame.

Finally, I managed to ask, "May I help you?"

This was probably the most southern accent he'd ever heard. It was far from French, but nonetheless, a hint of a grin tipped the corner of his mouth. I peered upward at him. At five feet tall myself, I guessed he had at least a foot on me. *A tall, strapping man* was how my mother would have described him. Blatantly sexy, his bedroom eyes and roguish smile lured me in. He wore a black fedora hat, and I must say he looked dashingly handsome in it.

"I'd be remiss if I didn't stop in your fine café while in town," he said.

He'd basically left the window wide open for me to have a tête-à-tête with him.

"Oh, you're new in town. Are you staying here long?" I asked.

"As long as they need me." A single dimple appeared in his right cheek when he smiled.

I exchanged a look with the blonde. I knew she'd been enthralled by my interaction with this stranger.

She grabbed her box of pastries and said, "I think your advice was good, Ms. Beaucoup. I just have to wait, and he'll walk right in the door for me too."

After turning her attention to the handsome stranger one more time, she winked and then strolled out of the shop with a spring in her step, glancing up at the sky. The rain had stopped.

"She is happy, no? You give advice too?" he asked while gazing into my eyes.

I felt the heat in my cheeks. "I wouldn't say *advice* per se."

"What kind of advice did you give her?" he continued.

No way would I tell him what I'd said moments earlier.

"I gave her a tip on a recipe," I said. "So what brings you to town?" Changing the subject was for the best.

"I work for Flaget Manufacturing. Paper products. Anything paper that you can think of, we make it. You've heard of it?"

I nodded. "Yes, I've seen the building. I drive by it on my way to work."

"We have an office in France too. They asked that I come here for continuing executive education. Allow me to introduce myself. My name is Antoine Dubois." He offered his hand, and I wasn't sure what to do.

Shake his hand or kiss it? No, that was in England. Or was it Spain? Or wait, the man kissed the woman's hand, not the other way around.

Where had I heard that name before? It seemed so familiar, but I knew I'd never met this man. I would have remembered someone as handsome as him. Nonetheless, I couldn't place the name or his face.

"*Enchanté.*" I cringed at my failed attempt at French and quickly switched to English, "It's a pleasure to meet you, Mr. Dubois." My words lacked confidence at the moment, and I hated that.

Normally I had no problem making eye contact with customers, but this man made me nervous. In a good way, though.

"Please call me Antoine." He watched me intently.

"Oh, where are my manners? I'm Marci . . . Beaucoup."

Now that I said my name out loud, I once again thought about how comical he'd find it. What had possessed my mother to name me Marci? Yes, it was clever but, in this situation, extremely awkward.

Sure enough, he chuckled. I figured I should just go with the awkwardness. On the other hand, I tried to own it these days. My name was my name. There was nothing to do to change that right now.

"Marci Beaucoup?" he asked with a raised eyebrow.

"It's a perfectly good name. I think it's clever." *Change the subject, Marci.* "Anyway, I'm glad you're here. I mean, thank you for stopping by La Belle Patisserie. What can I get for you?"

Even though my French was abysmal, I just had to roll with my lack of ability. *Keep your chin up and shoulders back*, I reminded myself. *You are a confident woman, Marci Beaucoup.* At least I gave things my best shot, and that had to count for something.

No doubt Antoine had eaten some of the crème de la crème of pastry in the world. Now I had to compete with real French bakeries. Antoine studied my face for several moments before shifting his gaze to the chalkboard menu above my head. What was going through his mind? Too much chocolate on the menu? Not enough cream?

He shifted his focus toward the glass display case to his left. This was like the county fair all over again. I'd entered the pie contest, and my crush Eric Reinhart had been a judge. This was even worse than that. At least I'd won the pie contest.

"Do you have any madeleines?" he asked.

I glanced over to the corner of the room, where Mrs. Dobson was lifting the last madeleine I'd sold her to her lips. "I'm sorry, but we're all out this morning."

"Oh, what a pity. My grandmother used to make them for me. I miss her."

Why hadn't I made another batch of those this morning? Ugh. "I'm sorry about that. We will have more tomorrow." With any luck, he'd come back.

"In that case, I will take two *choux au chocolat*." He held up two fingers.

His mouth tilted up on the right side as he offered another grin with a wink. Maybe it was my imagination, but was he interested in me romantically? He was smiling a lot and being kind of flirtatious. That could only mean one thing.

Okay, maybe there were other explanations for his behavior. He might be that way with everyone. After all, he hadn't offered to kiss my hand. He seemed like the type of smooth, debonair man who would make an advance like that. Surely if he'd wanted to woo me, he would have tried that move. Any girl would swoon over such a romantic gesture.

More than anything, I was nervous knowing that he was from France and would be eating my pastry.

"Is this your bakery?" he asked.

"Yes, it is," I said, feeling a little self-conscious and proud at the same time.

"Well, it's nice meeting you. Maybe we could talk more sometime? Here's my card." He pulled out a card from inside his coat pocket and handed it to me.

"Yeah, I'd like that," I said, stumbling over the words.

Couldn't I have come up with something more clever than that? Perhaps I could have tried to sound more eloquent?

As I placed the pastry in a pink box with red velvet ribbon secured around it, a woman's voice caught my attention. The shrieking sound cut through the quiet like a sharp knife.

"I found you, Antoine. What are you doing here?" The woman placed her hands on her hips.

I glanced up to see the woman standing next to Antoine. With a flick of her wrist, she pushed the platinum-blonde locks from her shoulder. It was a small, flippant movement, but it spoke volumes on her current state of mind. A hint of black mascara had run from her eyelashes and now rimmed the bottoms of her bright-blue eyes. Had she been crying? Had Antoine made her cry? Maybe he was nothing more than a heartbreaker.

With her Cupid's bow lips covered in red lipstick and her rosy cheeks, she looked like a doll. Although an angry one. It was like the artist had mistakenly painted her brows into a permanent scowl. My gaze moved to the delicate butterfly necklace around her neck. I touched the chain at my own throat. We had the same necklace. Apparently, we had something in common.

The woman must have felt me staring, because she looked my way, eyeing me up and down as if I were somehow guilty of something. Was this his wife? I saw no wedding band on his finger, but maybe she was just a girlfriend. Yes, I'd surreptitiously checked for the gold ring. Who could blame me for my curiosity?

"What do you want, Kellie?" Antoine asked around a sigh.

"You know what I want." Her tone was so harsh that surely Antoine physically felt the sting.

If they were going to argue, I'd have to ask them to leave my shop. Other than the cat and dog, I'd never had anyone fight in here before. Not even cranky Mrs. Shirley when she came in for the leftovers that she fed to the ducks. If I didn't get them to her fast enough, she complained and wanted to speak with the manager. I always told her I was the owner, but she never believed me.

Antoine handed me cash for his pastry and then took the box from the counter. "Thank you, Ms. Marci."

At least he'd thanked me in English and hadn't said *merci beaucoup, Marci Beaucoup.* I'd heard that lame attempt at humor too many times to count. When Kellie heard my name ooze from Antoine's lips like decadently gooey chocolate, she glared at me.

A pinkish hue colored Antoine's cheeks. Clearly, he was embarrassed by the incident. What could I say to make this better for him? Nothing. It wasn't my job to help, and it was doubtful there was anything I could say that would ease the tension.

"You're welcome, Antoine," I said, feeling completely awkward.

Without saying another word, Antoine walked toward the exit. Kellie lingered by the counter for a moment to glower at me before turning on her heel and stomping across the room after Antoine. He stopped at the door and held it open for Kellie. Still a gentleman, even after the scene she'd made. She stood there for a few seconds, giving him an angry glare before she hurried out onto the sidewalk.

"Bon appétit," I called out in their wake.

The couple stopped in front of my shop, and of course, I watched out the front windows as they argued. Well, mainly it was just her waving her arms while Antoine listened. The other customers watched too, enthralled by the soap opera playing out on the sidewalk in front of my shop.

"I wonder what that's all about," Aunt Barb said. "She's madder than a wet hen."

"Guess it's a lovers' spat," I said.

After a few minutes, Kellie turned and stormed away. Antoine walked in the opposite direction, never looking over at my shop again. Would he ever return?

# Chapter Three

"Y'all know who that is, right?" Gordon Dumensil asked as he wiped icing from his mouth with a napkin.

With his salt-and-pepper hair and short, trimmed beard, Gordon reminded me of Ernest Hemingway. Minus the fisherman's turtleneck, though. Gordon wore a plaid button-down shirt and khakis. His eyes radiated warmth despite their icy-blue color. Even with his graying hair, Gordon had a youthful quality about him. Maybe it was his round, rosy cheeks.

Gordon came in every morning at the stroke of eight and stayed until ten forty-five. No one knew why he kept this schedule. No one had directly asked him either—it seemed rude to pry into his business. The better way to find out was to sneak around and ask everyone else in town why he did it. Surprisingly, no one knew. He remained a mystery, though I hadn't given up on one day finding out what made Gordon tick. I'd never been one to let a mystery pass me by without at least some attempt to solve it.

"No, we certainly don't know who that is," Aunt Barb said in her booming voice.

She talked that way because she'd learned to mimic the way the drill sergeants talked to the soldiers. I tried to remind her she wasn't at Fort Knox anymore. My shop looked like strawberry milk and marshmallows had exploded inside, not tanks or guns. We used inside voices here. Aunt Barb never listened to me, though, bless her heart.

"Her name's Kellie Lowry. Been renting a room at Naomi Perry's."

"I sense there's more to this story," Aunt Barb said with a click of her tongue. "I think we should get to the bottom of this."

"The bottom of what? As far as I can tell, she's done nothing wrong other than be a bit cranky with her boyfriend. Maybe he did something to deserve her being that mad," I said.

"Oh, he's not her boyfriend," Gordon said matter-of-factly.

Gordon was a gossip too. That was just small-town life. Aunt Barb and I whipped our attention back to Gordon.

"How do you know that?" I asked.

Okay, my interest was piqued now. All right, all right, my interest was a lot piqued now. A handsome single Frenchman? *Oh là là.*

*Get ahold of yourself, Marci.* Just because he wasn't Kellie's boyfriend didn't mean he wasn't someone's boyfriend.

"Ms. Naomi and I are friends," Gordon said.

Aunt Barb and I exchanged a look. Gordon had a girlfriend? That was adorable. If anyone found out he ate the same love-infused almond croissant every morning, the rumors about my pastries would really spread.

"Just friends?" I asked with a smile. "You mean girlfriend?"

"Why lordy, no," he said. "We're just friends and that's all. I have my eye on someone else."

Had his cheeks turned red? "What happened with the couple?" I pressed.

"They called it quits," he said.

"They broke up?" I repeated, to make sure I'd heard him correctly.

"Yes, ma'am. I guess he broke up with her, and now she can't seem to let it go."

"That's tragic," I said.

"Yes, isn't it terrible that the man's single," Aunt Barb said in a singsong voice.

I knew she was mocking me now. Her voice rarely took on that tone.

Gordon stood from the chair and headed toward the door. "Well, I'll see you some other time."

He always said that too, as if he'd be back in a month or even a year. That never happened. As sure as the sun rose and set every day over Paris, Kentucky, Gordon came into my shop. I couldn't complain, because I loved the business. Plus, Gordon really was a sweet man, even if a bit enigmatic. I was disappointed that I wouldn't get the chance to ask Gordon more about the couple.

Gordon walked right out the door. I looked at my watch. It was exactly 10:45. How had he known it was ten forty-five without looking at a watch? I didn't have a clock on the wall anywhere. It was like he had an internal clock and the alarm went off at the exact same time every day.

"There's more to that man that I want to know about," Aunt Barb said. "He remains a mystery."

"I don't think you're going to figure Gordon out. You shouldn't even waste your time trying. We just have to let Gordon be Gordon," I said.

Aunt Barb watched Gordon through the window for much longer than I expected. What was she thinking?

"Oh, look at you talk," she said. "You were the one trying to figure out his relationship with Naomi."

"Yes, well, I gave up, and I guess you should too."

"If you say so," she said. "Do you think he's really dating Naomi Perry?"

"It certainly seems that way to me," I said.

Aunt Barb sighed. Maybe she didn't like my answer, and I wasn't sure why. Pepé Le Pew streaked by in a blur with Fifi running after him. Both had been running through puddles and tracked water in with them that messed up my clean floor. Pepé jumped onto the front windowsill and peered outside, completely ignoring Fifi. Something had captured Pepé's attention. Fifi pawed at Pepé Le Pew's tail, but he was having no part of her attempts at playtime.

"Now what are you going to do about that Frenchman?" Aunt Barb asked, drawing my attention away from the cat and dog.

"What do you mean?" I asked. "What am I supposed to do?"

"Well, I think you should talk to him. If you're not going to give Maverick the time of day, then the least you can do is talk to this handsome chap. Now fix your hair up a little bit and dab on some lipstick. Maybe you'll get a date."

"I have a business to run, Aunt Barb. There's no time for dating."

"You can tell yourself that, but I don't think you really believe it," Aunt Barb said as she followed behind me toward the kitchen.

"I believe just fine," I said. "You don't need to question me."

"Aren't you curious as to why they broke up? I mean, after that public display, I think we need answers. That was like a scene right out of one of those reality shows."

I picked up the spatula to get back to layering icing on the mille-feuille. That was French for "one thousand petals," a reference to the many layers of the pastry. I took in a deep breath, catching a whiff of fresh-from-the-oven croissants. In spite of the aroma, my insides churned and bubbled, forming a big ball of anxiety in the pit of my stomach. Customers said my croissants had a special way of making them feel comforted, as if they'd just received a warm hug from magic hands. Maybe I needed one of those magic-filled croissants right now.

"I think it's none of our concern." I swirled chocolate icing over the vanilla to make a zigzag pattern.

Aunt Barb remained silent. I felt the penetrating stare from her big brown eyes. Focusing on the pastries seemed virtually impossible with that sensation forcing its way into my psyche. She could stare a hole through a rock.

Finally, I looked up at her. "Okay, yes, I'm curious. Are you happy now? I'm dying to know. Did you see how gorgeous that man was?"

I released a big breath. It felt good to get it out. Pepé Le Pew and Fifi strolled up and sat at my feet. Pepé meowed and Fifi barked, as if agreeing with my assessment of the stranger's looks.

"Did I see? It couldn't have been more obvious if someone had knocked me over the head with a boulder. I might not date anymore, but I'm not immune to noticing a fine specimen of a man when I see one."

I sprinkled some of my special blend of sugar and spices over the top of the pastry for the finishing touch. "Why do you swear off dating, Aunt Barb? I just know the right man is out there for you somewhere. Here, have one of my pastries."

She waved her hands and stepped back. "I don't want a date. Therefore, I don't want one of those things."

As I placed the pastries on the display case tray, I shrugged. "Suit yourself. This batch is exceptionally magical tasting."

The day passed with no other sightings of the Frenchman or his jaded ex-lover, though they crossed my mind several times. What had happened between them that had led to this? It was none of my business. Just because I thought he was handsome and was intrigued by his accent didn't give me reason to give their situation further contemplation.

I kept busy, though, because a swarm of customers had descended on the bakery. Of course, that was always a fabulous thing. A frenzy of baking produced puff pastries, croissants, and even delectable macaron cookies for tomorrow morning. Yes, keeping busy would be the best medicine.

I continued my work by feverishly mixing batter for petit fours. These bitty cakes were popular, which was understandable because they were quite cute, with pastel-colored icing. Inside was pound cake, buttercream, and jam.

As I put the dish into the oven, the sound of clattering metal caught my attention. I spun around to find Aunt Barb scrambling to pick up the pots and pans from the floor. If she was going to keep hitting those, I needed to move them.

"My goodness, Aunt Barb, what are you doing?"

"Sorry, Marci. I'm just flustered by the influx of customers, but I have everything under control. Per usual."

It seemed as if she was trying to sound confident, but I wasn't sure I believed her.

"I'll take your word for it," I said.

Aunt Barb rushed behind the island and placed the pans back onto the rack above the island. "They're going through those petit fours like they're the last desserts on earth."

I wiped my hands on my apron. "Well, don't worry, we'll be just fine. I have another batch coming. As for the other chaos, we just have to do what we can."

Aunt Barb pushed the hairnet around on her head to keep it from falling off. "You're giving me pep talks now? This is bizarre."

Aunt Barb did a little bit of everything around the pâtisserie—cooking, customer service, marketing. For anything I needed help with, she was there. Lately, though, she'd seemed distracted. She'd also seemed a bit stressed, and I wondered if there was something she wasn't telling me. One thing Aunt Barb was never lacking in, though, was bon mots. She always had witty remarks at the ready.

"Hey, I learned from the best." I winked.

"Can I get help?" a customer called out.

"Coming," Aunt Barb said in a singsong voice.

She had a voice loud enough for people to mistakenly think she was using a bullhorn. How had things turned so chaotic so quickly? My mom was right: at least I had Aunt Barb. If not for Aunt Barb, I'd have been standing in this kitchen alone and confused. She might make me feel like I was at boot camp sometimes, but I trusted her more than anyone. Aunt Barb was a dichotomy, a mix of steadfast and capricious. It ran in the family, apparently.

A couple minutes later, Aunt Barb returned. "Okay, I think things are settled for the moment. Have you added more of that magic to the petit fours lately? Maybe that explains why they're loving them so much."

"There is no magic, Aunt Barb," I said. "Did you ever think that maybe they just love the scrumptious taste of them?"

"If you say so," she said.

"I say so."

"Do you *really* think Gordon is seeing that Naomi?" Aunt Barb asked as she handed me a new container of flour.

Wow, that was a big twist in the conversation. She was coming back to this question again? Why such an interest in his dating status? I paused and studied her face for a moment.

"He said no, but I thought yes, now I'm not sure, but why do you ask?"

"Oh, I was just curious," she said with a wave of her hand. "It's just that . . . well, I think Naomi is bad news and he should probably just stay away from her."

I raised an eyebrow. "And what makes you think she's bad news? Did she do something specific?"

"Well, she's a busybody, and she's always in everyone's business," Aunt Barb said.

I wouldn't mention to Aunt Barb that she was doing the same thing.

"Yes, well, I guess you have a point about that. But it's really none of our business who Gordon is friends with, right?"

"Well, I still would like to know more about him. Why is he so mysterious, anyway?"

"Maybe you should ask him," I said with a wink.

"Oh." Aunt Barb turned on her heel.

She headed back toward the counter. It seemed like maybe I'd touched a nerve. I glanced out into the dining area and saw the long line of customers waiting for their goodies. It made me smile but nervous at the same time. Fifi stood guard by the door, sniffing everyone's legs as soon as they walked in. Pepé Le Pew sat on the windowsill by the front door, licking his paws. He was probably waiting for someone to do something wrong so he could give them his typical condescending glare. Yes, the cat totally had a glare that he gave people, but everyone usually just called him a cute kitty, ignoring his grumpy face.

The sun soon melted in the sky, spilling a yellow glow over the late afternoon, and I headed for home. Aunt Barb had mentioned she was going to see a movie. She never went to the movies. When I questioned that she snapped at me a bit saying that she just wanted to change her routine. I wasn't sure what had gotten into her lately. I suppose changing the routine sometimes though would be a good idea. Perhaps I should do that more often.

Soon I'd have to get to bed—three AM came awfully early. Every morning before the crack of dawn, I made my way into the bakery. The pastries had to be fresh when customers wanted them with their morning coffee. And the morning treats certainly wouldn't make themselves. I needed my rest so I could add just the right amount of love into each delicious baked treat.

Across the sidewalk I spotted a couple walking. Was that Maverick? This proved my point: Maverick was walking with a woman. They were laughing and appeared to be having a great time. Therefore, I could only assume it was a date. She even touched his arm. The proof was in the pudding. I looked away. I didn't even want to watch more of their romantic stroll down Main Street.

My home was only a short distance from the bakery. In fact, it was only a couple of blocks, and I usually walked to work, though sometimes I liked to ride my bike. It looked *très parisien* when I carried baguettes in the bike's basket. That helped me burn off the calories from all the taste-testing. How could I resist the croissants, macarons, and éclairs? The sweet smell was intoxicating and spoke to my soul. For me, it wasn't just baking. It was art mixed with therapy, completely cathartic. Fifi and Pepé Le Pew enjoyed the walk too. Fifi walked on her leash, but Pepé actually liked being in his carrier.

Holding on to the leash, I tossed my hand up at Mrs. Jenkins. The widow sat on her front porch at 4:35 every evening when I walked by her home. Well, I wasn't there at exactly 4:35 every day, but more than once I'd seen her sitting on her porch swing at that exact time. She usually asked me about any new yummy desserts, and I asked her about her ten cats. Today they sat perched on the windowsill, lined up like little furry trophies watching her as she swayed back and forth on the porch swing. Their heads shifted from side to side in rhythm with the swing. Fifi growled as usual, but I managed to keep hold of the leash.

Today Mrs. Jenkins didn't ask about the pastries I'd made. Instead, she said, "I heard there was a big argument at the shop today. Like a fight broke out, or should I call it a brawl?"

See how things get twisted? Word had spread about the incident in front of my shop, but now people had made it much worse than it really had been.

I paused in front of her house. "Oh, no, it wasn't a brawl. It was just a disagreement between two people. No fighting or anything."

It amazed me how things got blown out of proportion, but that was small-town life.

"I heard it was that girl who's staying at Naomi Perry's. There's more to that story. It's a good thing you kicked her out of your shop."

"Oh, I didn't kick her out. She just left. There was nothing that happened in the store."

"Well, she was agitated at her ex-boyfriend." Mrs. Jenkins was determined to tell me something I didn't know, but Gordon had already informed me about the status of Kellie and Antoine's relationship. "I heard they broke up."

I wondered if the biggest town gossiper in front of me had any new information that would enlighten me as to what had happened between the mysterious couple. They'd taken their spat public, so they shouldn't be surprised if people talked.

"I heard he asked her to marry him and she said no. Or was it she asked him to marry her and he said no? Well, either way, they're not getting married, obviously."

That was kind of a big discrepancy. I mean, if he had asked her and she'd said no, then why would she be angry with him? So maybe it was the other way around and she had asked him and he'd said no. I kind of wanted to know, but what difference did it make? I knew nothing about either one of them, and it was really none of my business. I didn't know why I was so curious. Maybe it was just because he was from France and I was a teensy bit obsessed with all things French. Okay, a lot obsessed. Nevertheless, I wouldn't want to get to know someone just because he was from France. That was ridiculous.

"Speaking of getting married, when are you going to marry that handsome Detective Maverick Malone? He's quite a catch, you know. All the ladies in town want him."

"I'm not dating Maverick," I said. "Er, Detective Malone," I corrected myself.

"Well, you certainly should be. He's had a thing for you for years, honey."

"I don't think he has a thing for me."

I was absolutely finished with this conversation. I did not want to have a debate on why I wasn't marrying a man who seemed to have no idea I even existed. Why she would say he had a thing for me was beyond me. Was it because he occasionally came into the shop and bought a pastry? That was hardly a reason to think he liked me. He hadn't given me any indication he thought of me in a romantic way.

"I don't understand why you make all those love pastries if you're not going to use one for yourself."

I laughed and shook my head. "They're just regular pastries."

"If you say so," she said with a raised eyebrow. "Though maybe you're right to avoid that man. He is a ladies' man."

So other people knew that too. That just further validated my thoughts.

"I'll talk to you later." I tossed my hand up in another wave and hurried down the sidewalk to end the conversation.

# Chapter Four

The next morning, heat had already settled over Paris. The sun hadn't even come up yet, and it was already hotter than the devil's underwear. I knew today would be another scorcher. I'd decided to come in to work early this morning because I had to perfect my recipe. I'd made mille-feuille before but never with roasted strawberries and mascarpone. Since I'd already placed an ad announcing the strawberry-and-mascarpone would be available today, I had no choice but to make it work.

I worried that the buttercream pastry wouldn't turn out right. Or the strawberry sauce would be too runny. One bad experience and a customer might stay away forever. If they stayed away, they might tell their friends and family to stay away too. The next thing I knew, I'd be locking the door on my bakery for good. The windows would be boarded up and it would look like some haunted attraction.

I'd already made croissants, financiers, and éclairs by the time the sun rose, plus I'd started the mille-feuille. Fifi and Pepé Le Pew walked to the front of the shop with me as I went to turn the sign in the window. I pulled the earbuds from my ears. I loved listening to music while I baked. My music taste was all over the place. Today my choice of music was pop eighties.

As I flipped the sign to OPEN, I looked out and saw someone lying on the sidewalk. I recognized her long blonde hair, even though I couldn't see her face. Kellie Lowry was right there in front of my shop. And she wasn't moving. Panic surged through my body as I fumbled for the keys to unlock the front door. Aunt Barb hadn't come in yet. Of all days for her to have her yearly checkup.

"Stay here, Fifi and Pepé," I called out.

When I finally got the door open, I ran out onto the sidewalk. A few cars moved up and down the street, but no one seemed to be noticing Kellie; it hadn't quite gotten light yet. She wore black leggings, a white T-shirt, and running shoes. Had she been out for a run and been hit by a car? Surely I would have heard something like that.

"Are you all right, Kellie?" I yelled.

She offered no answer. When I saw the blood, I knew she was definitely not okay. I immediately ran back inside to get my phone to call for help. I couldn't believe this was happening. Why was she on the sidewalk in front of my shop, and what had happened to her? I dialed 911 and waited for the operator to answer. When she did, I frantically explained the situation.

"Are you sure she's not breathing?" the operator asked. "I need you to check her for me."

"Based on the way she looks, I don't think I need to check to know she's dead." I stared out the front door window at the body.

"I need you to check to make sure. Do you know CPR?"

Now my mind raced even more—did I know CPR? Sadly, the answer was a big no. Nevertheless, I did as she asked. With shaking legs and hands, I walked back to the sidewalk and checked the woman for any signs of a pulse.

"She's cold to the touch and slightly blue," I said.

After listening to my breathless account, the operator said someone would be out immediately.

I hoped that was the case, because I didn't quite know what to do. Should I stay with her or go inside? I had pastry in the oven, but that seemed insignificant compared to the dire situation on the sidewalk. But what if those pastries smoked up the whole place and set off the fire detector? That would be bad. I had no choice but to go back inside. I'd just have to hurry.

I ran across the shop, almost tripping over a table to get to the oven. After shoving my hands into the oven mitts, I pulled out the pastries, turned the oven off, and ran back through the shop to the front. No one had noticed Kellie. She was still there, motionless on the sidewalk.

As I stood there waiting for the police to arrive, unsure what to do next, I looked around. What was I searching for? I had no idea. Maybe any sign of what could have happened to her? Then it hit me. What if someone had done this to her? What if this wasn't an accident? A killer could be anywhere around here right this second. This was a terrifying thought. I tried to reason with my racing thoughts. She could have had an epileptic fit or hit her head.

*Stop thinking of the most sinister scenario, Marci.*

As much as I hated to look at her, I stared at her for several seconds. She still wore the gold necklace around her neck. The same as mine. I wondered what else Kellie and I had had in common. We were probably alike in similar ways. Oddly enough, at this moment I felt a strange connection to her. I wished I could have been here to help her sooner.

Was that a bullet wound on her head? Surely not. Surely this was just another one of those times where I was letting my imagination run wild. I stared a few more seconds.

Yup, definitely a bullet wound.

Now I was panicking. It had been a while since we'd had a murder in town. Not since Bruce Addison went into a jealous rage and shot Henry Maupin for having an affair with Bruce's wife.

Had Kellie been murdered? It certainly looked that way. I hadn't heard a gunshot, but I'd had the earbuds in, so maybe I wouldn't have heard the sound.

Could Antoine have done this? Immediately he'd come to mind—obviously because he'd been out here arguing with her just yesterday. Well, it was more her arguing with him, but still . . . it had been a conflict, and it had been in the same spot where she was now lying dead. That was very odd. Why was she back here again? The mysterious Frenchman Antoine was nowhere in sight, but I supposed that after doing this to her, he wouldn't stick around. Unless he came back to kill someone else.

The police would suspect handsome, charming Antoine. The ex-boyfriend was always the first one interrogated. However, if I was being honest, I didn't want to believe he'd do something so horrific. I couldn't have a crush on a killer. If it turned out he'd done this, my daydreams about a particularly dashing Frenchman would fly out the window.

Could there just be a random killer around? Were we all in danger? Awful thoughts flooded my mind. It was taking the police forever to arrive. Why hadn't the police arrived yet? I wanted to help Kellie, but I knew there was nothing that could be done. I just had to stand here awkwardly with a dead body while people passed by unaware. Soon customers would show up, though. I hoped the police arrived before that happened. People would be walking over her dead body just to get inside and get some pastries.

Sirens sounded in the distance. Thank goodness, the police were on their way. I felt like I might collapse myself if I had to stay here with Kellie much longer. They'd find two bodies on the sidewalk. I waved down the approaching police cars.

When the first one screeched to a halt in front of the shop, I recognized the man behind the wheel right away.

Detective Maverick Malone was on the scene. There was something about the man that I'd never been able to pinpoint—he had a certain je na sais quoi. His slate-gray eyes held a mysterious and mischievous sparkle. That lopsided grin of his made me weak in the knees. He had the face of a Greek god. I'd given up on him years ago, though. That didn't mean he didn't still make my heart go pitty-pat every time I saw him. Wow, he looked sharp in his black uniform. The fabric fit perfectly to his athletic frame.

Along with other officers, Maverick approached Kellie's motionless body. I stood back to give them room as they instructed. The flurry of activity made me dizzy.

After what seemed like an eternity, Maverick made eye contact with me and headed in my direction.

"Good morning, Marci," he said in his southern drawl.

"Bonjour, Detective Malone," I said.

"Are you all right?" he asked.

I nodded. "Yes, as well as can be expected, I guess."

"Obviously it was quite a tragic thing that happened here, and I'm sorry you had to experience this." Maverick searched my eyes.

"Thank you, Detective. I'll be fine."

"Can you tell me anything?" he asked.

"After I arrived to bake this morning, I found her. I don't know what happened. Do you know what happened to her?"

"That's what I'm working on now. What time did you arrive this morning? Did you hear anything?" he asked.

I released a deep breath, trying to calm down and allow myself to recall the details. It was hard to think straight. "I don't remember exactly what time I arrived. It was probably around three thirty AM. Long enough to bake brioche, croissants, and financiers. I made the call right after I found her."

"Can you think of anything else?" Maverick asked.

Nothing came to mind at first, but then it hit me again. "Well, there was the thing that happened yesterday."

"Oh, really? What thing happened yesterday?" he asked.

I was surprised Maverick hadn't heard about the fight.

"Kellie and her ex-boyfriend Antoine had a fight when they were in my shop. They left, and it looked as if the conversation got heated, because it spilled out onto the sidewalk. They eventually went their separate ways. Coincidentally, it happened right where she was killed. Seems suspicious to me."

After saying all that, I realized I sounded like the town gossip.

"No, I hadn't heard that. What was the fight about?" He studied me with those beautiful yet haunted eyes.

I shrugged. "I'm not entirely sure. Maybe it was because he broke up with her. At least that's what I heard."

Again I sounded like a gossip. I didn't want to be seen as a busybody.

"Do you know who the man is?"

I shook my head. "No, I don't know him personally, only his name, but I don't think he could be the killer, Detective."

Maverick's left eyebrow rose in a look of surprise.

"What makes you say that?"

"Well, he just doesn't seem the type." I was embarrassed that I'd said it as soon as the words left my mouth, but nonetheless, it was out there now. Plus, it was really what I thought.

"What?" Maverick asked in shock.

"He just really didn't look like a killer."

"Well, Marci, we can't really tell who's a killer just based on their looks."

"No, I know that. I'm just saying, shouldn't he have a scowl and beady little eyes?"

I was joking. Sort of.

"Not by the beady eyes either," he said.

I shrugged. "Well, I realize that, but it's just a feeling I have."

"Nonetheless, I'll be looking into him. Thank you for the lead." Worry flashed through his eyes, making them seem a much darker shade of gray. Almost like charcoal.

The way he said it made me wonder if I shouldn't have told him about the fight. No, of course I'd had to tell him, because I didn't truly know the Frenchman at all. He very well could be the killer. I had to keep that in mind. The thought sent a chill down my spine. Could the killer have been in my shop buying a pastry the day before murdering his ex-girlfriend?

"I'll need to ask you a few more questions soon," Maverick said.

I nodded. "I'll be right here baking."

Maybe it seemed strange that I would bake right now, but besides the fact that I had orders to fill, baking was cathartic for me. When I was stressed, it helped me feel better. Did I have a magic touch that seeped into my baked goods? Perhaps I did, but it was something I hadn't fully discovered yet. I often wondered what people meant when they said my pastries were magical. No doubt about it, though, I felt a rush of energy each time I baked. Perhaps there was an unseen force at work that I knew nothing about.

I watched as Maverick walked away and rejoined the other officers. They moved around the scene like bumblebees. Instead of collecting pollen and nectar, they were collecting clues. I stood by the door for a while watching the officers, fascinated. I wondered what would happen next.

Peering behind the crime scene tape, I noticed that a group of people had gathered and were gawking at the scene in front of my shop. Gordon stood by himself at the corner of the building. I glanced back at the shop. Fifi and Pepé Le Pew watched from the window. All this action wouldn't be good for business.

When I looked to my right, I spotted something on the ground. A scrap of paper had been discarded nearby. It looked like a card. Why hadn't the police noticed this? Why hadn't I noticed it before?

# Chapter Five

After checking to see if anyone was paying attention to me, I walked over for a better look. The paper wasn't close enough for the officers to notice what I was doing. Glancing down, I realized it was someone's business card. I waved at the officers.

"Excuse me?" I said.

Nobody looked over, and I scooped up the card before it blew away entirely.

Once I had the business card, I tried again to wave over a police officer. Everyone ignored me. I'd have to give it to them when they were less busy, I supposed. I stuffed the card into my pocket, turned around, and headed back into the bakery. I needed to bake the pastries and more croissants. Regardless of what was going on outside, I had catering jobs later this morning, and they had to go out. So as distracted as I was at the moment, it was still necessary that I work.

Would the police be finished soon? Aunt Barb would be here within a matter of minutes. I could only imagine what she'd say about the police presence. I tried to distract myself with the baking and hoped it would help ease my mind. When that didn't work, I pulled the card from my pocket. George Gustavsson, CFO, Flaget Manufacturing. Hmm, interesting.

Just as I read the card, the door opened and in walked Aunt Barb.

"What in blue blazes is going on out there?" Aunt Barb asked. "I almost couldn't get through. I had to practically bribe the police officers to get me inside."

"I asked Officer Abbott to make sure you got in."

"Well, he ignored me when I tried to talk to him. Thank goodness that handsome Detective Maverick let me in." Aunt Barb gestured over her shoulder.

"That was sweet of him, but he knows you work here. He absolutely should have let you in," I said.

"No doubt because he's smitten with you," Aunt Barb said. "Has been for years. I don't know why you don't give him a chance. I think you're just scared of commitment."

"Now is not the time to discuss this." I focused on the business card in my hand.

"You never want to discuss it. Not picking you up for prom was an accident."

"He could have found a way to be there."

"After all these years, you're still going to hold that against him?" Aunt Barb asked.

"Pretty much, yes," I said.

"It's time to let it go,"

"I can't discuss this right now. There was a murder, Aunt Barb. Right here in front of the bakery." I waved a pot through the air in a dramatic motion.

"Well, I assumed that by the body laying covered up on the ground."

"I figured the news would be all over town by now and that you'd know about it."

"Haven't heard a peep about it yet. Though it is early. Give it time and it'll spread like wildfire. Who was killed?"

"You're not going to believe this," I said. "But it's Kellie, the woman who was in here yesterday. The one who was arguing with Antoine."

Aunt Barb's eyes widened. "I knew something was wrong. He killed her, didn't he?"

"I don't think so," I said.

Aunt Barb looked at me suspiciously. "Well, who else could it have been? We don't have murderers roaming around town."

"Obviously we do. Someone has been murdered out there."

"And it's Antoine. He was her boyfriend, and he was arguing with her." Aunt Barb punctuated the sentence with a jab of her spatula.

"Oh, Aunt Barb, that's preposterous. No way," I said as I placed croissants in one of the pink pâtisserie boxes.

"Not preposterous at all. Don't let his good looks sway you," Aunt Barb said.

"That's not what it's about," I said, peeking outside the window. "He just doesn't seem like someone who would do this."

"How do you know that?" she asked.

I shrugged. "I guess I just have a feeling."

"Well, the crime won't be solved on a feeling," she said.

"We need to get the orders ready," I said, changing the subject.

It still bugged me that Antoine's name sounded familiar. Antoine Dubois. Why did it seem as if I'd heard that before?

"I'm guessing we won't be able to open today," Aunt Barb said. "With a murder scene right outside the front door, the police probably won't let anyone through."

"They said they'd be finished with the crime scene investigation in a few hours," I said.

"That seems soon," Aunt Barb said.

I felt guilty even worrying about baking at a time like this, but I really needed the money to pay bills. It was hard keeping the place afloat even with busy days—I had to pay back the loans I'd gotten to buy all this stuff. When the day came that I didn't owe anything, things would be much easier, but that day hadn't come yet.

Still, when a flash of Kellie's lifeless body came to mind, I knew I had to press pause on the baking. Out of respect for the deceased, closing was the right thing to do. Plus, the cops in front of the shop would no doubt be bad advertisement.

"At least for today, we'll stay closed. I mean, crime scene tape and a sheet-draped body on the ground aren't good for business," I said.

"I suppose you could change the macarons sign to read, *Macarons Can Be Murder*." Again Aunt Barb ended the sentence with a jab of the spatula in her hand. She liked to use utensils to add dramatic flair to her conversations.

"Not funny, Aunt Barb," I said.

"I'm just trying to be an entrepreneur and savvy. You gotta stay on your toes when you're in the army, you know?"

Oh no. Now I'd get the lecture about staying on my toes. I'd been hearing it since I'd barely been able to stand on my literal toes as a toddler. At least it seemed that way.

"Yes, ma'am," I said.

I'd just taken pastries out of the oven when a knock on the front window glass startled me. I screamed and tossed the pan of croissants in the air. Fifi barked. Why hadn't she warned me? I looked over at the window, clutching my chest.

Thank goodness—I was safe. Maverick motioned for me to let him inside. Pepé Le Pew meowed loudly. It seemed my kitty liked the detective.

"He's such a nice guy. I don't know why you two kids don't get together." Aunt Barb flicked a pinch of flour my way.

Luckily, the powder missed me as it rained down toward the floor like a snow shower.

"We're not interested in getting together, Aunt Barb. I've told you that repeatedly, like every day." I removed my oven mitts.

"Oh, nonsense. I see the look that you two give each other. The spark is there, so don't fight it anymore."

"No spark, Aunt Barb. There's no spark." I waved the spatula. Was there a spark between us? I already knew the answer to that.

"I know you got the hots for Antoine, but let's face it, he could be a murderer. Maverick is the best option."

"Who says I have the hots for anyone?" I asked.

"Open the door for Maverick." Aunt Barb gestured.

I marched across the shop and opened the door for him. He gazed at me with those sexy eyes, and I wondered what was on his mind at that exact moment. Finding a murderer, I supposed.

Catching movement outside, I spotted Gordon. He'd moved closer and was standing near the crime scene tape. However, he stood next to the building as if using it for protection.

"Hello, Detective Malone," I said, trying to sound professional.

"Ms. Beaucoup," he said. "I just have a few more questions for you."

Fifi sniffed Maverick's leg, and Pepé Le Pew rubbed up against his other leg. He reached down and petted them.

"I'll try my best to answer," I said. "But I told you everything earlier."

"Yes, well, sometimes things come back to you that you wouldn't remember otherwise."

Aunt Barb coughed. I wasn't sure what she was trying to convey, but she was obviously invested in our conversation. Maverick looked at her and around the shop as he talked to me. He glanced down at the counter and noticed the business card I must have taken out of my pocket earlier. Oops. I should have already given it to him, but I'd completely forgotten because I'd been busy with work.

"Why is this here?" he asked.

Should I lie or tell him the truth—that I'd been snooping around out there and taken potential evidence? I guessed I had to tell him the truth. Though I hadn't kept this from him intentionally. It was a simple mistake, right?

"It's a card that was outside on the ground. I picked it up."

He looked at me with wide eyes. "This was outside? Just now?"

"Yes, that's right," I said with a nod. "Was I not supposed to touch anything?"

"No, you weren't supposed to touch anything."

"Well, they shouldn't have had me out there if they didn't want me touching things."

Guiltily, I realized I was trying to take the blame off myself. Maybe I should just accept my mistake and not put it on anyone else. That was the more mature thing to do. It was probably too late now.

He studied my face for a couple seconds. "So this was at the crime scene?"

"I guess you could say that," I said.

"Where at the scene did you find it?" he asked.

"Close to my door on the sidewalk."

"I need to take this. I'm going to have a talk with this person."

"I highly doubted a murderer would leave their business card at the scene of the crime," I said.

"You'd be surprised," he said as he tucked the card into his pocket.

It didn't matter if he took the card, because I had already seen the address and the name: George Gustavsson at Flaget Manufacturing. I was good with names, but I didn't recognize his.

At that moment, it hit me. I remembered where I'd heard Antoine's name. Why hadn't I thought of it sooner? My landlord had left me a message saying she was selling the building that housed my shop to a man named Antoine Dubois. That meant a murder suspect would now be my landlord? What did that mean for me? What if he went to jail and lost the building? Would I be kicked out on the street along with my macarons? It hadn't been easy to find an available spot for my bakery, let alone a fantastic location like this one on the cutest, busiest street in town.

Antoine couldn't be responsible for such a horrendous act. I mean, sure, he was new in town, so of course everyone would point fingers at him. Plus there was the fact that he'd been fighting with the murder victim the day before she was killed. But those were minor details.

No one would want to be in the middle of a murder investigation, but here I found myself right in the thick of it. I couldn't possibly have been any closer. I didn't want to end up as the next victim, but since we didn't know who the killer was, we were all in danger. What if I was the real target? What if they had been looking for me and they'd thought I'd be here at that time in the morning? Or maybe someone was trying to rob the bakery and Kellie just happened to be in front of the shop at that time.

There were a lot of possibilities. I wondered if a local could have done this, but it could be an outsider too. Anyone could have come to Paris to kill her. Maybe it was a hired hit. She could be a spy, for all I knew. Though what was there to spy on in Paris, Kentucky?

That was neither here nor there. I was sure there were some hidden secrets around here.

When Maverick finished rubbing on Fifi and Pepé Le Pew, he looked my way and said, "Thank you, Ms. Beaucoup. If I have any further questions, I'll be in touch. And please try not to contaminate the crime scene any more."

"I have no reason to go out there, Detective Malone," I said.

He studied my face for a moment, and my stomach flipped. Maybe it was just because I hadn't had breakfast. I *was* feeling a little light-headed. I'd grab a croissant and some coffee, then I'd be good to go. That should take care of the butterflies.

Okay, who was I kidding? I thought Maverick was hot, but I wished he acted differently. I wasn't sure why he was still staring at me. Yes, people said he was into me, but was that the only reason?

"Well, I'll see you," I said.

That was the hint that it was time for him to leave.

"Right," he said.

After another pause, he turned around and headed for the door. He looked back over his shoulder as he walked out. Once he closed the door, I hurriedly locked it behind him.

"Oh, great, Marci, look what you did. You chased the handsome detective away," Aunt Barb said.

"He was done talking," I said, grabbing a croissant.

"No, he wasn't done. I saw the look he was giving you. There's magic in the air."

I took a bite of the croissant. "There's no magic. I don't believe in magic."

"Oh, please, yes you do. You know magic is around, and you just need to learn what to do with it. Don't ignore the magic."

"If you say so," I said. "Now let's finish getting the orders ready."

Yes, I was changing the subject. There was nothing left to discuss.

40

"I'm just saying you should give your first love another chance."

"He wasn't my first love, Aunt Barb."

"Yes, he most certainly was your first love," she said.

Okay, so Maverick had kissed me on the cheek in third grade. It happened during recess. Back then he had a crush on me, I guess. I suppose I'd had a little crush on him, too, but it was third grade. That wasn't considered love.

"There was no great romance, Aunt Barb. You're exaggerating again."

"Don't take that tone with me." She pointed a warning finger.

"He's a ladies' man. A playboy. He will never settle down, and I'm not interested."

Aunt Barb placed macarons in one of the shop's pretty pink boxes. "You have no proof to back up that claim."

"I have plenty to back it up," I said as I put the last croissant into the box.

"All I know is that you won't give him a chance and he's had a crush on you since third grade."

"I don't need to talk about this anymore," I said.

I stuck by what I said. My thoughts hadn't changed one bit. He truly was a ladies' man—I'd seen him around town with a different date every other night. Maverick would never settle down; therefore, I wasn't interested in anything slightly romantic with him. Although I had to admit his strong jawline, dark eyes, and full lips that turned up in the cutest little smirk were the best I'd ever seen. He made me feel as if a chorus line were doing the French cancan in my stomach.

Fifi and Pepé Le Pew stood guard next to me as I looked out the window and watched Maverick speak with other officers. It appeared they were wrapping things up. They had removed the body. Detectives had been out there all morning, taking photos and collecting evidence. Now it looked as if things might be almost back to normal.

What was I saying? Things would be far from normal. There would always be that memory of finding Kellie there and being helpless to do anything to save her.

Maverick climbed into his car. Maybe it was just my imagination, but I thought for sure he was watching me. He sat there for the longest time, and I couldn't tell if he was looking at the window or at something else. Butterflies continued to dance in my stomach at the thought, so I moved away from the window. This was no time to think about something like that. A woman was dead.

I knew the police would interrogate Antoine soon. I mean, they always accused the boyfriend. They might even take him to jail. I wanted to talk to him before anything like that happened. I couldn't help but be curious. I wasn't a police officer or detective, but I had some skills. I'd read a lot of mystery books, and I watched those true crime shows. I was a smart woman. If I could run a business, then I could solve a crime if I tried hard enough.

What would I ask him? *Did you kill your girlfriend?* It wasn't like he would confess to me, and I was sure he hadn't done it anyway. He wouldn't confess to the police either, even if—*especially* if—he'd done anything wrong. Call it instinct, but as I'd told Maverick, I honestly didn't think he'd done this.

Maybe I was being swayed by Antoine's lovely French accent. I couldn't lie to myself and say I didn't love it.

I thought about Maverick. I supposed maybe he did have a crush on me. But why would I go out with him when he was chasing every other woman in town? I thought of that soap opera I'd watched with Aunt Barb last week. This could be like a scene from that—if Maverick liked me and thought I was interested in the

Frenchman, then maybe he would do everything in his power to make sure Antoine was behind bars, staring at cold steel the rest of his life.

I stopped my train of thought. I couldn't assume Maverick would do something like that, but he would definitely be focused on the ex-boyfriend first. There were no other leads that I knew of.

Understandably, Maverick was being tight-lipped about the case, though. I hoped he was looking at someone else. Like George Gustavsson, the name on that business card. Why had that card been at the crime scene?

I spotted Gordon walking by the shop. He paused and looked around. Was he searching for something? What was he up to? He glanced my way, and I waved. Gordon didn't wave in return, so I assumed he hadn't seen me. Or had he ignored me on purpose?

# Chapter Six

A short while later as I headed for my car, my phone rang. When I checked the screen, I saw that my landlord was calling. My anxiety spiked right away. I normally wouldn't think anything of this, but after the morning's events, I was a bit nervous. Though I supposed maybe she just wanted to find out what had happened. Why did I feel as if she would blame me for this morning's events? Maybe she'd ask me to get out of the building. What if I lost the bakery?

"Hello?" My voice wavered just a bit.

"Marci?"

"Yes, hi, Mrs. Williams." Nervousness still filled my words.

"Please call me Chantelle."

She said that all the time, but I felt I should keep the phone calls on a professional level. But I didn't want to make her mad. I was always on edge that I might lose the shop.

"Hi, Chantelle. Is everything okay?" I asked.

It wasn't a coincidence that there had been a murder and now I was receiving a call from her. I waited for her to drop the bomb.

"Well, dear . . ." She paused.

This wasn't a good sign. The tone of her voice said it all. I braced myself for the bad news. But could I really ever be prepared for this? I supposed it was best to get it over with so I could plan something else. If she asked me to leave the building, what would I do? Where would I go?

"Did you get my message letting you know that I'm planning on selling the building?" Chantelle said.

Yes, I'd gotten her message, but I'd hoped it had all been a mistake. I hadn't called her back because I'd needed time to process the news. Plus, I was now in the middle of dealing with my business being the scene of a crime. I didn't know what to say to Chantelle.

"Why are you selling?" I asked, trying not to sound too upset.

"Like I said in the message, I received an offer for the building, and I decided to sell because I need the money. I wanted to give you notice. The buyer, Antoine Dubois, said he will continue your lease. At least for now. I'm sorry, and I hope you understand I had to sell, Marci."

For now? Chantelle was saying Antoine would let me stay *for now*. But for how long? That might all change if he was sent to prison.

"Do you think everything will be okay?" I asked.

"Yes, of course. What makes you think everything wouldn't be okay?"

Why was she acting so confused?

Had she not heard the news? I'd thought everyone in town had heard by now.

"You don't know what happened?" I asked.

"No, I have no idea. Please tell me what's going on."

"Antoine is being charged with murder. Well, I'm not sure he's being charged. But it sure looks that way."

"Why? He seems like such a nice man. Can you give me any more information?" she asked.

"Well, actually, I was the one who found the murder victim. It was his ex-girlfriend. I guess they had had a fight. He was in my shop the day before with her. And they were arguing."

"This is very unusual. He doesn't seem like the type who would do something like that," she said.

My landlord had always acted somewhat detached, but I had expected a bit more reaction from her over this shocking news.

"That's exactly what I thought," I said. "Will the sale to him still go through?"

"Not if he's charged with murder," she said. "If for any reason he can't complete the purchase soon, I have another buyer, who wants to tear the buildings down and put in that chain sandwich shop that also sells baked goods. I can't remember the name of it now, but it's super popular. I think it would go over well in town."

Was she seriously telling me this? Was I dreaming? Why would she do this to me?

I wasn't sure how to react or what to say. Should I just tell her thank you for letting me know? What else was there to say? It was too late to convince her not to sell. After all, it was her building.

Would I have to find a new spot and move everything in the shop? I knew there wasn't another good location available in town. Would this be the end of the bakery for me? Things had just started to take off. Sadness overwhelmed me.

"Thank you," I said shakily. "I appreciate you telling me. Please let me know as soon as possible. I will have to immediately start looking for a new place."

We said good-bye, and I rushed toward my car. I needed to do my catering orders for the day regardless of what was going on with the murder or my building.

If the sale to Antoine did go through, would he want me to move too? Maybe he'd just let me stay. At least there was a *chance* if Antoine stayed the buyer.

My landlord had said the sale had to go through soon—and the cops would be focused on Antoine, wasting time and potentially opening the door for the bulldozing buyer. If I wanted to keep my business open, I had to prove his innocence.

How could I prove that Antoine wasn't the murderer? If I wanted to take a stab at it as soon as possible, I needed to speak with him as soon as I finished my catering orders. And I had to locate him in order to speak to him. Maybe someone in town would know where he was staying. Gossip spread through town like butter on a hot croissant, and Antoine and Kelly would be all the buzz.

I'd just delivered the final catering order and was headed toward my car when I was stopped by Mrs. Angelina Foley, the second biggest gossip in town. She knew things I'd thought only God could see, and I'd wondered if she had a bug in people's houses. The woman knew what kind of shampoo I used and that I always had a small glass of almond milk before bed. She didn't know everything, though, and she was way off base if she thought she'd already solved this murder.

"Yoo-hoo, Marci." She waved magnanimously as she hurried across the street.

I knew why she wanted to talk to me, and it wasn't because she wanted to order macarons. Of course the murder would be the talk of the town—there was nothing I could do to avoid that. Plus, I was in the middle of the crime. Surely everyone in town wanted to speak with me to get a firsthand account of the morning's events. I didn't want to hear her theories about Antoine being the murderer. I gave a halfhearted wave and continued toward my car. Maybe I could tell her I was late for an appointment.

She probably already knew my schedule.

As I tried to open the car door, she hurried up to the door and blocked me. My southern manners struggled to stay intact. My mama would have a fit if she found out I'd caused a scene in the middle of town, even if Mrs. Foley completely deserved it. I'd just have to get through this conversation.

"I heard the news, Marci. It's just terrible, isn't it?" Mrs. Foley asked.

"Yes, Mrs. Foley, it's tragic." I looked around for someone who might save me.

"I heard that the stranger in town did it. That doesn't surprise me one bit. I mean, a drifter just wanders into town. The police had better arrest that man soon." She searched my face, waiting for my response.

She wanted me to agree with her, but there was no way I could do that. If she found out I didn't see eye to eye with her, though, she'd make things much more difficult for me.

"I'm sure the police are working diligently to make sure an arrest is made." I climbed behind the wheel.

She held on to the door, refusing to let me go until she was ready. "I heard there were witnesses who saw Antoine at the scene of the crime."

My eyes widened. "Who saw him?"

Was this the truth or just a rumor? If someone had seen him, then I wanted to speak with the witnesses myself. Now I had to make sure Mrs. Foley gave me the names.

"Mrs. Bobbie Mansfield and Mrs. Jacqueline O'Neal. They were out walking their yippy little ugly dogs and spotted that creepy stranger rushing by," she said with a smug look of satisfaction. "Antoine Dubois."

48

I knew by that look that she thought she had the case wrapped up. A conviction was just a matter of time.

"I met him. He seemed like a nice gentleman," I said.

She scoffed. "He's rude. The French are known for that, you know. I can tell by looking at him that's he's guilty. He looks low class, if you ask me. I heard he has a tattoo on his arm. Probably got it in prison."

She was the rudest woman I'd ever met. It was hard for me to bite my tongue and not tell her what I thought of her too. The last thing I wanted was to continue this conversation with her. Now that I had names, I had to speak with those women. Perhaps it had been dark and they'd just *thought* it was Antoine. Whatever the case, I wanted to find out as soon as possible. I knew I'd find the women together at Honeybun's Diner—they went there every morning for coffee. I'd once made a faux pas and called the diner a café. I'd been swiftly corrected and told it was a diner. *Pardonne-moi.*

"Okay, Mrs. Foley, I need to go now. You take care, okay?" I cranked the engine and drowned out her words.

I assumed she was complaining about the Frenchman or asking more questions to confirm her theory that he'd committed the murder. I'd told her all I wanted to share. I hoped she didn't try to step out in front of my car. I shoved it into drive and tapped on the gas pedal. She scowled at me as I inched forward. Thank goodness she didn't try to stop me, but I knew she was unhappy with me. I just hoped she didn't tell everyone in town not to come by my bakery just because of the crime.

Though even if she did, I wasn't sure they would believe her right away. Lately people had seemed obsessed with my pastries, and I wasn't sure what it would take to make them not want them anymore. But I had no doubt that if Mrs. Foley really wanted to hurt my business, she'd be successful. She wasn't the type who let anything stand in her way. When she'd wanted Peter McPherson out as mayor, she'd found an old technicality and taken him to court, rendering him ineligible to run for office. If she set her sights on something, she didn't stop until she got her way. She gnawed on it like a dog chewing a thigh bone.

I maneuvered my car through the center of town and headed for the diner. The cars around me traveled sedately as they made their way around downtown. Everything seemed to move slower in Paris—except the gossip.

Seconds later, I pulled up in front of the diner and shut off the car. I stared at the building for a couple of minutes, contemplating what I would do when I entered. It wasn't like I could strike up this conversation quickly. This was something I'd have to ease into. The sign out front advertised grits, eggs, and bacon as the daily breakfast special. I had to admit my stomach was rumbling at the thought. The croissant I'd had earlier wasn't lasting as long as I had hoped.

It was now or never. The place would likely be full of people wanting to gossip about the tragedy outside my bakery door. That would slow down my quest for real clues that could help me save my business.

Nevertheless, I had to get out of the car and go inside. That was the whole reason I was here, so no more delaying.

After exiting the car, I walked along the sidewalk toward the diner's front entrance. Cars were driving at a steady pace around the courthouse in the middle of the town square. Brick and stone buildings lined the streets, accommodating charming boutiques— an antiques shop, a coffee shop, and a café, to name a few. Planters bursting with chrysanthemums in rich shades of burgundy, yellow, and red decorated the sidewalks.

The back of my neck prickled as I walked. It felt as if someone was watching me. When I glanced around, I noticed that several people sitting in front of the barbershop were in fact staring. I supposed they had heard what had happened. But it wasn't like I could stop the gossip. I just had to ride out the storm.

As I continued walking, I spotted Gordon headed right for me. I wasn't sure if he knew I was in front of him, though. He peered down at his feet as he walked. We were on a collision course with each other. Before I let him bump into me, I decided I would move to the right. I wasn't sure if he'd notice me at all. But he looked up at the last moment and met my gaze. A slight smile crossed his face.

"Good morning, Ms. Marci," he said with a slight nod.

"Hello, Mr. Dumensil. How are you?"

"Fine, fine," he said, looking up at the sky. "Just fine."

"Yes, it is a good day, I suppose, weatherwise," I said.

I wanted to ask him about the scene out in front of my shop, but then again, maybe I didn't want to bring it up and scare one of my best customers away. Though he'd obviously been curious about what was going on. Why else would he have been hanging around the shop so much this morning?

"Where's your aunt Barb?" he said, looking around.

"Oh, she isn't with me. I'm just heading into the diner." I gestured.

He nodded. "Well, good. I hope you have a great day. I'll see you."

"See you later, Mr. Dumensil." I waved.

Without saying anything else, he hurried down the sidewalk. Maybe I should have asked him if he'd noticed anything unusual at the bakery. A man who came to a pâtisserie every morning at eight sharp certainly wasn't the type to be skulking around town in the middle of the night, so he wouldn't have been around when the murder occurred. But maybe he'd noticed something out of the ordinary this morning that the cops or I had missed. I needed to just hurry up and get in the diner to ask the ladies what they'd seen. That would further my investigation better than anything else I could do at the moment.

I stepped up to the door and walked inside. Immediately the smell of bacon and eggs hit me. I wasn't sure if I would be able to resist having food before I left. I supposed that could serve as my reason for being here. I mean, why else would I be in a diner?

I looked around for Mrs. O'Neal and Mrs. Mansfield and immediately spotted them in the corner of the room. Of course, everyone in the diner was gaping at me, including the two women. Now I had to act as if they weren't the reason for my visit. I spotted an empty table nearby. Thank goodness. The uneasiness of being watched was awfully strange. I tried to smile and be friendly, but everyone was just staring at me as if they'd never seen me before. It wasn't like *I* was the murderer. Or was that what they thought? That wouldn't be good. Or if the women really had seen Antoine at the scene of the crime, maybe they thought I was his accomplice. They'd certainly think that if they knew I was trying to get him off any charges that might be pending against him. I had to make sure they didn't realize *why* I was asking about what they'd seen.

I sat down at the table and tried to pretend the women weren't staring at me. How long could I tolerate them watching me like this, though? It was becoming painfully awkward—but this was my opportunity; I just had to pretend to notice them and say hello.

Seconds after I picked up the menu, Darcey Matthews, Honeybun's short-tempered brunette waitress, approached the table. She stood beside the table for several seconds without speaking. Darcey and I had attended high school together. She'd always said my love of all things French was ridiculous. As if her collection of porcelain clowns wasn't downright creepy. Small wonder she was short-tempered; she was probably possessed by a ghost.

After a little more awkward silence, she said, "Well, I haven't seen you in here for years. What made you decide to grace us with your presence?"

Her smirk told me there was a bit of attitude behind that remark. Had I done something wrong again? Was I supposed to be in here more often? When had that become a requirement of citizenship in Paris?

"Things have been busy with work," I said with a forced smile.

"Yes, I've heard that your fancy bakery is doing well. I heard it's because of all those love pastries you're making."

"My pastries are made with *amour*, if that's what you mean."

"Everyone seems to be crazy about them. A lot of customers don't even come in here anymore because they just go by your place and get baked stuff for breakfast."

"Well, I know there are plenty of customers in Paris for both of us."

So that was what the hostility was about. She thought I was taking away business. I ordered the daily special and handed her the menu, glad to be ending the confrontation.

Mrs. Mansfield and Mrs. O'Neal were still watching me, though not quite as much now because they had their food. I should just start a conversation. I shouldn't ask about the murder right away. I could start with the weather.

"Beautiful weather today, isn't it?" I said.

Both women turned and peered out the window, as if they needed confirmation that the sun was still shining.

"Yes, it's lovely," Mrs. Mansfield said. "As nice as it can be after such a horrifying crime in town."

"We're surprised to see you here," Mrs. O'Neal said.

"I just came in for some breakfast," I replied.

Mrs. Mansfield eyed me over the scarlet-colored cat-eye eyeglasses she wore pushed down the bridge of her nose. "Well, I bet you do have quite an appetite after what happened to you this morning."

They had segued into my topic for me. Now was my chance to start talking about the murder.

"Yes, it was a stressful morning. I heard you saw some things too." I focused my gaze on them.

Mrs. Mansfield and Mrs. O'Neal exchanged a look.

Then Mrs. O'Neal said, "We certainly did. We saw that man come right away from Main Street when we were out for our usual walk last night."

"Meaning Antoine Dubois?" I asked.

"Yes, the new man in town. He was her boyfriend."

"I think they had broken up," I said, my face warm.

"If you believe that rumor." Mrs. Mansfield nonchalantly stirred more sugar into her coffee.

"Are you sure it was him? That you really saw him? I mean, it was dark. It could have been anyone," I said.

"Oh, no. We're positive. It looked just like him." Mrs. O'Neal spoke with authority for both of them.

"Can you describe him for me?" I asked.

"He was tall, wearing dark clothing. And handsome." Both women nodded in agreement.

"That seems pretty vague. I mean, it could have been anyone from town who's tall and handsome."

"We're sure it was him."

I still didn't believe them, but it looked as if I might have no other choice. I wondered if there was any surveillance video from anywhere in town that would confirm what they'd said. I was sure the police were working on that, but I needed to figure this out before they made an arrest.

Considering everyone was still watching me, I didn't really feel like staying here to eat the food. When Darcey brought over my order, I asked her if I could get it to go. Of course, she probably didn't like this one bit; her knuckles were turning white against the plate. However, she brought it back in a bag, and I quickly grabbed it so I could get out of there.

Now the police would have eyewitnesses placing Antoine at the scene of the crime. I wondered if he knew about the witnesses. What was I saying? He was probably already at the police station being interrogated. Unless, of course, he'd fled the state. How would I find him? Maybe I should swing by the police station. No, that would probably get me arrested. I mean, they could very well think I'd done it if I kept snooping around. Maybe I needed to stay far away from the police station. Though wouldn't it be nice if Antoine knew someone in town cared and was rooting for him?

# Chapter Seven

I was torn on what I should do. I'd driven away from the diner and was getting close to the police station now. I supposed taking a look at the parking lot wouldn't do any harm. Maybe they'd let Antoine go for now and I'd spot him on his way out.

My phone rang, sending a chiming sound throughout my car. When I looked at the screen on my car's dashboard, it read *Unknown caller*. Should I answer the call? I certainly didn't have time to listen to someone ask to speak to me about my car's extended warranty. What if it was an important call, though?

Reluctantly, I picked up the phone. "Hello?"

No response. I checked the phone to see if there was still a connection. It looked as if the call was still active.

"Hello?" I repeated.

Still, no one said a word. Seconds later the call ended. I supposed it was a wrong number. The silence on the other end had been creepy, though, under the circumstances.

When the phone rang again, the sound startled me so much that I almost tossed it out the window. Caller ID identified the person this time. My friend Kristina owned the local clothing boutique. She'd likely heard the news about what had happened.

*Likely?* Who was I kidding? Everyone in town and the surrounding towns had no doubt already caught the news.

"Oh my gosh, I heard what happened. Are you okay?" she asked immediately when I answered.

I released a deep breath. "Yes, I'm fine, but obviously this scared the bejeebus out of me."

"I can only imagine, Marci. I mean, a dead body right there on the sidewalk? What did you do?"

"Well, I panicked, of course," I said.

"But it seems like you kept yourself under control. I heard you were right on the scene when it happened," she said.

"I bet you heard a lot. Well, I wasn't on the scene when it happened. I found the body and that was it."

"Are you sure you're okay? That's traumatic."

"I'm fine, really, I am." My voice wavered slightly.

"Listen, I just wanted to call and make sure everything was fine. I've got some customers coming in, but I'll check on you later, all right?"

"Thank you, Kristina," I said. "Hey, before I let you go, I know you're really good at this kind of stuff, and . . . well, I just thought maybe you could keep your eyes and ears open for me. Let me know if you find out anything about what happened. Or if you think of anything that might be a clue as to who did this. To be honest, I'm kind of freaked out, since it happened in front of my shop."

"Honey, I don't know what I would do if it had happened in front of my shop, but you can count on me. I'll call you soon."

"Thank you, Kristina. Talk to you later."

I was glad that I had her in my corner. She really was good with the FBI skills.

About ten minutes had passed when I caught movement at the police station. Someone was coming out the front door. It was him.

Wow, he really was handsome, even from this distance. Apparently, the police had taken him in for questioning. Now they were letting him go? That was a good sign. He walked across the parking lot and slipped into a black Mercedes. I slid down in my seat a bit so he wouldn't notice me when he pulled out of the lot.

So what would I do now? My business depended on Antoine not going to prison. If he went to jail, the other buyer would get the building and it would be lights-out on my little bake shop. I had to prove his innocence by trying to find the real killer.

I turned the ignition and pulled out onto the road to follow him. I just hoped he wouldn't see me and think I was crazy. If he did see me, I could just tell him I'd happened to be driving this way. He wouldn't know I was following him. I mean, this was a small town. It wouldn't be that much of a coincidence to run into him, right?

But what would I do after I followed him and found out where he was going? How could I make it look random if I went up to him and started a conversation? I supposed that now that he was going to be my landlord, I could talk to him about that. Yes, that was the perfect excuse. I'd ask him if he'd let me stay in the building while I was at it. And maybe he'd ask about the murder. Although he probably didn't want to discuss that at the moment.

When we pulled up to a red light, I was right behind him. I thought for sure he was onto me. He was looking in the rearview mirror. Did he recognize me?

When the light turned green, he took off. I punched the gas in pursuit.

# Chapter Eight

Antoine pulled up in front of a white brick house and got out of the car. I didn't know what to do now. Approach him as he walked up the driveway, I supposed. Whatever I was going to do, I needed to hurry, because soon he'd be in the house, and it would be even more awkward to knock on the door. Right now I could just pretend I was walking along the sidewalk or something.

I pulled the car up along the curb, shoved it into park, and turned off the ignition. I quickly grabbed the keys and hurried out from behind the wheel, rushing up to the sidewalk. He'd almost made it up the path and to the front door when I reached the driveway. I had to call out to him before he got inside.

"Excuse me, Antoine." I couldn't believe I'd actually called out his name.

Maybe I should have pretended I couldn't remember his name. Now he might think he'd been on my mind for a long time. Although maybe something like that would impress him—that I was smart enough to remember his name.

I was overanalyzing again. Nevertheless, I had captured his attention, because he looked my way. Recognition hit his face right away.

"Marci Beaucoup," he said in his lovely French accent.

I hoped I didn't giggle, because I felt like a giddy schoolgirl. What was I thinking? This guy could be a murderer, for heaven's sake. Although the police hadn't arrested him, so maybe he had given them a solid alibi. I would sure like to know what that was.

"I'm surprised to see you here," he said.

"I came by because I heard you're buying my building." I studied his handsome face. His eyes seemed sadder now, like happiness had melted out of his chocolate-brown eyes.

He ran his hand through his thick hair. "I was going to come and talk to you about that."

"I don't want to leave," I said.

"I'm not going to ask you to leave the building," he said.

Well, that was a relief. I wondered if he'd put that in writing.

"You wouldn't have a problem signing a new lease?" I asked.

"Absolutely not. I would prefer that, if that's all right with you?"

"Yes, I would like that. We can discuss the details of the lease soon?"

"Sure, as long as I'm not arrested," he said around a nervous laugh.

"I don't want that to happen, because obviously you didn't do it."

"No, of course not, Marci." The nervousness lingered in his words.

Discussing the lease might make him talk more. Maybe then he would tell me his alibi or something. But he didn't offer any explanation right now. Maybe I could help him out of this situation, but he had to open up and tell me everything.

"Look, Antoine, I like to think I'm a good judge of character, and something tells me you're innocent. I want to help you. I know this is a tough question, but where were you this morning?" I asked. "I know you don't have to talk to me about any of this, but you need someone to talk to, right? Someone who will be on your side. This is a small town, and I know the residents can be unwelcoming to newcomers. Especially ones who might be murderers. You need a friend in this town."

I tried not to sound too abrasive. I meant everything I'd said to him.

After a pause, he said, "I was home alone."

"That isn't a good alibi, is it?" I asked. He really did need help clearing his name.

"Not at all," he said, looking down at his feet. "Nevertheless, it's the truth, and I won't lie. But I'm certain they'll figure out I had nothing to do with this soon enough."

"I hope that's the case. I just wanted to ask you some questions, because I'm a bit confused why Kellie would be there at that time of the morning."

"I answered all the questions the police had, and I just don't know why she was there."

I stared at his face to see if he was being sincere. I honestly had no idea.

"Well, some women in town—I won't name names—said they saw you leave the scene of the crime."

He raised an eyebrow. "They are mistaken. It wasn't me."

I didn't want to push it. After all, he was hopefully going to be my landlord now. He could ask me to get out of there immediately.

It seemed there was nothing left to say, since I had no other questions right now. Maybe that would change the more I looked into the crime.

"If there's anything I can do to help, please don't hesitate to ask," I said.

"I appreciate that, Marci. Thank you." He handed me another card. "Call me if you need anything."

Butterflies danced in my stomach as I took it. "I will."

"I'll make sure to stop in the shop. Your *choux au chocolat* was the best I've ever had."

My eyes widened. "Are you just telling me that to be polite?"

"No, I mean it. They were absolutely perfect. I've never had anything so great in Paris, France. To think I had to come all the way to Paris, Kentucky, to get the best."

"That is ironic, isn't it?" I sensed by the tone of his voice that he was only being kind. I mean, me making pastry better than authentic Parisian fare? That seemed impossible. I felt he was genuine in his desire to make me feel better, though. That wouldn't be a quality a murderer would possess, would it?

# Chapter Nine

The next day, bright and early, I arrived at the bakery. Thank goodness, this time I didn't discover a crime scene, though an eerie feeling hung over me and the whole area.

Glancing around, I wondered if there was something more making me feel this way. I supposed it would fade as time went by. Or at least I hoped that would be the case. Still, something seemed off. I chalked it up to the emotional trauma I'd experienced from finding Kellie Lowry.

Somehow, I'd felt connected to her because of the butterfly necklace she'd been wearing. I'd given my cousin Jennifer one just like it for Christmas two years ago. Jen and I had been best friends since childhood. Little had I known that Jen would be killed in a car accident a month later. Having her suddenly taken from my life was something I'd never gotten over.

Something like Kellie's murder couldn't be forgotten in a matter of hours. My life would never truly be the same now. I checked over my shoulder again, feeling like someone was watching me. It was as if a trace of the killer's bad energy had been left behind. I hoped Fifi or Pepé Le Pew would let me know if danger was headed my way.

I'd spotted Aunt Barb down the street chatting with Gordon again last evening. Curiosity was getting to me, and I wanted to know what they had discussed. I thought I'd actually seen Aunt Barb laughing, and she had touched Gordon's arm. If I didn't know better, I'd have sworn she was flirting with him. Though if I asked her, she'd totally deny it.

Once Aunt Barb arrived, she and I both worked busily in the kitchen. She didn't mention her chat with Gordon and stayed extremely focused on the baking. Soon everything fresh was placed in the display cases and the coffee machine was ready for the morning. I flipped the sign on the door to OPEN. Peering out the window, I realized there wasn't a line on the sidewalk waiting to enter. That was odd. Usually a line of customers filed into the shop in the morning. My stomach turned at the thought. What if I never had customers again? The best I could hope for was that the slowdown would be temporary.

I'd just stepped back behind the counter when the bell above the door chimed. Gordon was the first customer of the day. At least *he* hadn't abandoned me. I could always count on him. I started preparing his coffee—black, with none of that fancy stuff added, as he always said. While I waited for the fresh coffee to grind, I placed his pastry on a dish.

"Good morning, Mr. Dumensil. How are you?" I tried to sound perky, as if a murder hadn't occurred here a day ago.

Would he mention the elephant in the room? Maybe *I* should, just to get it out in the open.

I placed his coffee and pastry on the counter. "This one is on me, Mr. Dumensil."

"Oh, no, I can't let you do that." He waved his hand and then pulled out his wallet.

"No, I really want to," I said, pushing his wallet away.

"You think my money isn't good?" he asked.

"No, that's not it at all," I said. "It's just that—well, okay, I'll be honest with you. After what happened here yesterday, I'm not sure I'll have customers, so it's just my way of saying thank you for staying loyal."

"Well, if you're not going to charge your customers when they come in, then you won't have any business. And you won't be able to stay open. That kind of defeats the point, now, doesn't it?"

Sure, but I'd thought giving him something for free was supposed to be a good thing. Now I was feeling guilty about it.

"I guess you're right about that," I said.

"All right then, let me pay," he said.

I reluctantly took the cash. Hopefully, it was the thought that counted.

"And don't you worry, Ms. Beaucoup. Things will die down. You'll have customers again. People around here know when to do the right thing."

I hoped he was right about that. Gordon said nothing else as he took his plate and coffee. He turned and headed toward his usual spot over in the corner of the room next to the window. He liked to sit there, I thought, because the sunshine came in at the exact time in the morning when he visited the shop.

Gordon hadn't mentioned anything about the murder. I wondered what he thought about it. Perhaps I needed to ask instead of letting him bring up the subject. I made my way over to his table, pretending I was cleaning tabletops, although I was probably being kind of obvious as I inched toward him.

"So, Mr. Dumensil, what do you think about what happened?"

"What do I think about what?" he asked.

"About the murder. Do you have any idea who may have done this?" I asked.

"I wasn't here when it happened. Why would I know?"

"Well, I thought maybe you had a theory."

"I have no theories; sorry. I don't know what happened exactly," he said.

"You were here and saw the police, right? I saw you outside near the crime scene when the police were here."

He scowled. "I was just watching like everybody else. Doesn't mean I have any idea what happened."

"No, of course not. I didn't mean to imply that you would," I said.

Aunt Barb motioned for me to come back to the kitchen. I figured she just wanted me to leave Gordon alone.

It wasn't that I was trying to harass him, but I needed clues. Any little hint to help me get where I needed to be.

"I have no idea who would do this. But I have a feeling that Detective Malone will figure it out in no time," Mr. Dumensil said, punctuating the sentence with a lift of his coffee cup.

The mention of Maverick sent a spark through my body. Ignoring that feeling was grower harder each day.

"All right, Mr. Dumensil, I'm sorry for disturbing you. I'm going to get back to work before my aunt Barb has a hissy fit back there."

"You just get back to what you do best, making those pastries," he said with a wink.

"Will do." I started to walk away.

Gordon called out, "Everything will be fine, Marci. You'll see."

"Thank you, Mr. Dumensil. I appreciate that," I said with a smile.

Stepping through the kitchen door, I spotted Aunt Barb standing in front of the counter with the largest stainless steel mixing bowl I owned. The thing was big enough to use as a swimming pool. Okay, that was an exaggeration, but nonetheless, the thing was huge. The mixer whirled, adding a loud hum throughout the room.

"Why are we making all this stuff anyway?" I asked when I stepped back into the kitchen.

"What do you mean?" Aunt Barb asked.

"Well, apparently no one's coming in at all today."

"You have such little faith. Don't talk like that. Keeping a positive attitude is key. How do you think I made it all those years in the army if I didn't keep a positive attitude?"

I sighed. "I guess you're right."

Aunt Barb and I busied ourselves with mundane little tasks once all the baking was done. And since there were no customers to wait on at the moment, that left a lot of free time. I contemplated reading a book. However, just a few minutes later, the bell above the door chimed. My heart jumped into action, beating harder as I turned my attention to the front of the bakery. More customers? Maybe we were off to a good start after all. It was still early, but it looked as if things might turn around.

Okay, it was just one customer, but that was better than nothing. The woman didn't look my way, though. She immediately started looking around the bakery as if she was confused about where she might be. Couldn't she smell all the delicious pastries in the air? That alone was enough to draw anyone's attention to the counter and the display cases. But she seemed immune to it. What was her secret? No sense of smell? Yes, that had to be it.

Still, she had to know where she was. How could she have wandered into a building and not know what she was walking into? With signs clearly marking all the stores in town, it wasn't like she had stepped into the antiques shop across the street or the barbershop down the road. The fact that this was a bakery was clearly marked out front, and the window displays featured delicious treats. I wanted them to be obvious so that they would attract customers from the sidewalk.

The woman had short blonde hair and wore an expensive-looking black dress. Her Chanel bag made me long for a visit to the headquarters on Rue Cambon. Aunt Barb and I watched her move about the shop. She checked the walls as if she was looking for cracks or other flaws. Pepé Le Pew sat on the front window-sill, eyeing the woman's every move. I worried that Pepé might pounce at any moment and scratch the woman. Fifi sat nearby and growled every time the woman moved. Fifi rarely ever showed any signs of aggression—only when she felt we were in danger.

"What does she think she's doin'?" Aunt Barb asked.

"I don't know, but do you think I should go find out?"

"I think yes, you should ask her what she's doing, because this is strange."

"All right, I'm going to do it," I said.

I hated confronting weird people. It was always so awkward, and I never knew what they would do next. Nevertheless, this was my shop, and I couldn't let this woman just roam around and scare all the customers away. Oh, wait, there was only one customer, but that was neither here nor there. I wondered if this had something to do with the murder. Maybe she was looking for evidence. Was she a detective and I just didn't know about this visit? I'd have thought they would warn me in advance if they were going to do something like this.

The woman was now checking the floor, which seemed even more strange.

I glanced over at Gordon. He was watching the woman, but then he looked at me. He shrugged as if to tell me he had no idea what she was doing either. I noticed several customers headed toward the shop, and my stomach danced with excitement and anxiety at the same time, a hurricane of emotions battling inside my body. I wanted to get rid of this woman before she scared my few customers away.

I felt Aunt Barb's stare on me, so I glanced back. She pointed, indicating that I should hurry up and ask the woman what she was doing. I supposed I was dragging this out. In my mind, I was still running through what I was going to say and what the outcome might be. The woman hadn't acknowledged me. She hadn't even looked up to let me know she knew I existed.

# Chapter Ten

After helping the customers, I walked over to the woman and stood behind her. She still had no idea I was even there. Or if she did, she didn't let on. Maybe she thought I'd just go away. She acted as if she owned this place.

"Excuse me, ma'am," I said.

She completely ignored me. I was beginning to get angry. I'd have to ask her to leave if she wasn't going to buy something. She couldn't stand here and act weird. I tapped her on the shoulder.

She finally spun around and gave me an angry look. Fifi and Pepé Le Pew watched the woman, ready to leap into action at the first sign of any aggressive behavior from the stranger.

"Oh, nothing for me, thanks." She dismissed me with a wave of her hand.

I couldn't believe she was that arrogant.

"Excuse me, but what are you doing?" I asked.

She raised an eyebrow as if I should never have asked her that question—as if she was appalled that I would have the nerve to even speak to her. I was this close to calling the cops on her. And if she didn't shape up and get out of here soon, that was exactly what would happen.

"I'm sorry, but I need to know what you're doing," I said.

"Well, I'm checking out my investment, of course," she said.

I shook my head. "Your investment? You don't own this building."

"Not yet, but I'm buying it," she said matter-of-factly.

What was she talking about?

"Antoine Dubois is supposed to buy this building. He *is* buying this building," I repeated.

Maybe if I said it, then it would come true.

"The real estate transactions on this property are none of your business."

"Well, I feel differently about whether I should know about the real estate transactions."

The bell jingled and a customer walked in.

"This place is a mess. Did you even pass inspection?" the nosy woman asked in a loud voice.

The customer turned and walked back out the door.

"So exactly what are you doing by looking around? I mean, I'm running a business here. You can't just come in and act that way. You're scaring away the customers."

She looked around the room and over at Gordon. "Yes, I can see it's so busy here."

"You just scared that customer away. And I've had a few this morning. Normally it's not like this, but there was a murder here yesterday."

"Yes, I heard about that. Even more reason that we should make a change here."

"Exactly what do you mean by that?" She was making me mad, and I wouldn't wait two more seconds to tell her about it. She was being downright rude to me.

"What I said." She placed her hands on her hips.

"What do you mean, it's time for a change?" I asked, placing my own hands on my hips to mimic her.

"Antoine Dubois clearly can't buy the place now. And it's time for a change here with this building. I plan on buying it and tearing it down. I've run the numbers. I can get more rent from a newer building. We'll put in a nice strip mall and some businesses that will actually benefit the community."

This woman was my landlord's backup buyer. I felt my blood course hot through my veins. Soon it would bubble over and spew out in the form of physical anger. Actually, I wanted to pick her up and toss her out of here. How dare she say that the bakery wasn't good for the community! Everyone loved my pastries. They thought they were magical, with love added. Of course, few customers were coming in today now that word of the murder had spread around town, but that was only temporary. Most people probably thought I was still closed. And now I was beginning to think maybe I *should* have stayed closed another day. That was neither here nor there. People loved my food, and I wanted to continue to provide that for the town, this town that I loved, and I wouldn't let this woman stop me from that.

"You have no idea what you're talking about," I said. "This building has to stay. It's been here a long time."

"It's not on the historic register," she said. "If it's so important, then why isn't it?"

"Well, I'll see to it that it's added," I said.

She scoffed. "Good luck on getting that done. Especially before I buy this place. It'll be nothing more than a memory by the time they even look at the paperwork."

She really was making me furious. I felt the rage coming off me in waves. She had to sense it as well. It probably practically smacked her in the face. She deserved it too. I glanced over my shoulder, because I knew that if Aunt Barb got a load of what was happening, she would most likely lose her temper. If she got angry enough, she'd act like a Tasmanian devil and this place would end up a disaster area. I didn't want a big scene.

The more I thought about what was happening, the more I started to panic. Last night I'd thought things were better, but they had taken a turn for the worse this morning with me coming face-to-face with this woman.

*Okay, calm down, Marci. Don't let the crazy thoughts get to you.* So what would I do now? First thing I needed to do was ask the woman to leave.

So that was exactly what I did.

"You want me to what?" she asked, as if she was in complete shock that anyone would ever ask her to leave an establishment.

Something told me it couldn't have been the first time this had happened to her.

"I'm going to need you to leave my bakery right now."

"You don't own this place, so I don't have to leave."

"I don't want you here, so please go away. This is a business that I own, and I can certainly tell you to go away," I said.

I couldn't believe she was arguing with me about this. Did I have to call the police? I would if I had to, and it was looking more and more like that would be the only option soon.

I felt a presence behind me, and I knew Aunt Barb was approaching. This would not end well for the lady. I needed to get her name and find out who exactly I was dealing with. I would try to keep Aunt Barb from getting too angry before I got her out.

"What is your name?" I asked, glaring at her.

"I'm Audrey Timmons. You'd better get acquainted with that name, because you'll be dealing with it a lot when I buy this building. That is, until I tear it down."

"I told you that you're not tearing it down."

"You want to do what?" Aunt Barb asked in the loudest voice I'd ever heard.

It was so loud that it almost knocked me down as she stood behind me. How could I keep Aunt Barb from attacking this woman? Aunt Barb was really strong. I didn't even know how many push-ups she could do. A lot.

"Okay, everybody needs to just calm down," I said. "No one's tearing down any building."

"Oh yes I am," Audrey said. "You just wait and see."

"I want you to leave right now, before I call the police," I said.

"Before someone gets hurt," Aunt Barb said.

"Oh yeah? What are you going to do about it?" Audrey asked in a mocking tone. "You're not so tough."

She really shouldn't have said that. Aunt Barb turned and ran back toward the kitchen. What was she going to do? Get a sharp object and use it as a weapon? Oh my gosh. What if we had another murder on our hands? No, Aunt Barb would never murder anyone. She just wanted to scare this lady.

The next thing I knew, macarons were whizzing by my head.

What had gotten into Aunt Barb? She wasn't acting like the former drill sergeant I knew. A pink strawberry macaron popped Audrey right in the forehead as if she'd had a bull's-eye in the center. She screeched like she'd just been hit by a boulder. Fifi barked and Pepé Le Pew hissed. They weren't used to this kind of drama in the bakery.

"I can't believe you did that. I'm going to file charges."

"What are you going to tell them happened? That you were attacked with a macaron?"

Audrey turned around and stomped toward the door. Her ego was more injured than her forehead. The macaron had crumbled when it hit her head and fallen to the floor. There was no way it had hurt her. Now, it possibly could have if it had hit her at the right angle, but even then it would only have caused a little scratch. She could never have been seriously harmed. But the way she was acting, it was the end of the world. Aunt Barb threw a mean macaron.

Audrey turned and glared at me one last time. Fifi barked a warning to her, then proceeded over to the macaron remnants and started eating the crumbles.

"You'll be hearing from my lawyer," Audrey said through gritted teeth. "You hit me with a cookie."

I rolled my eyes. I had expected her to say as much. Finally, she opened the door and marched out, letting it slam behind her as she went.

"Well, that was quite a scene. I didn't know I would get a show today," Gordon said.

I didn't even respond to that, because what could I say? It *had* been quite a scene. The murder was already horrible, but now to have had this happen publicly? Word would probably spread pretty quickly that the building would be torn down. I wondered what the rest of the town would say about that. I wanted to think they would like to keep the building here and not have something new built in its place—but not if this building was the site of an unsolved murder. People would want to get rid of any reminder of a dark event.

"What exactly did she say?" Aunt Barb asked as she went over and swept up the crumbled macaron.

"She said she was going to buy this building and tear it down. Then put in a strip mall."

Aunt Barb gasped. "That is preposterous. She can't do something like that. I can't imagine anyone in town would want that either."

"My landlord told me about this too. That woman is the buyer if Antoine can't buy the building."

"Well, we won't panic just yet," Aunt Barb said. "We have to keep a positive attitude. Remember?"

"Yes, keep a positive attitude," I said, giving a sloppy salute. "That's how you got through the army."

Aunt Barb took me by the arm and showed me the correct way to salute. "That's right. Now suck it up, buttercup, and let's get this taken care of."

I felt like I was working with a drill sergeant. Which, technically, I was. But at least she kept me on my toes and kept me moving. Never mind that I might have wanted to just go home and crawl in bed and pull the covers over my eyes.

She grabbed a tray of croissants and headed for the glass display case. Apparently, Aunt Barb was ready to get back to business as usual.

As I stared through the window out onto the street in front of the shop, the knot in my stomach churned as if I'd eaten one of my burnt canistrelli. Yup—sometimes it happened. Canistrelli were a shortbread cookie from Corsica. They were crunchy and delicious when not overcooked. Nothing specifically caught my attention as sinister, but that eerie feeling stuck with me like burnt butter on a cookie sheet.

When I wasn't looking, Aunt Barb had slipped over to Gordon's table and begun chatting with him. She always had been a talker. She might be a little aloof at first, but when she got going, she was quite the charmer. I wondered what they were talking about. When they laughed, I wondered if they were discussing my latest goof-ups.

As I headed back toward the kitchen, the bell above the door caught my attention again. Had Audrey Timmons returned? I certainly hoped not. Aunt Barb and I whipped around to see that Detective Maverick had stepped into the shop. My heart sped up a bit. I hadn't been expecting to see him.

He sure was Mr. Tall, Dark, and Handsome. He wore a white dress shirt and a red tie with tailored black slacks. I had to admit I loved his short, mussed hair and strong jaw. Had he always had that scar above his right eye? A closer inspection was in order.

"Oh, Detective Malone," Aunt Barb said. "Isn't it nice to see you here!"

What she meant was that she was happy to see an opportunity for him to flirt with me. But I had a feeling he wasn't here to seduce me. He was here because a murder had taken place. Or because that woman had just left. What if she'd called the cops and told them she had been attacked with a cookie?

"What are you doing here, Detective Malone?" I asked.

As if I needed to ask that question. Sometimes I was so awkward around him and didn't know what to say.

"We just got a call about a disturbance here. I wanted to make sure you're okay and see what happened. Considering there was just a murder here."

So Audrey had called after all. How rotten of her.

"Yes, well, this woman came in and said she was going to tear down the building," I said.

Maverick's eyes widened. "Tear down the building?"

"Yes, she wants to buy it and tear it down."

He shook his head. "That won't happen."

"I wouldn't be so sure about that, Detective," I said.

"Why did she call me? What happened in here?"

"Well, because Aunt Barb hit her with a macaron," I said.

He laughed. "Oh, Aunt Barb, please don't hit customers with cookies."

"That 'cookie' couldn't have hurt her," Aunt Barb said.

"Well, if everything is all right here, I guess I'll let you get back to the macarons," he said.

"Yes, everything is just fine. Thank you, Detective Malone," I said.

"Wait just a minute," Aunt Barb said with a wave of her hand.

Oh no. Was this when she'd ask him if he wanted to go out on a date with me?

"I wanted to give you a pastry," she said, trying to sound innocent.

Aunt Barb was just stalling for more time so she could ask him more questions about being my potential boyfriend. I knew what she was up to. When he glanced away for a split second, Aunt Barb motioned with a tilt of her head for me to move closer to him.

"Oh, well, thank you, Aunt Barb," he said, turning his attention back to her. "I really shouldn't."

The way her name rolled off his tongue made me melt a little. He acted like he'd been a part of my family for years, and I liked it. He sounded so sweet calling her Aunt Barb. Nevertheless, I knew nothing could ever come of us, so there was no point in even thinking about it.

"Oh no, sir, I insist you take one," Aunt Barb said. "Plus, after the murder yesterday, things aren't exactly hopping around here. We're going to have a lot of extra pastries."

"I'm sure customers will be fine with coming back soon. Most people probably think you're still closed for the day," Maverick said.

"I hope that's the case," I said.

"I wouldn't worry about it," he said, giving me a wink.

Of course I felt a little giddy when he did that. Hoping he didn't notice me blushing, I hurried back behind the counter to help Aunt Barb prepare pastries for him. I felt him watching me as I placed a palmier, an éclair, a croissant, and a few assorted macarons into a pink box. I knew my cheeks were probably red because I'd felt the heat rush to them. It wasn't because of the oven either.

I sensed that maybe Maverick wanted to ask me something, and I had a feeling it wasn't about the murder, just by the way he watched me. Was that desire in his eyes? Or was I imagining it? Yes, probably my imagination. I tried not to look at him, but I kept glancing over in spite of myself. His stare was making butterflies flutter in my stomach. I had to remind myself that he made all the ladies around town feel that way—and he knew it—and I shouldn't fall for it.

I handed Maverick the box. "I hope you enjoy them."

"Let me pay you for that," he said as he reached for his wallet.

I waved my hand dismissively. "It's a thank-you."

"For what?" he asked.

"For being so great with the investigation so far."

He chuckled. "I haven't done anything other than my job. We don't have the killer yet."

"Don't I know that," I said. "Should we be worried walking around town? I mean, what if the killer comes back?"

"The chances of him coming back here are slim. Besides, I think we know who the killer is."

"You don't mean Antoine?"

He raised an eyebrow. "I can't say anything else."

"You have no evidence against him."

"What makes you so sure he didn't do it?"

"I just have a feeling, that's all."

"Well, we can't go by feelings, can we?" He followed the words with a frown.

"No, but I also have a feeling that the real killer will be exposed soon enough."

His eyes snapped to mine as if he was wondering what I was talking about, but I wouldn't say a word about what I had planned.

Maverick held the box and continued to stare at me for what seemed like forever. He didn't say anything. Was I supposed to do something else now? He had that funny look on his face.

"So I was wondering," he started, finally breaking the silence. He didn't take his eyes off me. I wanted to look away, but I held my gaze on his.

"I wondered if you would like to have dinner soon. As soon as you're available . . . tonight, tomorrow night?"

Aunt Barb made a noise, something like an *aww* sound. She was practically swooning back there. But I couldn't go out with him. I wouldn't put myself through that.

"I'm sorry, but I have a lot of work. I just don't think it would be possible."

His smile instantly turned. He looked disappointed, but probably just because he wasn't getting his way.

"Right, well, I can see you're busy, so I'll get out of your hair. I'll be in touch with you soon, and thanks for the pastries, ladies." He turned around in a hurry and headed out of the shop.

That had been an awkward end to the conversation. I felt kind of bad, but I had to stand my ground. I'd set those boundaries, and I wouldn't back down now. I was sure he'd find another date soon enough. Although, unlike the city with the large Eiffel Tower, our town had a small replica Eiffel Tower and a small population to match. Maybe the few other ladies would catch on to his ways too.

Perhaps he would go to Lexington and find a lucky lady there to date. It just wasn't going to be here in Paris and in my bakeshop. Besides, I had other things to worry about.

But if I truly thought this way, why did I feel like someone had punched me in the stomach when he walked out the door and didn't look back? I fought back the tears welling in my eyes.

# Chapter Eleven

"What in the name of country-fried chicken are you doing?" Aunt Barb yelled.

It was like when I was a child and I used to sneak cookies from the jar during visits to her house.

I whipped around to look at her. "What do you mean?"

"You turned down that gorgeous man. He obviously adores you, and he would be a wonderful husband. And you're just going to toss that away like a day-old éclair."

"I'm sorry, but I'm not sure he's serious. Look at the way he acted in high school."

"The man was a teenager. Give him a chance. He's a grown adult now. People change."

"No, people don't change. Have you changed one bit since you were a teenager?" I asked.

"Why yes, I am older and wiser now," she said. "That's change."

"Older, wiser, and set in your ways, that's all. You're just more stubborn than you were. Nothing has changed. Your personality's still the same bubbling one you had back then."

She stared at me in contemplation. "Well, I suppose you're right about that. I am bubbly."

I'd been sarcastic with my comment, but she was ignoring that. If by bubbly she meant crude oil bubbling from the ground, then yes, she was bubbly. But I wouldn't point that out.

"Besides, Aunt Barb, I have other things to worry about, like getting business back into this shop."

"I wouldn't worry about that," she said, motioning toward the door.

When I looked over my shoulder, I saw customers headed toward the front door. Mrs. O'Neal and Mrs. Mansfield, two peas in their nosy pod. Also Mrs. Jenkins, minus all her cats. The bell jingled repeatedly as customer after customer filed into the shop. I couldn't believe it. They had turned my bad day around quickly. The customers had been late, but they'd shown up. I guessed they'd figured out that the bakery was open after all. And they still couldn't refuse my love pastries. Joy made my stomach tingle with excitement.

Then again, the townsfolk were probably only here to get the latest gossip. The giddiness subsided with the thought.

Fifi and Pepé Le Pew stood by the front door, watching as customers left. Pepé Le Pew wore her usual irritated scowl, while Fifi was hoping someone would drop a few big crumbs on their way out.

Unfortunately, Aunt Barb was still mad at me. She made that perfectly clear throughout the day as we waited on customers and kept busy. It was a flurry of activity, so I didn't have a whole lot of chance to think about her anger, but I felt it every time she glared at me. She was still upset that I had turned Maverick down. But she'd get over it. She'd have to, because I wasn't going to change my mind. There was nothing Maverick could do to make me—not even if he gave me that lopsided grin or that little wink with his beautiful steely eyes. None of that worked, even if he did make my heart dance a little.

When the crowd had settled down and it was almost time to close for the day, I had time to talk with Aunt Barb and find out if she was still upset with me. She couldn't stay angry for too long over something as simple as turning down a date. There were much worse things she could be mad about. Like when I didn't add enough butter to a recipe—she liked to come along behind me and add extra.

I turned to face Aunt Barb. She wasn't looking at me as she stirred batter in the bowl, pretending she was too busy to talk.

"Aunt Barb, are you going to ignore me all day?" I asked.

She didn't speak.

"I can't go out with him," I said.

"And why not?" she asked, putting the wooden spoon down and staring at me.

"I told you why."

"That's not a valid reason," she said.

"It is a completely valid reason. I want someone who's going to be faithful and loyal, not a womanizer," I said.

"He is not a womanizer, and I don't know where you got that idea other than what you think you know from years ago."

"He took another girl to prom and stood me up," I snapped.

I needed to get a hold of my feelings. That had been years ago, and I was over it. Okay, maybe I still held on to anger, but that wasn't even important right now. I had other problems at the moment.

"His car broke down, and he said that girl just gave him a ride to the dance," Aunt Barb said.

"Well, thanks for the recap, but it's neither here nor there right now, because I have other things to do."

"Like what?" she asked.

"Like making sure this building isn't sold out from under me. I'm going to call Antoine."

"Oh, Antoine, the Frenchman. *Oh là là*," she said, mocking me.

I rolled my eyes. It was pretty clear who she wanted me to date, even though she had thought Antoine was handsome.

"I'll go out with Maverick when *you* have a date," I said.

"Oh, don't say such things," Aunt Barb said with a wave of her hand.

After closing shop and cleaning up, I decided it was time to call Antoine. I would tell him about Audrey and see if he had any updates on his defense, but I wanted to do it in a quiet place where Aunt Barb wouldn't interrupt me with talk about Maverick or anything else she thought was urgent at the moment. And it just so happened that Aunt Barb was taking Fifi and Pepé Le Pew to the pet store for treats and toys.

After locking up and saying au revoir to the three of them, I went out to my car. I had driven to work today because I figured it would be safer.

I sat inside my car to call Antoine. Unfortunately, after several rings, he didn't answer, so now I was forced to leave him a message.

"Um, this is Marci Beaucoup. Will you please call me back as soon as possible, please? Talk to you soon. Thank you."

I had to be realistic and at least consider the idea that Antoine was Kellie's killer. And that thought was terrifying, because who wanted to be around a murderer? Had I just left the killer a voice message? Would he come after me next? All I knew was I needed to get to the bottom of this.

But really, Antoine as the killer? I mean, he just didn't have that vibe. How would I find out, though? Maybe I should have done this already, but I needed to know more about Kellie Lowry. She might just lead me right to her killer.

The first person I thought of visiting was her landlord. By going to her house, perhaps? That would give me a lead on other family members or friends. I could get to know Kellie more and find out exactly what she'd been doing leading up to her death. Perhaps someone had been stalking her or she'd had an enemy. Obviously, since she'd been murdered, someone didn't like her.

Luckily, I'd brought a box full of macarons with me. I'd been planning to give them to my neighbor, Mrs. Biggs, as a thank-you for bringing me back an Eiffel Tower snow globe from her recent Paris trip. I would just have to wait and do that tomorrow. Instead, I would give them to the landlord Naomi Perry, a peace offering so that maybe she would give me the information I needed. A bribe, if you will.

I pulled up in front of the white two-story house. It was older, probably built around the turn of the last century. Gordon had told me Kellie had been renting the top floor.

The owner of the house lived at the bottom, so I parked my car and got out. I walked up the path to the front door with the box of cookies in hand. I stood on the wide front porch in front of the door. Yellow and burgundy chrysanthemums took up most of the porch floor. I pushed the doorbell, and nothing happened. It must not be working.

I pounded against the door and waited, but I heard nothing on the other side. Now I worried that maybe no one was home. I'd just have to come back some other time. I knocked on the door again, and to my surprise, I heard footsteps sounding from inside the house. I got a little nervous as I went over what I was going to say in my mind. I waited for the door, and a few seconds later, after a couple of unlocks, it cracked open just a bit. The gray-haired woman eyed me up and down.

"Good evening, ma'am. My name is Marci Beaucoup. I'm here to speak with you about your tenant Kellie Lowry."

She got ready to close the door, but I thrust my hand forward and forced her to stop.

She eyed the pink box, and the promise of macarons must have worked, because she opened the door farther. "What do you want to talk about? I've already talked to the police."

"Yes, ma'am, I know, but I just have some questions for you. I won't take up much of your time. Plus, I brought you these macarons from my bakery. I have the bakeshop in town."

"Oh yes, I thought I recognized you," she said. "I've been meaning to stop by there, but it looks awfully fancy, and I'm not sure it would be a place I would want to come inside."

"Oh, it's not that fancy," I said. "I think you would like it. You should come in sometime. Anytime." I thrust the bakery box at her again, and this time she took it. "Though I am worried how much longer I'll be in business, after what happened. That shop is my livelihood. I have everything invested in it."

She studied my face for a moment, and her expression softened. "Would you like to come inside?"

She still didn't sound that enthused at the prospect, but she'd invited me and I wanted to ask questions, so I agreed. I followed her into the dimly lit house. We moved to the right and into a parlor filled with antique-looking furniture covered in burgundy and gold velvet.

"Please have a seat anywhere you'd like," she said.

She pointed at the sofa by the window, though, so I assumed that was where she really wanted me to sit down. I perched on the edge of the sofa, placing my hands in my lap. I waited as she took a seat in the big wingback chair by the fireplace. She held the box of macarons in her lap, opened it up, and took one out, then immediately took a bite. I smiled at her eagerness, hoping she was enjoying it. I waited until she finished chewing before I started talking again.

"I just have questions about Kellie, like I said—if you knew any of her friends or family."

She shook her head. "I don't think she has any living relatives anymore, and I guess the girl doesn't have any friends. I never saw anyone with her. She was always alone, and she never spoke of anyone either."

No friends and no family. That would make this very difficult. "There was no one she was around?" I pressed.

"Just that handsome fella, but apparently, they had a fight, because she came home crying and stormed upstairs the day before she was murdered. I asked her what was wrong, and she said he had broken her heart and she didn't want to talk about it."

"Well, that's sad," I said. "Do you know what he did?"

"No, I'm not positive. Wait. You know, as a matter of fact, there was one other person who came around quite often."

I sat up a little straighter, suddenly curious. "Who's that?"

"Her boss, George Gustavsson. Since she was his assistant, I guess he felt like she was always at his beck and call. He was always coming over to see her, I'm assuming bringing more work to her, which didn't seem quite fair, considering she shouldn't have been doing anything during her off-duty hours. The manufacturing company has been doing well, so I guess it added some pressure to George's job to keep that going. I guess she was really driven and wanted to get ahead in the company, so she would agree to anything George wanted."

"Anything else you can tell me about him?" I asked.

"I don't know." She shrugged. "I saw him sitting outside, staring at the house sometimes. Which seemed kind of odd, but maybe he was waiting for her to come outside."

"Did she go out and talk to him?" I asked.

"He usually left before she went outside. It was a strange situation."

"That is interesting," I said. "Did you tell the police about this?"

She shook her head. "No, I forgot, and I didn't think it would be important. After all, they seemed focused on the ex-boyfriend as the suspect. It seems like a cut-and-dry case."

"Yes, I suppose that is what they're focusing on, but I have reason to believe it's not him."

"What's your reason?" she said with a raised eyebrow.

Could I tell her it was just a feeling? I knew there were witnesses who supposedly had seen him. So what was my reason? My only reason was because he seemed like a nice guy. Had I only imagined his sweet demeanor? Holding doors open for people and saying *s'il vous plait* or *merci* didn't equal a nice guy. Was it because I thought he was handsome and that he wasn't really a murdering lunatic? Ugh. I was going nowhere with this. Sometimes my thoughts were all over the place.

"I guess it was just how he interacted with her. He seemed nice and kind even though she was quite angry with him. He remained calm and never acted as if he was angry at all."

She eyed me for a moment, then said, "Well, that makes sense, I suppose. I guess if he was really mean, he would have lost his temper right away."

I nodded. "Yes, that's what I believe."

She took another macaron from the box and took a bite. I smiled again. Apparently the macarons were a success. Not to brag, but I had to admit they were quite good. With just the right amount of sweetness, each wonderful flavor brought a subtle burst of taste. Actually, I wished I could sell them nationally. Everyone would love them better than Ladurée macarons. My favorite flavors were pistachio, chocolate, and strawberry, though the vanilla ones melted in my mouth too. The almond meal and confectioners' sugar blended into a perfectly puffy, smooth surface. Then I stuffed the jam, buttercream, or ganache in the middle.

"I appreciate the information. Thank you. I'm just so worried that I will lose my shop because of this. Customers might stop coming in. Is there anything else you can think of?"

She finished chewing the macaron and shook her head. "Nothing that comes to mind. I'm sorry I can't help more."

"You've been a lot of help," I said.

At least I had something to go on now. I would talk to Kellie's boss. Based on the information on Mr. Gustavsson's business card, he worked at Flaget Manufacturing, same as Antoine; did that mean Kellie and Antoine had been coworkers? At any rate, surely her boss would know her better than Naomi knew her. He could give me more details of her life. I hoped he didn't just agree with the police and say he thought Antoine had done it.

I wanted to speak with Mr. Gustavsson as soon as possible, but since I assumed he was gone from work for the day, I would probably have to wait.

Though I guessed it wouldn't take long for me to swing by the paper plant and see if perhaps he was still around. All I had to go on was a name. I didn't have a car type to see if his car was even in the parking lot or anything else. I wondered if they would even let me in the building. I assumed there was a security guard or something.

I pushed to my feet. "Thank you for everything, and please stop by the bakery sometime."

"The cookies are delicious. Thank you so much."

"You're quite welcome. I'll see myself out."

Ms. Perry nodded and continued to nibble on the cookie as I headed for the door.

As I hurried across the street toward my car, a rustling noise caught my attention. Furthermore, I thought I caught movement out of the corner of my eye. It sounded as if it had come from the nearby bushes. Though I saw nothing now, I felt as if someone was watching me. I rushed my steps—the feeling gave me the creeps. When I reached the car door, I looked around, but I saw no one. I looked back at Ms. Perry's house, thinking that maybe she was watching me, but she wasn't at the door. I guessed I was just spooked after everything that had happened and tried to shake the feeling off, but it wouldn't go away. It stuck with me like glue.

I opened the car and slid inside, locking it behind me. I felt somewhat safer now. I released a deep breath. At least I was in the safe haven of my car, and no one could get to me. Why did I feel like someone was ready to attack me? It sent a shiver up and down my spine.

I cranked the engine and hurried away from the curb, getting out of there before someone had a chance to get me. I looked in the rearview mirror to see if anyone was following me but noticed nothing out of the ordinary. There were no cars back there, so it had to have been my imagination. Maybe I needed some rest—my mind was seriously starting to play games with me now, and that wasn't a good sign. I would never solve this puzzle if I was too busy having strange feelings and being paranoid that someone was following me.

# Chapter Twelve

I tried to enjoy the ride to the building where I hoped to find Kellie's boss. Enjoying the trip wasn't easy, though. The only reason I wanted to enjoy it was because I felt like I needed to destress before I had a huge panic attack. The anxiety in my stomach had already settled in; that was the first sign that my feelings could soon turn to full-fledged panic mode. I'd made it this far, so I didn't want to let my anxiety take over. After all, I'd managed to get through finding a murder victim on my front doorstep. Surely this couldn't be worse than that. No more dead bodies, please.

I tended to let my anxiety get the best of me sometimes. Maybe that reaction came across as flighty, but it was just the way my brain handled stress. With this situation though, I felt my anxious feelings were valid.

Thank goodness the place wasn't that far. Less than a mile and I'd be there. I flipped the radio off, and silence filled the car. This left me with my thoughts, so I turned it on again. I was so antsy that I was getting on my own nerves.

Up ahead the building came into view, and then I started to worry even more. The place was so large that I wondered if I would be able to locate the man, even if he *was* still here. Would someone point me in the right direction, or would they tell me to get lost? It was getting late too, and with each passing second, I ran the risk of him no longer being at work.

The factory complex took up the entire block. One section housed the manufacturing facilities, and the other held the offices. I headed for the office section. I had no plan for this visit, as usual, so I decided to wing it. Part of me wished Aunt Barb was with me. I wondered whether, if I called her, she'd come over right away. She could be my backup. But I figured she was busy. Likely she'd just tell me not to get involved.

So I'd just have to do this on my own. *This* being one of the craziest things I'd ever done. Although there was that one time when I'd helped my friend locate her missing boyfriend—turned out he had passed out from drinking too much. We found him in the middle of a cornfield and had to drag him all the way to the car, then lift his body up into the back seat. It had looked as if we were kidnapping him when we stuffed him into the trunk. No one had come along to help him either.

Since it had been such a remote area, we should've just left him out there. It would have served him right. But he'd ultimately learned his lesson—she finally broke up with him. It still boggled my mind how long she'd stayed with him. In her defense, though, the dating pool in Paris sure was awful. I mean, don't get me wrong, there was a dating pool, but it was murky and dangerous. I'd gone on some terrible first dates, no second date required. Like the time my date showed up wearing a Santa costume and then got drunk. I had to call an Uber for him. I mean, who wants to deal with a drunk Santa? Fake beard falling off, stuffing from his belly coming out, and he lost his bag full of empty wrapped boxes. Sure, it had been close to Christmas. A week before Thanksgiving.

He knew I loved Christmas. I supposed the sentiment was nice, but just the same, I'd rather my date had worn a nice pair of pants and dress shirt. No costumes, please. I didn't want to be Mrs. Claus.

Up ahead, I spotted the sign for the main entrance. Should I use the main entrance, though, or be less conspicuous and use one of the back entrances? Furthermore, there was still time to back out. I could just drive past, turn around, and head back to town. No one was forcing me to do this, and I was having second thoughts. However, when I came to the turnoff to the main entrance, I whipped into the drive, hoping that I'd gain access to the inside of the building. I would just be honest with Mr. Gustavsson, get straight to the point, and tell him why I was here.

With any luck, he would understand and answer all my questions. Hey, maybe I would even solve this murder right away. Stranger things had happened. I had to keep a positive attitude, like Aunt Barb said. If not, I might lose the business I'd worked so hard to grow, and my innocent Antoine could go to prison.

It was all about having the time to do it. Right now, I was forcing myself to find the time. It wouldn't be easy, though. I'd have to get to work on baking before the sun was even up tomorrow.

My hopes at this going smoothly and quickly were soon dashed. I'd come upon a huge block in my investigation. Literally. I stared at the large silver metal gate barring me from the main entrance. It looked as if there would be no way I'd be able to get through, and I could see a security camera pointed straight at me.

What had I just been saying? Even though I'd been thrown a bit of a curve ball didn't mean I couldn't find another strategy. I hadn't gotten this far in life only to let something like this stop me. What was a little metal? If there was a way around this, I would find it, I thought—wondering how many pep talks I would have to give myself today. I scanned my surroundings to see if there was a guard or another employee, but no one was in sight.

This was kind of a good thing, but kind of a bad thing at the same time. A security guard would probably stop me in my tracks, but another employee might actually help. Maybe I could charm my way inside and get them to open the gate for me. Plenty of cars were in the parking lot, so I held out hope that I might run into someone. I just hoped it was the right someone.

At this point, I didn't have a way to conceal my identity—or my car, for that matter. I was right out there and exposed for everyone to see. I'd made no attempt at stealth. Could I climb the fence? Oh, what was I saying? I could barely climb on the counter at work to reach the top shelf for the extra supplies Aunt Barb always stuck up there. If she ever wanted to keep something out of my reach, all she had to do was stick it on one of those shelves.

Hmm. What other plan could I come up with? I couldn't ram my car through the gate to get inside.

I'd just have to look for another way in. There had to be more than one entrance; this was a big place.

I put the car in reverse and backed out onto the road once again. I hoped that if I found another gate, it would be open, although that seemed highly unlikely. At least I could tell myself I'd tried.

I drove around the side of the building, looking for another way into the lot. When I came to the next gate, I stopped and just sat there on the street. What had I been thinking? Of course all the gates would be closed. Why would they leave them open? It looked as if the only way in would be if I had a card to scan or a code.

Just as I was ready to give up, a new wave of energy swept through me, as if something was telling me not to give up. Not yet. My mama said I was stubborn, and her assessment was proving to be true.

My phone rang, and I looked at the screen. Aunt Barb was calling. Somehow I felt guilty, as if she knew what I was doing. Did she know? Of course there was no way she could know—unless someone had seen me on the surveillance cameras and told her I was here. I didn't think she knew anyone who worked here, but it was a distinct possibility, because Aunt Barb knew a lot of people in town. A lot of people knew her too. She had the kind of personality that commanded attention without being too harsh.

Should I answer the call or let it go to voice mail? I knew Aunt Barb wouldn't text. She never texted. It wasn't like she didn't know how, but if I texted her, she would call me back. On the other hand, if I didn't answer her call, she would just call me over and over again. Maybe even at a time when it would be inconvenient or bad for me to get a call, like when I was talking to Kellie's boss inside the office.

I reluctantly picked up. "Aunt Barb, is everything okay?"

She usually called only if there was a problem.

"Where are you?" she asked.

Oh no. Now I really felt as if she knew. How could she know?

"I'm just running some errands."

A pause settled between us. She sensed I wasn't telling the truth. I didn't know how she did it, but she could always tell. She knew I was making something up, but I wouldn't let on that I knew she knew. I would keep up the facade. Aunt Barb asked a few more questions about my errands, but finally she just asked me straight out.

"Now why don't you tell me the truth?" Aunt Barb asked.

"I am telling the truth, Aunt Barb," I said with my fingers crossed.

While still on the call with Aunt Barb, I sat there for what seemed like a half hour, contemplating what I would say or do next. In reality, only a couple of moments passed. How long would I wait before giving up and finally admitting defeat—admitting to Aunt Barb that I was attempting breaking and entering, and then driving back home without finding Mr. Gustavsson?

Movement caught my attention, and then I spotted a red car approaching the gate on the other side. The driver waited for the gate to open. Since the gate moved slowly, could I take the chance and slip inside once it was open? I had to. It was my only shot. There was no other way inside. I'd wait until the car was out of the way, then drive through to the other side before the gate closed. I had to drive fast enough to get through, but whether I could pull it off depended on how fast that other car got out of my way.

"What is that noise?" Aunt Barb asked. "Sounds like a car."

"Well, I am driving, Aunt Barb." My voice was shaky, like I was out of breath.

My heart beat faster at the thought of getting caught, either because someone knew I wasn't supposed to be there and came after me or because I'd gotten stuck in the gate as it closed. Then they would surely call the police on me. How would I explain that to Maverick? I might not want to date him, but I certainly didn't want to be embarrassed in front of him either.

Finally, the gate was fully open, and the car drove through. I inched forward just a bit, hoping they wouldn't realize what I was doing. Then, as soon as they turned to the left and drove out, I gunned my gas pedal and zoomed right through the open gate.

"Are you speeding?" Aunt Barb asked.

I was inside the fenced-off parking lot. I'd done it.

"Yes!" I yelled.

"Oh, for heaven's sake, you scared me. Why are you yelling?" Aunt Barb asked.

Oops. I'd forgotten I was on the phone.

"I made the yellow light," I said.

"You need to slow down," Aunt Barb said.

Now what? Now that I was in the lot, I drove toward the office building. I decided I didn't want to find a spot right up front, though.

"I'd better go, Aunt Barb, so that I can concentrate on driving. I'll call you," I said.

"You'd better," she said, before ending the call.

Now I could focus on getting inside. I kept to the back of the lot, as if that would conceal me from cameras. It was a risk I'd have to take. I found a spot close to a shade tree and decided that would be the best place for me to park, as I'd be somewhat out of sight. No one would be suspicious if I got out of the car and headed to the building. With any luck, I'd find Kellie's boss quickly. I'd ask him a few questions, solve the case, and then we'd all put this behind us. As much as possible. I mean, I'd never truly forget about what had happened or get over finding Kellie's body.

After parking, I sat in the car for quite some time, thinking about my next move. I had to prepare my plan of action. If I didn't get this over with soon, I would miss the opportunity. Maybe Mr. Gustavsson would be leaving soon, if he wasn't already gone. Thinking about not losing the shop kept me motivated. I opened the car door and got out.

My phone rang again. Aunt Barb was calling back.

"Are you sure you're not up to something?" she asked when I answered.

Walking away from the car, I hurried across the lot, nervous that I would soon be caught. I looked around to see if someone might be in the parking lot with me, but I noticed no one, just cars and plenty of open parking spaces.

"I'm just parking," I whispered.

"Why are you whispering?" she asked with suspicion in her voice.

"Am I? I hadn't noticed."

"You're still doing it," she said.

It looked as if a lot of people had gone home for the day. It was already kind of spooky around here. I almost felt as if someone was watching me, but surely that was only because someone *could* be watching from inside the building via the security cameras. They would be wondering why I was here. I hoped they'd think I was just an employee. After all, it looked like plenty of employees were still working at this late hour of the afternoon.

"Do I have to come looking for you?" Aunt Barb asked.

I headed for the first door I saw—it didn't matter if it was the main one or not. I just wanted to get inside the building and track Mr. Gustavsson down. The longer I put it off, the worse it would get.

"No!" I said a little louder than I'd intended. "I mean, I'm fine, Aunt Barb. I'm just a little distracted. I'll call you back, though."

I ended the call and decided I'd just have to not answer if she called again. Though she might truly come looking for me.

I'd reached the door by now and looked around one last time to see if anyone was really spying on me. The eerie feeling of being watched stayed with me, but I reached for the door handle anyway.

When I checked the door, it was locked. Had I really expected anything less? Of course the doors were locked. Why would they leave them open? They probably wanted to keep people like me out of a secure area. Maybe they had money in there; I didn't know all they did here at this company.

As I headed around the building to look for other doors, I looked back to see if there was some kind of keypad for entrance or a lock that opened in some special way, but I saw nothing other than the keyhole below the handle. That meant someone needed a key to get in, and that someone wasn't me. I had no key.

Movement caught my attention. When I looked over my shoulder, I spotted a security guard walking toward the building. My heart rate sped up. Was he coming for me? He wasn't looking in my direction, so I wasn't sure if he had noticed me yet. Maybe they'd seen me on the surveillance feed, stalking the building, and that was why he was coming over here. Either way, I needed to get out of there before he actually caught up to me. There was no telling what he would do. Handcuff me? Throw me in a holding cell where they kept all the trespassers? Maybe there was no way out of here. Maybe I would even get so far as to talk to Kellie's boss and then still not get away from here.

*Positive thinking, Marci, positive thinking. Remember what Aunt Barb said.* All those negative thoughts weren't getting me anywhere.

So far, he still hadn't noticed me. I stopped walking, and as I stood watching him, he made a shift to his left. Then I realized he was headed my way. We were on a collision course.

# Chapter Thirteen

I didn't think he'd noticed me yet. And I wanted to keep it that way. What would I do now? If I ran toward my car, he would surely see me. Could I hide from him? My anxiety had reached an all-time high. I dove behind a nearby evergreen bush. Tiny needles on the branches poked at the exposed skin of my arms and face, and I landed on the ground behind the bush. That dive was definitely going to leave a bruise in the morning. The scent of pine and earth surrounded me. A branch full of sharp leaves slapped me in the face.

There was nothing I could do about it right now, though. I had to stay behind the bush so the security guard wouldn't see me. Though I really wanted to know what he was doing. Maybe I could peek out and watch him. Would he notice me? There was no way to predict the future. I'd have to hope for the best. I tried to stay as quiet as possible, like a mouse hiding from a cat.

Noticing that I was holding my breath, I reminded myself to breathe. Then, mustering my courage, I slowly eased up from behind the bush and peeked his way. I prayed that he wouldn't look mine. He stood in front of the door. I watched as he pulled a ring of keys from his pocket and shoved one into the door lock. Just as he reached out to grab the door handle, he looked over his shoulder. I immediately ducked down behind the bush again. He had to have seen me, right? There was no way he'd missed me.

I remained completely still, bracing myself for the worst. No need to get my hopes up and expect that he wouldn't rip me out from behind the bush.

How long should I wait before checking to see what he was doing? If he hadn't gone in and he hadn't grabbed me, then what was he doing? I figured I would count to ten and then peek out for another look. I tried to steady my breath as I counted. Maybe I was even dragging out each number. I didn't want to wait too long, though, because I had to know what he was up to.

When I finally reached ten, I kept my promise to myself and peeked up once again. It took every ounce of my courage, but I did it.

He was standing there, looking for something in his pocket. He pulled out a couple pieces of paper and then shoved them back when he'd decided they weren't what he was looking for. One of the papers dropped to the ground. He didn't notice. Instead he grabbed the door handle once again and then walked inside. He never looked my way.

Honestly, he didn't seem like a good security guard. If he'd been good, he would have noticed me. He would have sensed me watching him. He disappeared inside the building.

Now was my chance to do something. I had to at least try to see if he'd left the door unlocked. Plus, I needed to pick up that piece of paper he'd lost on the sidewalk. My curiosity burned—I really wanted to know what was written on the little slip of white paper. It looked smaller than a receipt. I rushed out from behind the bush, trying not to trip and land face first back in the branches.

I maneuvered around the bush. Thank goodness I was still standing. Although I smelled like a Christmas tree. I probably had a few pine needles in my hair too. I had to hurry up before the man decided to come back outside. My heart beat faster as I reached the sidewalk and leaned down to pick up the paper. It was a business card.

In small black font, the name MICHAEL ELMWOOD was written on the front with the title HEAD OF SECURITY underneath. Wow, he was head of security? He was even worse at his job than I'd thought. But that was neither here nor there now. I'd found a card like this at the scene of the crime. Of course, that card had given Kellie's boss's info. Nevertheless, it was strange that this man had dropped his card as well. He would have worked with Kellie too—were they all butterfingers here? Would the security guard have been at my bakery? Could he have dropped Mr. Gustavsson's card?

Perhaps I needed to question him too, since he'd worked with Kellie. He was on my radar now. Though I supposed that dropping a business card wasn't enough evidence to put him on the suspects list.

I moved so fast for the door handle that it was like I was in a race for my life. As I ran, I checked all around to see if anyone else was nearby. Perhaps another security guard?

I hoped to get inside before Mr. Elmwood returned. This was my only opportunity. I prayed that he wouldn't look back and notice me entering the building. I was out here in the open without the pine bush to conceal me. Nevertheless, I pushed forward. Being caught was a chance I had to take.

When I reached the door, I grabbed the handle and yanked. I almost fell backward onto the sidewalk. The door wasn't as heavy as it looked, and he'd left it unlocked.

With the door open now, I slipped easily into the building. I couldn't believe I'd made it this far. Hallways stretched out in front of me. Doors lined each side as far as I could see. Where had the guard gone? This wouldn't be easy. I couldn't try every door. I had no idea what was in each room. Offices, probably, and people wouldn't be happy with me just barging in.

Even though the security guard was nowhere in sight, and I should be thankful for that, I kind of wanted to catch up to him. For starters, if I knew when he was coming back, then I could determine how much I'd be able to accomplish during this visit. But catching up to the security guard could also get me kicked out of the building, and I didn't want to risk it. Kellie's boss might be able to answer a lot of questions for me, and it was imperative that I speak with him right away.

Now that I was in the building, though, the thought hit me: what in the world would I really do next? It wasn't like I could stop someone and ask them for directions. No doubt any verified, invited visitors were encouraged to check in at the main entrance. I had doubts that I would have been allowed entrance, though, because who would I say had invited me or given me a pass? Therefore, I'd felt I had to sneak in. Had I lost my marbles by doing this? What would Aunt Barb say? What would Maverick say?

The middle of this hallway looked like it crossed with another hallway. Was that where the security guard had gone? Maybe I'd be able to figure out where the main offices were located. It was worth a shot. I supposed it was my only option.

If anyone was suspicious of me, I'd tell them I was looking for a company to print menus for me. Maybe they'd know I was lying right away. I wondered if my picture had been in the newspaper— I'd forgotten to even check. If so, I just hoped people didn't think I'd done something so horrific as murder. The thought that people around town might look at me as a suspect was horrible to think about, so I had even more reason to find the killer. I should have checked the newspaper's afternoon edition. With news this scandalous, they'd have wanted to run to the presses with an account of the happenings right away.

There was no sign of the security guard, and I had no way to know where he'd gone. For all I knew, he was going to the exact spot I needed to go. How would I explain that away if I showed up in the same room as him and he'd actually seen me outside? Maybe he'd only pretended not to see me so he could find out what I did next. I still hadn't changed out of my uniform—pink-and-white-striped shirt with matching pants—so I'd be easy to remember. I looked like a stick of chewing gum. The security guard would think I was dressed for Halloween. I should have changed my clothes to something less conspicuous.

I pushed my shoulders back and held my head up high. Acting as if I belonged here could only work to my advantage. Now that I was in the building, I had to figure out where I was going. I had no idea where any of the offices were. It would be easy for me to get lost in here if I wasn't careful. Then I'd definitely be in big trouble.

Another question popped into my head. How would I get out of this building? My shoulders slumped again with that thought. My confidence waned. What if I needed a key code to open the door? Surely they wouldn't lock all the doors. That would be a fire safety issue. If I was stuck in here all night, the security guard would surely find me. Then I'd be arrested. Dragged out of the building in handcuffs. That would probably make the front page of the newspaper. What would my mama and daddy say?

I decided that aimlessly roaming around wouldn't do me any good. I was just wasting time. I needed to look for an office directory. Perhaps that would tell me where to find Mr. Gustavs-son's office.

I eased down the hallway, my anxiety so high that I thought I might hyperventilate. So much for looking like I belonged and that I had copious amounts of confidence. Now I was just try-ing to make it through. I kept close to the wall, as if that might conceal me. Like I'd blend into the wall before anyone actually spotted me. Too bad they didn't have pink-and-white-striped wall-paper. At any moment, someone could come out of one of the rooms. I hoped they didn't open a door when I was right next to it. I didn't want to be smacked in the face.

With each step, my anxiety grew. The longer I was in this building, the tighter my chest felt and the more my stomach churned. I seriously needed a Tums.

Finally, I came to the intersection of two hallways. This had seemed like the longest hallway ever—although, now that I thought about it, this building *was* as long as a football field. I paused at the corner so that I could look both ways before proceeding. On the count of three, I peeped around the edge of the wall to the right into the other hallway. That corridor was shorter and had a glass double door at the end. Based on where I was in the building, I assumed it led to the back parking lot. I didn't need to go there. Not yet at least. It was nice knowing another way out, though. Quickly I looked to the left. A set of double doors stood at the end of that hallway too. I spotted a glass display on the wall. Aha. That could be a directory of names. Thank goodness—something that might lead me in the right direction.

I dashed from the longer hallway into the shorter one and over to the glass case on the wall. Much to my chagrin, a lot of names were listed, and they weren't in alphabetical order. Who had arranged this, and what had they been thinking? Now I had to search through every single name to find the right one.

I ran my finger over the glass display case to help me keep track of which names I'd already looked at, moving down and up the columns. I came to the last name in the first column and started to panic. But halfway down the last one, I finally came to GEORGE GUSTAVSSON.

Based on the signs on the wall with arrows and office numbers, Kellie's boss's office would apparently be upstairs and to the left when I stepped out of the stairwell. Now I just needed to find that stairwell.

Once at the hallway intersection again, I turned to the left and raced down the hall toward the end. This might be the craziest thing I'd ever done, even crazier than when I'd sneaked into the high school gym and hidden the mascot's giant beaver costume. In my defense, it had been a dare, and I couldn't turn down a dare. Since my parents had worked a lot, I'd spent a lot of time with Aunt Barb during the summers, and she'd put me on kitchen duty for a month over that caper. It was just as well, though, because I'd learned to love cooking because of that. Now look at me. Well, maybe right this second wasn't the best example of my personal growth, but the point was that I had a successful business.

At least for now. If I didn't solve this mystery, that was all likely to change.

After reaching the staircase, I hurried up to the second floor. Trying to catch my breath, I slunk down the hallway like a cat burglar. All I needed was black clothing and I would fit the part. Counting down the office numbers, I hoped I would end up at my destination soon. Finally, I reached the door marked with George Gustavsson's name.

This was what I'd wanted. But now I wasn't so sure. What if I'd made the wrong decision by coming here?

Should I knock on the door? I supposed Kellie had been Mr. Gustavsson's assistant. Who was helping him now? A man's voice traveled through the door, and I paused. That had to be him. I wanted to eavesdrop on his conversation so badly that I could almost taste it. I had no idea if someone was in the room with him or if he was simply on the phone. It would be best if he was on the phone; that way I could wait for him to end the call and then knock. I wanted one-on-one time with him.

What if he took too long on the call? I shifted from foot to foot, impatiently waiting for him to stop talking.

A shuffling noise came from my right, and I spotted the security guard walking down the hallway. He was headed straight for me. Fortunately for me, he wasn't looking up from his phone at the moment. Once again, he was being a terrible security guard. The whole building could be on fire and he probably wouldn't notice.

It was too risky to stand out here, though. Soon he would spot me.

I moved closer to the door and rapped it with my fist. While I anxiously waited, I hoped for the best. I glanced to my left to see if the guard had noticed me yet. Nope. He was still occupied by his phone. If Kellie's boss didn't answer me soon, I'd have to enter the office without his invitation. What would he do if I just burst into the room? I hoped I didn't have to find out and rapped on the door again.

"Come in," the man said in an irritated voice.

Now that he'd told me to come inside, I was even more worried about this being the right decision. Glancing down the hallway, I saw the security guard look up from his phone. At that second our eyes locked, and he frowned. Uh-oh. I was in trouble now.

"I said come inside," he repeated.

He sounded agitated now. The last thing I needed was to start this encounter on the wrong foot. I had to get over my fear and just go in there. The security guard was gaining on me. There was no more time for debate.

As hard as it was to carry out, I acted as if I knew exactly what I was doing and was supposed to be here. I wrapped my hand around the doorknob, pushed the door open, and walked right into the room.

The man sat behind a huge wooden desk in front of double windows. Sun streamed into the room, bathing the space in a yellow glow. If I tried to work in here, I'd probably want to take a nap. The space was definitely cozy.

Two leather chairs sat in front of the desk, and a credenza occupied the wall near the door. Bookshelves lined the walls to the left and right, but they weren't full of books. A few classics rested on the shelves, but a collection of small statues took up most of the space. Some of them were tall and others short; some were metal and others clay. Maybe he'd collected them from different places around the world. Or maybe he just wanted it to appear that way.

"Who are you?" The snap in his voice almost knocked me over.

"Marci Beaucoup. I own the French bakery in town," I said timidly. "I have a few questions for you."

He gestured toward the chairs. "Have a seat."

I remained quiet as I perched on the edge of the cushion like a tiny sparrow in front of a hawk.

"I guess I know why you're here," he continued, studying my face. "I assume you're not here to deliver croissants to me. I see no croissants."

*Did* he know why I was here? I wasn't even sure *I* knew why I was here. Oh yes, of course—I had to ask about Kellie and his connection to her murder. Did Kellie have a creepy stalker? An enemy? Or had it been a random attack? He seemed like a successful man, and after his initial hostility, his tone had somewhat improved. I mean, he'd snapped at me, but he could have told me to get out of here. Instead, he was talking to me, and that had to mean something.

I shifted in the leather chair but remained on the edge of my seat, ready to leap up if I needed to run away. I wasn't sure why I felt so uncomfortable—maybe because I had no authority to ask him questions. Not to mention he'd want to know why I was asking about Kellie. I was behaving like I was a police officer or something.

Did that even matter, though? It was in my interest to solve the case; I had things at risk here. Not only might I lose my bakery—everything I had worked hard for could be gone in an instant—but I feared the killer would come after me next, since I was trying to solve the murder. I hoped this man would want to help me find out who had killed Kellie. Obviously, he'd been close to her, if they'd worked together and he'd been visiting her at her home. But I wanted to know more about their relationship.

Should I have given him my name and told him I ran the bakery? Though making up a name probably wouldn't have worked either. Sooner or later, he'd have discovered who I was. Besides, what was the worst that could happen if he knew my real name?

He eyed me suspiciously. "What questions do you have?"

I sat up a little straighter. "I'm trying to find out who killed Kellie. After all, she was found in front of my bakery. I want to know where she was going when she was murdered."

He had no reaction to my statement. Did he not care? Maybe I'd misjudged his relationship with Kellie.

"I thought maybe since you worked with her and you knew her well, you might have some idea who would do this."

"If I had some idea who would do this, I would have told the police, and they would have arrested the person already."

"I realize that," I said. "But I'm worried about losing business, so I'm investigating on my own."

He practically cackled as he leaned back in his chair. "What makes you think you can do an investigation? Do you have training in law enforcement?"

"No, I do not, but I'm not dumb. I can put clues together."

He chuckled. "Good luck with that. You're going to need it."

"What is that supposed to mean?" I asked.

"It means you're a baker and not a detective," he answered smugly. He was being less than helpful.

"Nevertheless, I hope you'll humor me and answer a few questions."

"Go right ahead," he said with a wave of his hand.

He was so cavalier about all of this. I would just have to push past that and continue with my mission.

"When was the last time you saw Kellie?" I asked.

"Like I told the police, the evening before her murder."

Aha. So he had been one of the last people to see her. Perhaps *the* last. This realization hit me like a punch to the stomach. A kick of panic raced through me. Was I sitting in front of the killer? Should I run for my life? *Breathe, Marci, breathe.*

"What time was that?" I asked.

"As I told the police," he said through gritted teeth, "it was around eight forty-five PM. After that, I have no idea where she went. From what I'm told, her car was found the next morning in the same spot where she'd parked the night I saw her."

"Where were you talking to her? At her home?"

Rose Betancourt

"In town," he said. "Right there on the square. I noticed her car parked, so I decided to pull up and ask if she was okay. She said everything was fine and that she was meeting someone."

"Meeting whom?" I asked.

"She didn't tell me. I'm not her babysitter, and I don't have to keep tabs on every single move she makes. All I'm responsible for is when she's at work."

"But yet you visit her at her home? That seems like more than work," I said.

He leaned forward in his chair. My question had wiped the smirk right off his face. Maybe it was my imagination, but he seemed a bit worried now. Perhaps he was shocked that I'd actually been checking up on him. How much more dirt on him could I dig up?

"I had some promotional items printed up, like tote bags for the office, and she was taking care of that for me. And I wanted to show her one of the possible prototypes. If she liked it, then I was going to order a thousand."

That explained why he had visited her, I supposed. Or did it? I had my reservations. Why would the tote bags need to be discussed outside of work? That didn't seem like an urgent matter. It seemed like something that could wait until the next workday. And why had he been lurking outside her house? Why not just walk right up to the door?

Mr. Gustavsson picked up a pencil from the container on his desk and then tossed it into the trash bin by his desk. Then he grabbed a pen from the same holder. I watched as he jotted down notes. I felt like leaning forward to find out what he was writing, but I refrained.

"You don't like pencils?" I asked.

"No, I can't stand them. I use paper notes because I like writing with a pen rather than typing on my phone," he said. "No pencils, though."

"You're in luck. They have something now that's like a pen for your phone. You can use it on your phone's screen. I can show you how to use it."

Why had I said that? Anxiety was making me ramble, and he might notice my nervousness if I kept up my blathering.

"I think I can figure it out on my own, but thanks for the info," he said.

"Right. Yes, of course you can," I said.

"I guess I'm trying to understand the real reason why you're here exactly. Why do you care about Kellie? Did you know her?"

He had me there. Did he think I was just being snoopy? Maybe to some extent I *was* snoopy sometimes, just like everyone else in this gossipy little town.

He started shoving files into his briefcase. "I think this conversation is over."

Some of the papers fell to the floor, and he scrambled to pick them up and shove them back into his briefcase. He really was kind of clumsy. He even knocked over the pen holder in the process, then hurriedly stuffed the pens back into the holder.

Wow. He seemed extremely flustered.

# Chapter Fourteen

I caught his shirt sleeve before he exited the room. "Well, sir, I'm interested in this case because, as I told you, Kellie was outside my bakery when she was murdered. I want to know why she was there. I have questions, and I want to find the killer. He could easily be coming after me next. Why was she at my bakery? So you can understand why I'm coming to ask what you know about Kellie and her last few hours here on earth."

He stared at me, and I knew he was contemplating what I'd said.

"I'm sorry, Ms. Beaucoup, but I have nothing else to tell you," he said.

"Any detail would help," I said.

"I have no other information," he said.

"Was Kellie a good employee? Did she seem distressed before her murder?" I pressed.

"Yes, of course she was a great employee. She seemed fine before her death."

Why had Kellie been parked by the town square? Had she met with someone after Mr. Gustavsson talked to her? Why else would she have been in town at that hour? In Paris people rolled up the sidewalk at nine at night. Could she have left and then returned the next morning? Maybe she'd thought I'd be at the bakery and she'd come to see me. But why? Was it just to get a croissant, or to confront me about Antoine's flirtations? She should have known my shop was closed. My bakery clearly wasn't open twenty-four hours a day.

I glanced around the room, taking in the surroundings one more time. I noticed a pair of crutches against the wall. On the table next to the crutches sat a black fedora hat. I'd seen Antoine holding one just like it the first day he'd come into my shop.

When I turned my attention back to Mr. Gustavsson, I realized he was still staring at me.

"Did you hurt your leg or foot?" I asked.

His eyes didn't move from my face. "Um, yeah, just this morning. I tripped over the curb coming in the building."

"Sorry to hear that," I said.

Mr. Gustavsson glared at me expectantly, as if letting me know he was ready for me to leave. So I took the hint and pushed to my feet.

"Thank you for your time," I said as I headed for the door.

"How did you get by security, anyway?" he asked. "Guests aren't allowed in this area of the building. Do you have a pass?"

I glanced back at him. "Was I not supposed to be back here? My mistake. I didn't realize. Oops."

That sounded kind of tough, and I liked it. I wasn't going to let him intimidate me. I marched out of the office and down the hallway, headed for the exit so that I could get back to my car. I wasn't going to let anything stop me. His lack of answers made me feel a bit defeated, but I was determined more than ever to figure out this murder. I'd never been one to turn down a challenge.

I wasn't scared at all until someone grabbed me by the arm. I let out a scream and spun around, ready to fight. The security guard maintained his grip.

"Where do you think you're going?" he asked.

"I'm leaving," I said, trying to yank my arm away from him.

"What are you doing in here?"

"I was visiting an employee, thank you very much," I said.

"I didn't see any visitors listed for today."

I still couldn't get him to let go of my arm.

"Let me go," I said.

"I want to know why you're here."

"I just told you I was visiting an employee. I don't owe you an explanation. Now let go."

He laughed. "I have to escort you out."

"Oh yeah?" I asked. "Thanks, but I can see myself out."

Wow, I really had gotten sassy. Maybe it would be better if I was nice to him. I'd probably attract more bees with honey, but he'd left me no choice but to show him my tougher side. I had to figure out how I was going to get away from this guy.

"I came here to see Mr. Gustavsson. He hurt his foot this morning, and I came to check on him."

"Nice try. You need to get your story straight. He hurt his foot two days ago," the guard said.

Hmm. That was odd. Why had Mr. Gustavsson told me he'd hurt his foot this morning? Was the guard lying or simply mistaken?

"If you don't let go of me, sir, I'm going to call the police and tell them you're holding me against my will." I tried to move my arm, but his grip was tight.

"I'll tell them you were here trespassing."

"You can ask Mr. Gustavsson about that. He'll say he talked to me. It's not trespassing when I had a meeting with him."

The man eyed me for a moment and then finally let me go. I yanked my arm away as if he were still touching me. I glared at him for a moment and then spun around. Without looking back, I hurried toward the door.

Thank goodness he didn't follow me. Although I supposed if he wanted to find me, it was quite clear from my uniform that I worked at the bakery.

When I reached the door, I pushed, but it didn't open. One of my worst fears. Was the door stuck?

Now what would I do? I pushed again, but of course, the outcome was the same. I felt the security guard's presence behind me. I could feel his breath on the back of my neck, and the tiny hairs there stood on end. He reached his arm around me and shoved on the door harder, and the latch clicked. I didn't look back at him. I didn't want to look into his icy-blue eyes.

He paused with his hand on the door. Would he open the door or not? I was starting to think he had changed his mind about letting me go. Just as I was about to say something, he pushed open the door.

"I'd better not see you around here again," he said.

I stormed out before he had a chance to reconsider.

As I hurried across the parking lot, I couldn't get to my car fast enough. Once I was inside, I'd feel safe. Although I supposed he could hunt me down and call the cops. I just needed to get out of here. I needed to give myself a chance to think about the conversation I'd had with Mr. Gustavsson.

When I looked back to see if the security guard was still at the door, sure enough, he was standing right there, so I turned around quickly to quicken my steps. However, I bumped right into someone. The smack knocked the wind out of me, and I tumbled to the ground.

"Are you all right?" the man asked as he helped me up.

I peered up at the dark-haired man. He took me into his arms and helped me get on my feet again.

"I'm sorry," I said. "I didn't see you standing there."

"That's quite all right, but where are you going in such a hurry?" he asked.

The man wore a gray suit with a red tie. I assumed he worked in the offices here. Should I give him the real reason I was here or lie and just say I was lost? Why did I have to tell him anything? I was tongue-tied, though. His gaze was fixed on me. He was probably getting more suspicious by the second.

"Is that security guard bothering you?" he asked.

I shrugged. "Oh, um, no, there was just a misunderstanding."

This guy seemed sincere. For some reason, I thought I could open up to him.

"Can I help you with something?" he asked.

"Do you work here?"

"I'm head of the IT department." He flashed a small grin.

"I'm Marci, by the way," I said.

"The name's Blake," he said as he thrust his hand out.

"Nice to meet you, Blake. I own the bakery where Kellie Lowry was killed, and I'm trying to find out who murdered her. She worked here. I'm assuming you heard the news that someone in town was murdered?"

He nodded. "Yes, I'm aware of what happened. I'm sorry that happened at your bakery."

"Thank you," I said. "But I just want to get to the bottom of this. I was talking with her boss, George Gustavsson. That didn't go well. And to top it off, the security guard doesn't like that I'm here."

"Well, he doesn't like anyone, so I wouldn't take it personally."

"Do you know anything about the guy? Why is he so mean?"

"I'm not aware of anything in particular about him, but I do know Kellie's boss." He shook his head. "I don't know how she worked for that man."

"What? What about her boss?"

"The last time I saw her at work, I was walking down the hallway and overheard Gustavsson tell her that if she didn't do what he wanted, he would fire her."

"What did she do that made him want to fire her?" I asked.

"I'm not sure about that," he said. "Although there was something else going on with Kellie."

"What's that?" I asked.

He looked around as if someone might overhear. This guy had an awful lot of information. Was he the company gossip? I sensed that he really didn't like Mr. Gustavsson.

"Were you friends with her?" I pressed.

"Well, we had offices next to each other, so we talked quite a bit. Sometimes we went to lunch together."

"Oh, so you *were* friends, then?"

"Yes, I guess you could say that. I mean, we weren't close. We didn't talk outside of work, but while we were here, we were friends."

"So what's the other thing?" I asked.

"She thought she had a stalker," he said.

"Really?" I said with surprise. I wondered if Maverick knew about this. "What made Kellie think she had a stalker?"

The thought sent a shiver down my spine. Was someone stalking me too now? Would I meet the same fate?

"She said someone had been following her."

"How did she know?"

"Well, she'd seen a car and the person following her," he said.

"So she knew who it was?"

He nodded. "It was someone she met on a dating app. She'd been recently trying to find someone new after she and Antoine broke up."

"Why did they break up?" I asked.

"She said he just broke up with her for no reason."

I didn't believe it was for no reason, but maybe she just hadn't told this guy. Or she didn't want to admit the reason. Or maybe Antoine just hadn't told her why. But there had to be a reason. People didn't break up for no reason at all. I had to get to the bottom of this. I would never have guessed that my livelihood might come down to two strangers who had a bad breakup.

"So did she know this man's name?" I asked.

"All she had was a first name. His name is Hunter."

"She'd gone out on a date with him?" I asked.

"I think they met for coffee one day, but she didn't like him, so that was it. Right after that, she started seeing him everywhere she went."

"That's scary," I said.

I wondered if he was the person who had killed her. And how would I hunt Hunter down?

"Is there any other information you can give me about him? What does he look like?"

"He has light-brown hair, about five foot eleven and a hundred and eighty pounds. He has close-set eyes too. And they're a deep, dark blue."

"That's a lot of description. Did you see him?"

"She'd been excited to meet him at first, so she gave a good description of him. Plus, I saw the picture."

"So anything else that stood out to you?"

"No, not really," he said.

"Do you know where I can find him?" I asked.

He briefly peered down at his polished black shoes. "I'm not sure. I think she said he was a business owner. Oh, and he's from Lexington."

Well, that didn't narrow it down much. A man named Hunter in Lexington. Who also owned a business. Lexington was big, though, and would have a lot of men named Hunter. I guessed that was better than nothing. Now I had another person on my list of suspects. Did Maverick have this information? Maybe there would be some kind of video evidence.

"Kellie and Antoine have been broken up for a year now," he said.

My eyes widened. "I had no idea it had been that long."

"This happened when they were both in Paris, France. I told her it was time to move on. After a year, if you haven't gotten back together, there's no need to stick with false hope. I encouraged to her to try the dating apps."

"I suppose that was a good thing. Unless the person who killed her was someone she met on the dating app. That would be bad," I said.

"I'd feel really guilty about that. But I thought it was the right advice at the time." He ran his hand through his thick hair.

"How did she meet Antoine?" I asked.

"She worked with him at the France office." Blake loosened his tie. Beads of sweat were forming on his forehead.

"I didn't know she was French too. She didn't have an accent," I said.

"She's not. Kellie was from Atlanta. When Antoine was transferred here to this branch of Flaget Manufacturing, she followed him. They worked together at the branch in France, so she asked for a transfer too, even though they'd already broken up. Well, it took her a couple months to get the company to transfer her. Her time at the company was good and they wanted to promote her, so she asked to be sent to Kentucky."

"So they were already broken up when that happened?"

"Yes, that's right," he said.

It sounded like Kellie had been stalking her ex.

"Antoine didn't ask her to come to Kentucky?"

He released a deep breath. "No, I don't think so. I heard them arguing once, and he accused her of following him."

So maybe Antoine did have a reason for murder. Just because she had followed him, though? A sane person would get a restraining order, not kill the woman. I didn't think Antoine would want to take it as far as murder. I mean, she hadn't done anything to harm him.

"That makes sense, I guess. Do you know anything else about him?"

"We didn't go out for lunch or anything, but we exchanged pleasantries here at the office. Antoine works in a different area, so we don't have much interaction with each other."

This was certainly more information than I had gotten from Mr. Gustavsson and a pleasant surprise. Needless to say, I was happy about it. Now I felt invigorated and hopeful about solving the crime.

I pulled one of my cards from my pocket and handed it to him. "If you find out anything else, would you give me a call?"

"Sure, no problem," he said. "I'll stop in your bakery sometime."

"I'd love that," I said.

"I've heard good things about your place," he said. "You know, you really have an air about you. You're easy to talk to."

"Thank you. That's sweet of you."

If I was easy to talk to, that might come in handy when trying to solve a crime. I looked back at the security guard. He was still watching us. Now I really felt intimidated. He probably thought we were talking about him. Of course, we had been, but he didn't need to know that.

"Thank you again," I said. "I should be going."

I hurried toward my car. Blake watched me for a second, then walked across the parking lot, heading away from the security guard in the other direction. I almost fell tripping over my own feet as I watched him go. I stumbled to the car, pressed the key fob, and opened the door. I slid into the car like a race car driver. As I tried to shove the key into the ignition, I looked toward the building. The security guard still stood at the door, staring at me.

Would he be on the lookout for me? Would he get my license plate number and give it to the police? I'd done nothing wrong here. Well, other than a little trespassing. I was worried it would be his word against mine because, well, maybe I couldn't get Mr. Gustavsson to say we'd had a meeting after all. He definitely didn't like me.

With a squealing of my tires, I pulled across the parking lot. Oops. I hadn't meant to do that, but I was in a hurry to get out of there.

I wasn't sure the new information would do any good, but at least I had a bit more to go on now. Mr. Gustavsson had been upset with Kellie. Would that give him reason to kill her, though? He'd been near the scene of the crime. I'd found his card there. And now I knew there had been tension between the two of them. Though Antoine had a motive. And what about the stalker? This definitely warranted a conversation with Maverick. Of course, he'd think I was doing his job. Nevertheless, it wouldn't hurt to point out what I knew. A second set of eyes on the case wouldn't be a bad thing. At least in my opinion. I had to add Mr. Gustavsson and Hunter to the list of suspects.

I pointed my car in the direction of my house, thankful that I'd actually gotten out of there. But I kept glancing in my rearview mirror every so often to see if the police were coming after me. Maybe I should just tell Maverick what I'd done and get it over with instead of postponing what I knew I had to do.

No, I'd wait until the police talked to me about this. If they found out. If not, I wouldn't have to worry about it. They probably already had the info anyway. Talking to Maverick would cause too much distraction right now, especially after I'd just turned him down. Besides, they probably wouldn't like that I was doing my own investigation. Would they even take me seriously? Or just brush off anything I told them?

Yes, I'd wait until the cops approached me. In the meantime, I had a murder to solve.

# Chapter Fifteen

I made it home safely with no signs of being followed by the police. Or a call back from Antoine. Maverick hadn't called to ask me more questions about the crime either. Was I disappointed by that? Just a little, maybe, but I would never admit that out loud. No way would I tell Aunt Barb.

Being home didn't last long. Aunt Barb called and said she thought she'd left the dough out of the fridge by mistake. How was that even possible, given her level of experience? But I didn't dare say anything to her about it; I didn't want to make her feel bad. Was it the murder that had her so distracted, or was there another reason? Was something else bothering her? I forgot stuff all the time; it wasn't uncharacteristic of me to forget to check things before I left the shop. But not Aunt Barb.

This wasn't an emergency, obviously, because I could just throw the dough away in the morning. However, Aunt Barb would no doubt worry about it attracting pests. For her peace of mind and for mine, I would check; I knew she would keep calling until I found out. It was really bothering her, so I would go and get the answer. And then I'd head back home, I supposed.

I wasn't going to drive, though. It was a nice evening, and I needed the extra time to think. A walk would help me clear my head and go over everything I knew about the investigation. Though I grabbed a rolling pin for protection on my way out the door. Those things could cause some serious damage.

As I headed down the sidewalk, I neared Mrs. Jenkins's house. I saw that she was on the front porch again. Oh no. Now she would want to talk about her cats, bless her heart. Maybe I should cross the street.

It was too late, though. She'd looked my way, and we made eye contact. If I crossed the street now, she'd know I'd done it on purpose. She'd tell everyone in town that I was rude and didn't want to talk to her. She'd probably make it a one-woman mission to get everyone not to come into my shop. She and Mrs. Foley were like twins from different parents. Therefore, I smiled at her and continued down the sidewalk, on a collision course with a conversation with her. She would want to know all about what was happening with the investigation, and I had nothing to update her on. I sure wasn't going to tell her anything I'd discovered—not that there was much to tell anyway.

As I neared the house, I was surprised to see a man walk out the front door, speak to Mrs. Jenkins, and then head down the steps toward the sidewalk. He didn't even look my way. As far as I knew, Mrs. Jenkins had lived alone ever since her husband died. Only the cats occupied the house with her.

I was kind of curious, but I didn't want to be the typical nosy gossip. Oh, who was I kidding? I'd broken that nosy threshold a long time ago. My questioning might make Mrs. Jenkins uncomfortable, though. However, if she was going to ask me questions, it seemed only fair for me to ask her questions too.

As I got closer to the house, she waved and called to me.

"I'm surprised to see you this time of evening," she said.

"Yes, well, I just forgot some business at the shop, so I thought I would walk."

"It is a lovely evening for a walk. Unless, of course, you think about how there might be a murderer out there."

The words made me pause. I was all too aware that there was a murderer out there. However, Paris had always been a safe town where I felt like I wouldn't run the risk of being attacked and killed. I hoped that was still true.

"So tell me, has anything new happened?" she asked.

I looked down the sidewalk and watched the man walking away. I'd answer her questions if she answered mine.

"Nothing yet," I said. "But I know the police are still working on it. By the way, who was that man? I thought you lived alone."

"Oh, that's just my nephew. He's just staying here for a while until he gets back on his feet," she said with a wave of her hand. "Hunter is a good kid, though."

*Hunter.* The name stuck out in my mind right away. What were the odds that this was the same Hunter that Kellie had been talking to, and how could I find out? It wasn't like his aunt would know the answer. She probably had no idea whether he was dating someone, and she would certainly not know if he was a killer.

"He's a Jenkins?" I smiled.

"Yes, ma'am, he's my sister's son."

"How long has he been here?" I asked.

"Just about two weeks now."

"Oh, well, that's not long," I said. "Does he have friends here?"

I was trying to be selective with my questions, as I didn't want her to be suspicious.

"Well, as far as I know, he doesn't have any friends here. I told him he should get out more and maybe meet some people. He can't stay here with me and the cats all the time." She looked back at said cats, who were sitting in the window, as usual.

They didn't move. It was almost like they were guards, watching us, perhaps waiting for us to try to come inside. More than likely they just wanted us to give them a treat.

I had to know if this was the Hunter who had gone out with Kellie. He certainly matched the description. This guy had light-brown hair, was about five foot eleven, and I guessed weighed a hundred and eighty pounds or so. He had close-set, deep, dark-blue eyes too. Today he was wearing a light-blue shirt and jeans.

Where had he come from, and why exactly was he here? Maybe if I caught up with him, I could ask him directly. Although that would be an awkward conversation. A stranger trying to talk to him would be weird. Maybe it was better if I just continued to question his aunt. But she might be suspicious or get angry with me. I was torn on what to do.

Ultimately, I decided I'd just ask her nephew directly. I had no plan for how I would do that, but I decided would figure it out when the time came.

"Is he from Lexington?"

"Yes, dear. Why do you ask?"

"Just curious. Well, I'd better get going," I said. "It was nice seeing you."

I tossed my hand up in a wave, then headed down the sidewalk before she had a chance to ask any other questions about the murder investigation. I had business to attend to, and it couldn't wait another second.

I spotted Hunter up ahead and wanted to catch up with him, hoping he wouldn't walk too fast or get into a car. Where was he headed, anyway? I'd just hang back a bit and follow him for as long as I could. Hopefully I'd get to the bottom of this today.

What would I do if I found out he was the killer? I might panic. I was starting to panic now. Hunter could be the killer. Would I be confronting the killer? That was a scary thought. And not too totally wild, like some of the thoughts I had at times. Maverick would most definitely say this was a bad idea.

I followed along behind Hunter, keeping just enough distance so that he wouldn't get suspicious but also wouldn't get away. I noticed a spark of gold on his black loafers. Like a buckle? His jeans were a bit short, allowing a full view of his shoes.

I couldn't let him get too far in front of me. He was walking slowly, but I had to walk fast—he had a bigger stride than me. We'd almost reached downtown and I would be at the shop soon. I'd have to make a decision then—whether I would continue past the shop or let it go. Something told me it wasn't in me to let it go.

After just a short distance more, he glanced over his shoulder. He must have sensed me back there. He frowned and then paused and turned around right in front of me.

He eyed me up and down. "Are you following me?"

I didn't look away. I wanted to seem confident and as if I weren't scared of him, but I was completely scared of him. He was taller and bigger and had an angry look on his face that aided me in imagining that he might have had something to do with Kellie's murder.

"I'm just headed into town."

"It seemed like you were following me," he said.

"I'm just going to get some flowers and maybe vegetables down the road at the farmers' market."

I'd gotten nervous with his question and made up that lie on the spur of the moment. Why, I had no idea. I'd panicked.

"Right." He drew the word out as if he didn't believe me. "What are you doing afterwards?"

That was an odd question. Was it really any of his business what I was doing?

"I'm just going to my shop." I pointed in the general direction. But I immediately regretted doing that, because I really didn't want him to know who I was. I'd rather keep this anonymous if possible. Maybe it was too late for that. I knew his aunt, and I wanted to keep her name out of it too. But if I didn't tell him any of this, then how would I segue into a question about the murdered woman?

"Are you new in town?" I asked, trying to sound friendly.

Maybe he would think I was flirting with him. That was fine, as long as I got my questions answered. I'd quickly be on my merry way. Though after I had snapped at him, he might wonder about my odd way of flirting.

"I'm not from around here," he said. "And I'll probably be leaving soon. I just came to check out real estate property."

Most murderers took off right after they'd done it. Unless, of course, they wanted to hang around and reminisce about their handiwork. He might like all the attention that the murder was getting in town. He probably loved all the rumors and gossip, plus the police hunting for the killer.

"Well, how do you like Paris?" I asked.

He shrugged. "It's kind of boring."

"It is a small town," I said with a smile. "Do you have any friends here?"

"Would you like to be my friend?" he asked.

This guy was creepy, but how could I say no if I wanted answers from him?

"Sure," I said. "I guess everyone in town can use a friend. Especially after what happened."

His expression changed. "What do you mean?"

"I mean after the murder." I shook my head. "Poor girl. She never saw it coming."

"I don't know much about that," he said. "I just got into town."

He'd been in town long enough to commit the murder.

"We should hang out," he said, eyeing me up and down. "You're kind of cute."

If he was trying to ask me out, it was definitely time for me to get away. He was acting as if he didn't know Kellie, but I had to figure out if that was the truth. How would I do that? There was no way to get him to admit to it. I would have to be sneaky and trick him into telling me.

"You know," I said, pointing my finger. "You look familiar. I think I've seen you before."

"I don't think so," he said, shaking his head.

"Yes, I saw you with a woman. Actually, it was the woman who was murdered, now that I think about it. The other day you were with her."

"That's impossible," he said. "I didn't know her."

"I didn't even say who she was," I said, fixing my gaze on him.

He looked down at his shoes, and in that split second, I knew he was lying to me. Why not make eye contact with me? He had every time before. Now he just kept staring at his shoes with the shiny gold buckles on them. Finally, he looked up, but he still didn't meet my stare.

"I gotta go," he said.

He turned around and hurried away down the sidewalk. No way would I catch up with him this time. He was walking way too fast, but that was okay, because I'd gotten the information I needed. He was definitely acting suspicious. This had to be the same Hunter who had stalked Kellie and might have had something to do with her murder.

# Chapter Sixteen

Once I'd tossed the dough that had been left out, I returned home from the shop, I decided to get in my car and drive to Antoine's house. I felt like a creepy stalker myself as I sat out in front of Antoine's house, staring at the front porch, contemplating whether I should invite myself in by going to his front door.

What was I thinking? I could go to jail for a long time if I tried something like that.

That wasn't exactly how I'd worked it out in my mind. I'd envisioned that maybe the door would be open, and I would pretend I was looking for Antoine if anyone caught me. I would go inside on that pretense and then just happen to peek around at all the stuff while I was at it. But that was a fantasy. It would be burglary, right? I couldn't do that. My fantasies couldn't come true. Although I had to admit my fantasy about opening my own bakery had worked. But now my shop had briefly taken a wrong turn with the murder, so again, my fantasies didn't always work out. I hoped the worst was behind me now.

I had to make a decision, though. Sitting here forever wasn't an option. What if he came outside and saw me sitting here staring at his house? He probably already thought I was slightly strange, but I didn't want to give him even more reason to think that.

I tapped my fingers against the steering wheel, trying to work up enough courage to do something. I'd just go up to the door and start talking. There was nothing wrong with that, right? I'd act like I was just being friendly. Though he might think I was totally obsessed with him and that was the reason for my visit.

Would he think I was here only to ask him questions, or would he think I wanted more? What would he say if I asked him if he was a murderer? Or would he think I was only here about the building? Furthermore, I was walking into a potential murderer's house. This would be one of the craziest things I'd ever done. Doing crazy things seemed to be a recurring theme in my life as of late. My parents would not be happy with me. Aunt Barb would be extremely upset.

After a few more seconds, I decided there was no more time to waste. I opened the car door, climbed out, and marched toward the house. Of course, my nerves were at an all-time high, but I was brave and did it anyway.

I made my way to the front door and stood there for several seconds before finally pushing on the doorbell. Talk about antsy. I was pretty sure Antoine was home, since his car was in the driveway. Maybe he wouldn't even answer the door. The thought had barely come to mind when I heard movement inside. I knew he was headed this way.

Soon he opened the door. Wow, did he look handsome. He had that same sparkle in his eye, even if he was potentially a killer. He'd been under the stress of being accused, so how did he still seem so relaxed? At the same time, though, if he really had carried out a horrific crime, I needed to keep my guard up. Yep, coming here made me question my sanity.

"Bonjour, Marci," he said. "I was hoping to see you."

He hoped to see me? I hadn't expected him to say that. Now I was more than a little curious. On the spur of the moment, I happened to think of an excuse so it wouldn't seem so awkward to ask about the murder. I could ease into the questions so they wouldn't be so abrupt. He might be more likely to be truthful that way. I didn't know how it popped into my head. Maybe it was just that the pressure of it all helped me be creative when I needed it most. Whatever the reason, I was thankful.

"I just have a question about French cooking, and I thought, who better to ask than the expert? Maybe you can show me the great ingredient that I need."

He laughed. "Well, I'm not an expert on cooking, by any means. On the French part? Considering we're in Kentucky, then I guess you could consider me the expert this time."

"Perfect," I said. "That's all I need."

He laughed again. "Well, what was your question? Where are my manners?" he said. "Would you like to come inside?"

He motioned over his shoulder.

"Absolutely I would like to come inside."

There were a lot of things in there I might want to take a look at. His home could hold the clues I was seeking.

He stepped out of the way and gestured for me to come in. This was it. I was walking into his house, and there might be no turning back now. However, I did it anyway. I stepped through, mustering as much courage as I could.

"Please make yourself at home. We can have a seat in the living room if you'd like. I have something for you."

The large space was broken up into two separate areas for the living room and on the other corner a dining table for the dining room space.

He had something for me? What could it be?

The place was neat and orderly. It had a nice eclectic vibe to it, with a rich-blue sofa and gold-framed art on the walls. The sitting area by the fireplace looked like a good spot for me to take a seat. I would still have a view of the front door and the windows if I needed to find an escape. And my back would be against the fireplace, so he wouldn't be able to sneak up on me. I had to be prepared. As much as I wanted to think he was innocent, better safe than sorry.

Antoine followed me into the room.

"Please have a seat. I'll be right back."

My heart thumped faster. Should I get out of here while I still had the chance?

Seconds later, Antoine returned. He had his arms around his back. Was he hiding a gun back there in his hands?

I flinched as he pulled his hand from around his back. "I picked these from the flower garden out back."

"Oh," I said in surprise.

He thrust the flowers toward me. "I noticed you had those daisies in your shop when I was there, and I thought you must like them. So, when I saw these, I cut them for you."

I took them from his outstretched hand. How incredibly sweet that he remembered just by seeing them once. I didn't think I'd ever had anyone be that thoughtful before.

I sniffed the flowers. "They're beautiful, thank you."

He sat across from me in a tall white wingback chair. "What's your question, Ms. Beaucoup?"

Now I had to come up with something I wouldn't know. There was nothing I could think of offhand that I didn't know about baking, even if I wasn't French. I would never have opened a bakery if I didn't consider myself an expert on the subject. I scrambled to think of something, anything, that I didn't know. But then, he wouldn't know the difference if I *did* know.

"Well, it's kind of silly, actually, but I was wondering about the butter." I sniffed the flowers again.

"The butter?" His accent grew thicker with the words.

The way he said them sounded so sexy.

"Yes, well, I think maybe I'm not using the right kind. I imagine having the right butter makes the pastry taste much different."

"It's true. French butter is better." He laughed. "I wasn't going to say anything."

"So you did notice?" I asked. "Mine aren't the best you've ever eaten?"

Why did I sound so defensive all of a sudden? I wasn't really here about the pastry. Nevertheless, I guessed no one liked a critique of their work. But maybe he had a point. How would I get him out of here so I could take a look around for a bit?

"Yours are still delicious, though," he said, around a pitying smile. "The best in the United States."

"Would you happen to have that recipe for the butter?" I asked.

He stared at me for a second with that cute smirk on his face. "Maybe I could get something for you. I could make a phone call. My mother has something fantastic."

"A recipe passed down from your mother. I would feel honored. Thank you."

"I'll just go give her a quick call," he said. "She loves when I ask her for recipes. My phone's in the kitchen."

What time was it in France? Was he really calling her or doing something else?

"Should I come too?" I asked.

He held out his hand, mimicking a stop sign. "Oh, no, no. I'll be fast."

That made me even more suspicious.

"I'll just stay right here," I said.

If I couldn't go with him to the kitchen, then at least I would check things out here. Although I still wanted to see his kitchen, right now I'd check out his living room without him being around. I just hoped I didn't get caught. I'd have no explanation if he caught me red-handed. Antoine would think I was more than a little nosy if he saw me. It was a risky move, but spying was something that absolutely had to be done.

He moved from the chair and walked out of the room. As soon as he did, I hopped up from my seat, because I had just minutes to get this done. Where would I look first? A cabinet across the way had drawers. I would check there.

Placing my flowers on the end table, I hurried across the room and started pulling open the drawers. Then I rifled through everything. I felt bad about doing it—it was definitely wrong—but that didn't stop me. The sound of Antoine's voice as he talked on the phone carried into the room from the kitchen. I knew just enough French to pick out a few words, and he was seemingly doing exactly what I'd asked him to do: calling his mother about the butter. How sweet was that? He was being so warm with her too. I really liked that he had a close relationship with his mom. Would a killer really be that sweet to his mother?

I found nothing in the drawers, so I continued my search, moving over to a small desk across the room. I opened all the drawers but found nothing. I was losing hope that I would locate anything until I came upon a small book—a blue-bound book with no writing on the front. I had no idea what was on the inside, but I flipped the cover to find out. The writing was in French and appeared to include some addresses that Antoine had scribbled in with his daily entries. I really wanted to know what it said, but I didn't have time to find out, because I heard him telling the person on the other line he had to go. I knew just enough French to figure that out. How would I get this book out of his house? And then I would have to return it. How would I manage that? I guessed I would just have to come back for another visit.

How would I hide this thing? I shoved it in the front of my pants and pulled my Breton-striped shirt down over it. Now I had a big lump on the front of me. That was kind of obvious. It would be better if I put it behind me, and then I could maybe duck out of the room somehow without him figuring out what I was doing. He would probably notice my strange behavior, but I would give it a shot anyway.

I stuffed the book into the back of my waistband and held the shirt down over it. Then I hurried back over to the chair and sat down, careful not to let the book fall out. I would have to remember that when I got up as well, because if it fell out onto the floor, then he might get angry. And if he was the killer, that anger might lead to him killing me right there. He'd drag my body across the hardwood floors to the outside, stuff me into his trunk, and drive away with me, dumping my body somewhere far away where no one would ever find me.

*There I go again with my fantasies.* I needed to get rid of these negative thoughts. My mother was always reminding me that my imagination could get crazy and fanciful, but it wasn't always bad. In this situation, though, it wasn't helping at all. Would he really have given me flowers if he was going to harm me?

I pushed the frightening images from my mind and sat there, impatiently waiting for Antoine to return, tapping my fingers against the arm of the chair. A few seconds later, I heard footsteps, and he entered the room again.

He handed me a piece of paper. "Here you go. I wrote it all down for you. This should help you a lot. I hope you'll let me know how it goes."

This time he sat down on the chair beside me.

"Absolutely. I'll let you know what happens. Well, I guess I should get out of your hair, because I know you're busy."

"Oh, I really wasn't doing much. How do you say in English . . . a few odds and ends around the house?"

He acted as if he wanted to talk more, and maybe I should use this opportunity to ask him questions about the murder.

"Yes, that's the correct phrase."

He chuckled. "Sometimes I forget the right words."

"That's understandable. My French is not so good. *Je connais un peu.*"

I'd just told him I knew a little bit of French, but the words came out as if I had peanut butter stuck to the top of my mouth.

"I can teach you sometime. If you'd like," he said around a laugh.

"I'd like that a lot." Did I sound too eager? "So how are things?"

Instantly he recognized what I meant.

"As well as they can be expected, I guess, considering I am considered a murderer."

"Have the police said any anything else about finding the killer?"

"They're solely focused on me. But I can tell you I didn't do it. And I think you believe me, right?"

"Absolutely I do."

I tried to sound confident; I didn't want him to know I'd had second thoughts about that. But now he seemed so sincere that I wanted to believe him.

"I told them we'd been broken up for quite some time. I had no motive. Just because they're not focusing on anyone else doesn't mean I'm not focusing on people as suspects," he said.

"Oh yeah?" I asked, shifting in the seat.

I made sure the book was still back there. Thank goodness—it hadn't moved an inch.

"And who are you focusing on as suspects?" I asked.

I really hoped he would tell me. Maybe we could compare notes. Or maybe he had someone on the list that I didn't even have on my radar.

"One is a man Kellie dated. I guess she started dating again. She wanted to make me jealous, but it wasn't working, because when things are over, they're just over. There's no reason to be jealous. I wanted her to be happy."

That sounded extremely secure.

"So you think this new person may have killed her? What would be the motive for that?"

"I'm not sure. Maybe if she rejected him."

"Yes, I guess that would be enough reason for a crazy person, but then again, anyone who murders has to be crazy anyway, right?"

"Absolutely," he said.

"Is there anyone else on your list?" I asked.

"Not really. I still think there's something about that guy. I know she had problems with him in the past. We didn't talk about it, but I know he was creepy."

"I heard that about him too," I said.

"I just need to figure out who did this so I can get in the clear. I can't continue like this." His accent seemed to thicken as his frustration grew.

"I want to ask you again about the building. I know you're under a lot of pressure, but I don't want to lose my shop. Audrey seemed quite serious about getting the building."

"I know Mrs. Timmons is serious. I promise you she will not get her hands on the building. I'll take care of everything."

"But if you go to jail, then the sale to you won't go through. And there will be nothing you can do to stop her from buying it."

The thought had stayed in my mind, unfortunately, and I didn't have enough money to buy the building myself. Not without help. Right now, I was just trying to focus on finding out if Antoine was a killer. One thing at a time.

I supposed it was time for me to get out of there, but now I was nervous knowing that I had the book behind me. He was being so nice, and I hated to betray him like that.

"Well, I really should be going now, and thank you again for the recipe. And for the flowers. They're truly beautiful."

"Anytime. If you want to maybe have dinner sometime?" he asked.

He was asking me out on a date? Now I really started panicking. What would I wear? What would I say on a date? Would we make small talk about the fact that his ex-girlfriend had been murdered? *Stop with the racing thoughts, Marci.* I needed to focus on the task at hand. I wanted to say yes, but what would my parents say? When they got home from their cruise and found out the news, they would panic. My mother would say she couldn't leave the state for two minutes without me getting into trouble. Okay, I was an adult. It wasn't up to them. If I wanted to say yes, then I could say yes. Never mind a little thing like he might be a killer.

"I'd like that very much," I said, picking up the flowers from the end table next to me.

"Great. Are you free tonight? I can meet you somewhere or pick you up at your house?"

What a gentleman. Most guys nowadays wanted to meet for a quick coffee and go Dutch too.

"Yes, I suppose I could do tonight. What time? How about you come by my place around eight thirty? You know I'm a great cook."

"But I don't want you doing the cooking. That's not why I'm inviting you. I want to show you that I do have some skills in the kitchen."

"I'm sure you do," I said with a laugh.

I felt that book behind me slipping a little, so I grabbed it. He looked at me oddly.

"Just a little too much jogging this morning, and I tweaked my back."

What was I saying? I never went jogging. Couldn't I have said something different? Like gardening or anything that wasn't as active? He'd expect to see me running around town now, and that wasn't going to happen. Every time I tried, I got a pain in my side. Not that I didn't like exercise, but I was more of a yoga-and-light-weights type of girl, definitely not the long-term running-and-gasping-for-breath variety. My friends didn't call me Slow Motion Marci for nothing.

"All right, so I'll see you tonight," I said with a smile as I got up.

I tried to ease my back against the door nonchalantly, but he probably noticed my strange movements.

"Your back again?" he asked with a frown.

"Yes, it's the back again. I guess I just need to walk a little to keep it from hurting again."

He seemed a bit confused by that, but he didn't question it. He stepped in front of me and opened the door. At least for the moment I was safe, but I knew when I walked out of here that he would probably be watching me. So while his back was facing me, I slipped the book out from behind me. My heart thumped wildly in my chest. I put the book in front of me and then tucked the shirt over it. I held my arms in front of me and hurried out the door.

"See you at eight thirty," I yelled out.

What would Aunt Barb say when I told her about this?

I couldn't wait to get away so I could check out the book. I would have to translate that French.

I couldn't read it while I was sitting in Antoine's driveway, so I hurried into the car. Once behind the wheel, I pulled the book from my waistband and placed it on the seat beside me. I hoped he wasn't still watching me. With any luck, he couldn't see inside the car and wouldn't know what I was doing.

I hurriedly started the car and then pulled away from the curb. Glancing in the mirror, I spotted Antoine watching me as I headed down the street. I couldn't believe I had agreed to go out with him tonight. At his house too. Alone. But he seemed so nice that I just couldn't believe he was the killer. I felt safe with him. Being at his house again would give me a chance to look through the rest of his stuff for any evidence that would prove his innocence or guilt. I hoped his innocence, but the doubts lingered.

After traveling a good distance away from the house, I pulled over into a parking lot. I couldn't wait until I got home; I just had to make out what was in that book right away. I'd been able to read a few words in the first entry, but that was it. I knew I'd found his diary, though. Thank goodness he seemed to use it for other details as well. This was his aide-mémoire, I supposed. I needed to translate his words. But it was beginning to sink in how extremely personal they were, and now I felt torn. Part of me wanted to know, but the other part of me felt like I should take the book back without reading any of it.

I supposed a quick scan through the rest of the book wouldn't harm anything. After all, I already had the book. Getting my hands on it had been the hard part.

Thank goodness he had unknowingly invited me over, because otherwise I'd have tried to find a way to get the book back to him and would have had to make up another recipe question.

I started typing the French words into my phone. Soon the entries were revealed to me. Mostly Antoine had written about his daily workouts—nothing unusual about that. I flipped to the days leading up to Kellie's murder. Not that I thought he would admit to killing her in diary, but it was possible. After all, he might assume no one would ever read it.

Yesterday, the day Kellie had been murdered, was blank. That would make sense if he was truly the murderer. It certainly wasn't proof that he'd killed her, though.

*Pourquoi les choses ont-elles d se terminer de cette façon?*

My French wasn't great, but I thought for sure the translation went something like this: *Why did things have to end this way?* Again, I wasn't quite sure how to interpret the meaning. Had he meant things ending with Kellie's death at someone else's hands, or things ending when he'd killed her?

Over the days leading up to the murder, he discussed how Kellie had increased her attempts to reconcile with him and resume their relationship. Antoine was adamant that it wasn't going to happen, that he would do anything to stop it. That made my breath catch in my throat. It wasn't an admission of guilt, but it was definitely suspect.

Another odd thing I noticed right away was the fact that over the week leading up to Kellie's death, Antoine had written about her movements, like places she had been and what time she was there.

*September 5th: Saw Kellie at the park around noon. Then again at the post office at two. She wore those huge black sunglasses and hat like she was trying to be disguised.*

*September 6th: Kellie was outside the grocery store. She pretended not to see me.*

*September 7th: Kellie was suspiciously absent today. Where was she hiding?*

Had Antoine been following her, or had she been following Antoine? If he was following her, he might have seen her the morning of her death. I needed to tell Maverick about this, right? But how would I explain that I'd taken Antoine's diary from his house? I couldn't tell him. There was just no way. I would have to think of another way to get the information to him. Or just keep it to myself for my own investigation.

If I solved this murder quickly enough, then my problem would be solved. Antoine wouldn't be in jail and the building wouldn't fall into the wrong hands, meaning my bakery could stay right where it was at. But that was a big *if*. I would give it some time, but if I didn't solve the murder soon, I would let Maverick know what I'd learned.

As I sat there flipping through the pages, trying to make out some of the words, the sound of a car captured my attention. When I looked in the rearview mirror, I spotted Maverick's cruiser. He had pulled up right behind my car. Oh my gosh. What would I do now? I stuffed the book into my bag and opened the car door. Was he going to arrest me?

"Ms. Beaucoup," Maverick said.

He did not sound happy with me. He sounded like he had questions for me. Like what the heck I was doing in this parking lot. Although, why was *he* here? Had he solved the case, or did he have a new lead?

"Good afternoon, Detective Malone. What can I do for you?"

"Just stopping to see if you're all right. Are you having car trouble?" He glanced at the daisies on my passenger seat.

Had he been following me? Did he know I had been at Antoine's house or the paper company? It didn't matter. I was allowed to go anywhere I wanted. I wasn't under arrest yet.

"My car is fine. I was just doing a little bit of reading."

"An odd place to read," he said.

"Well, it was a letter, and I decided I needed to read it right away." Yet another lie to add to my list of fibs.

"And you're sure that everything's okay?"

He didn't ask me what the letter was about. I'd kind of expected him to, given his level of suspicion.

"Everything is fine," I said. "No need for you to worry about me. Have you been following me so that you can give me a traffic ticket, Detective Malone?"

By the look on his face, I knew he wasn't finding that amusing. At least I found my humor slightly funny.

"So I guess it's safe to say that you haven't made an arrest today for the murder?" I continued.

"What makes you think I would make an arrest today?"

"I guess I was just hopeful. Have you checked into the doughnut shop on the west side of the street? I'm just wondering if perhaps the killer got the wrong address. Maybe they meant to kill someone at the doughnut shop."

Maverick raised an eyebrow. "Yeah, I checked into it all right. They have doughnuts with double-fudge chocolate icing, They're really good. Except for the jelly ones. Not my favorite."

"Yeah, well, now you're just mocking me."

"What? I know what you're thinking . . . a cop and doughnuts." He winked.

"You always have liked doughnuts. Remember when you took a bite out of Mrs. Pitchford's chocolate doughnut? She chased you all around the lunchroom demanding that you give it back," I said with a laugh.

"Hey, I was thirteen and Bobby Kiel dared me to do it."

"Yeah, you were never one to turn down a challenge."

"I think we have that in common," he said, searching my eyes.

"Well, nevertheless, back to the topic of the doughnut shop. I think they make the doughnuts the night before, so no wonder you don't like them. They don't make them fresh."

Maverick sighed, and his tone abruptly shifted. "You know that I know you've been doing some research on your own. So let's cut to the chase here, and you can let me know what you've been up to, Marci." It was obvious he wasn't happy with the fact that I had been doing my own investigating.

"Um, I've just been asking a few people questions. Nothing wrong with that, right?" I said hesitantly.

"It's dangerous; that's what's wrong with it." Maverick's phone rang. "I need to return this call, but you're not off the hook in telling me everything you know."

"When do you have time to talk?"

"Well, I asked you out, but you didn't seem interested in that. If you want to reconsider, we could perhaps get together tonight for dinner," Maverick said.

He was asking me out on a date again? Now I'd been asked out for three dates in one day. I'd never been so popular. Furthermore, was it a good idea to say yes after I'd already said no? Actually, maybe it was. If I went out with him, then maybe I could find out more about his investigation. I was torn on what to do. I needed to see Antoine to return the book, and besides, I really wanted to go out with him. But I also wanted to talk to Maverick.

However, Antoine had asked first, so I had to keep my word and see him for dinner tonight. If I went out with Maverick, it would be for investigation purposes only.

"You know, I will reconsider. I can't tonight, but how about tomorrow night?" I asked. At least I'd given him an alternative.

Had Maverick just blushed? The tint to his cheeks and smile said that yes, he was blushing. The reaction was surprising to me in a womanizer like him.

"I need to check a few things, but I can let you know soon. Is it all right if I give you a call later?" he asked.

"Yes, that would be great. Thank you."

Unless he called when I was busy. Then he'd just have to wonder what I was doing and leave a message.

"Right." He studied my face as if he was trying to figure out what made me tick. "Well, I guess I'll let you get back to reading your letter, and I'll make my call."

"Oh, I'm finished now, and I'm going home," I said.

"I think that might be a good idea."

Was he suggesting I had to go home now? Maybe I wasn't ready to go home. "Although I have a couple errands I need to run, so I think I'll do that." I stared at his handsome face.

I didn't actually have errands; I'd just told him that to show him I was free to do whatever I wanted.

"You know, maybe we can go to the pumpkin festival in a couple days," Maverick said.

Was he asking me to both dinner and the pumpkin festival? Or would we have dinner at the pumpkin festival? Corn dogs and candy apples wouldn't be much of a dinner.

"Okay, sure," I said.

"Have a nice evening, Marci," Maverick said, before walking away.

# Chapter Seventeen

To say that I was nervous for my date would be an understatement. I didn't think I'd been this nervous since I was in the Christmas pageant in sixth grade and accidentally slipped and fell flat on my face in front of the entire school. I hoped nothing like that happened this time. At least I wouldn't have an audience, but then again, being alone could be a bad thing too. If Antoine turned out to be a killer, I'd seriously have to question my ability to judge others' character.

I stood in front of my closet, debating what to wear. What did one wear to a date with someone the whole town thought was a killer? I mean, something cute? I'd once read that men loved red, that they fell in love immediately as soon as they saw a woman wearing red. It had probably been in some dumb *Cosmopolitan* article, so I shouldn't give it much credence. However, someone somewhere along the way had decided this was accurate, so maybe I *should* wear red. Although did I want him attracted to me? I mean, yes, he was a handsome man and I would be flattered, and he had asked me over, but what was his motive? To kill me or to find out what I knew, or was he actually interested in me? I supposed I was about to find out.

Just in case, I decided not to go for the red. I didn't want a serial killer falling head over heels in love with me. I snickered at the thought. But hey, it could happen, right? I was a successful woman, not that bad looking, and had a pleasant enough personality. What was not to love?

I decided to wear a pink blouse and a nice pair of white slacks with my white sandals. This seemed like the perfect casual-enough outfit, yet not too casual. Plus, it was the colors of my bakery. I decided to put on some makeup—after all, if I wanted to get him to talk, maybe I did need to turn on the charm just a little. I added some lipstick, grabbed my bag, and headed for the door.

I had a feeling my nervousness would only get worse as I approached his house. I took my time driving, trying to calm down.

When I arrived, I sat in the car for several minutes, reviewing my game plan. Once I got inside Antoine's place, I'd be on the lookout for anything suspicious. Would he be dumb enough to leave anything else lying around his house like the diary?

I grabbed my bag, got out of the car, and headed for his house. The sound of a car turning off caught my attention. When I looked to my left, I saw a dark sedan parked along the curb. It looked as if someone was behind the wheel, but it was too far away and hard to see who was actually there. I had that weird feeling again. Why did I feel as if that person was watching me? Maybe it was just because I was nervous and at Antoine's house. Yeah, that had to be it. Nothing else to be concerned about. Just going inside was enough to worry about without adding to my fears.

I shifted from foot to foot as I waited for Antoine to answer the door. Why was it taking him so long? What was he doing in there? Perhaps he was still getting ready for the date, or the so-called date. I wasn't looking at it so much as a date as a mission to solve this murder. I wasn't sure what he was thinking.

I knocked again. Maybe he'd decided he didn't want to go out with me. Or maybe he'd just completely forgotten about it. But that thought had no sooner entered my mind than I heard the door rattle. He opened it wide and smiled. He sure did look dashing in his black pants and his blue button-down shirt. Butterflies flitted around in my stomach. This was not the time for that feeling. *Settle down, butterflies; dance some other time.*

"You look beautiful," he said.

The butterflies started again, and I was pretty sure I was blushing.

"Thank you. You look handsome," I said.

"Why thank you, ma'am," he said. "Please come in."

He gestured for me to enter. I walked inside, stepping into the living room I had visited just a short time earlier.

"I'm glad you decided to come over," he said.

"Well, thanks for the invitation," I said.

I had the diary in my bag. Reading through it had left me with more questions than answers. Now I had to figure out how to get the book back into the desk without him knowing about it. Perhaps he would go into the kitchen, but then, if we were cooking together, he would want me to follow him in there. This could be tricky. What if he had noticed it was gone and he knew I was the one who'd taken it? I hoped I could put the book back before he discovered it was missing—and definitely before I left for the evening.

What was the worst that could happen? Well, he could kill me, I supposed, but if I kept a positive attitude and didn't rouse his suspicions, this might just work out in my favor. I didn't sense anything malicious coming from him. On the contrary, actually. He seemed pretty easy to talk to, and I wasn't nervous like I had been when I was outside walking up to his house. And thank goodness that creepy feeling of being watched had gone too. I felt more relaxed, which had to be a good sign. That had to mean he wasn't the killer.

"So shall we get started with dinner? I imagine you're hungry. We could have an appetizer while we prepare. We'll nibble on those while we cook. Maybe a glass of wine too?"

"Sounds like a great idea, thank you," I said.

"Would you like for me to take your bag?" he asked.

I clutched my bag as if it were a life preserver and I was about to drown. "No, I'll just set it down in the kitchen."

I wanted to keep it in the same room with me so I could keep an eye on it. Plus, that way he wouldn't be poking around looking at the contents.

I followed Antoine into the kitchen, placing my bag on the table. What if it fell off the counter and the contents tumbled out? That would be awkward. And how would I explain it?

"So what are we having?" I asked.

He proceeded to tell me about the fancy meal he intended on us making together.

"Coq au vin. Rooster with wine. Have you heard of it?"

The way the words rolled from his mouth made my insides tingle. I nodded but was temporary speechless.

"Of course you've heard of it. Let's get started, shall we?"

"That sounds lovely," I said.

Antoine started gathering the ingredients and pans. "I'll braise the silky wine sauce and finish it off with butter."

"Red wine, right?" I asked when my voice finally came back.

"Yes, that's right." Antoine added in onions and mushrooms with a flick of his wrist.

My forte was definitely baking, but I felt comfortable with any dish in the kitchen. I was au fait with many French recipes.

Antoine pulled out a platter from the refrigerator. "I almost forgot the appetizers."

I took one of the pieces of toast from the plate. "They look delicious. Is this smoked salmon?"

He nodded with a smile. "Canapés."

"It's delicious. Everything smells wonderful," I said.

"Wait until you taste it. Shall we finish?" he asked.

I nodded. "Yes, just let me know what you want me to do."

As he gave me instructions, we settled in nicely, working next to each other. We nibbled on the appetizer too. This was kind of nice. I could get used to working in the kitchen with Antoine.

Even with things going well so far, I had to make small talk. I didn't want him to think I was here just for his cooking or perhaps just because he was gorgeous. Maybe he was onto me and knew I was trying to see if he was the killer. Especially if he'd discovered his diary was missing.

"So how are you enjoying the United States so far?"

"I'm enjoying all the American stuff. But I miss a lot about Paris," Antoine said. "Why did you open the bakery?"

Hoping I didn't sound too crazy, I explained about my childhood and how I'd fallen in love with French everything.

"But you've never been," he said with a laugh.

"No, I've never been, but I hope to remedy that someday soon."

"Perhaps I could be your tour guide," he said.

Wow. I was surprised he had offered. That wasn't something a killer would do, right? Maybe this was going somewhere after all. I had a bunch of other questions for him, though, and I proceeded to ask all of them. We were having a nice conversation.

"How about that wine now?" he suggested.

If I had too much to drink, that might put me off my guard. What if he decided to make a move as the killer? But I guessed one glass would be okay, and maybe it would calm my nerves. When I nodded, he poured us each a glass of Cabernet Sauvignon, and we settled in the living room again. Of course I brought my bag with me. I figured he considered this strange behavior. Maybe he thought I was worried that he would steal from me. Oh, if he only knew the truth. Yes, I was doing this to him, but I had my reasons.

I took a deep breath. I had to use this opportunity to ask about Kellie. As much as I hated to bring the mood down, it had to be done. He might not want to discuss it, but what else could I do? I had to know more.

# Chapter Eighteen

"It's been a crazy time for you here in Paris, huh?" I asked, then took a sip of wine.

He sat down across from me and nodded. "I'm sure you have a lot of questions."

Wow. I was glad he'd brought that up. Though maybe he'd brought it up to throw me off. I'd think he was innocent if he was so willing to discuss this.

"Yes, I suppose I do," I said. What exactly was he talking about? Did he mean I could ask questions about his murdered ex-girlfriend? My heart beat a little faster. This was it. Maybe now I would hear all the details. "Well, I suppose I wondered why you all were fighting in my bakery."

"Kellie didn't want to break up. Even after a year she still wanted to talk about our relationship. But I knew we weren't right for each other. There were just too many things we didn't see eye to eye on. That ultimately led to us bickering all the time, and no one wants to do that, right?"

"No, I certainly wouldn't want that," I said. "It seems odd that she was still talking about your breakup. Did that make you feel uncomfortable?"

"Sure, but she said she was moving on from our breakup and had a date with a man. Well, a couple dates, I guess. She told me he had been following her. Just my opinion, but I think maybe it was him. The police aren't having any of that."

I didn't bother to mention that I already knew this tidbit of information. Though I was glad to get confirmation that the police knew about Hunter.

"They can't find any evidence against this guy?" I asked.

"If they have, I'm not aware of it."

The police couldn't, but maybe I could.

"And you don't know anything about him?"

"Other than what she told me, like just his name. Oh, and I saw his picture."

"Don't you think it's odd that she'd show that picture to her ex-boyfriend?" I asked.

He shrugged. "It was almost as if she was warning me. You know, in case something happened to her. Then I could look for this guy."

"Well, if that's the case, I wish she'd given more details, like a last name."

Why not share every single thing she knew about him? It certainly would have been much easier than the way I was going about things now. But even though she might have suspected the man of following her, she'd probably never truly thought this would happen to her. I wished it hadn't. I wished I could have helped her. Though she probably wouldn't have wanted my help if she knew I'd had my eye on her ex-boyfriend. Since she still wanted to be with him, she would have been livid to find out.

"Do you think there's any way that we can find him?" I asked, taking another sip of wine.

Pretending to be clueless about Hunter might allow me to get more details.

"I've tried, but so far I've had no luck." He stared at me. "Maybe you would have better luck. I sense that you like that kind of thing."

He smiled and took a drink. I waited for him to say more.

"What makes you think that?" I asked.

"Just an air about you, I suppose. You have that mysterious vibe underneath everything. You don't like anything to go unanswered, do you?"

"I guess I don't," I said.

Fear that he knew what I was up to crept in. Although I had other reasons for wanting to solve the murder as well. I supposed his assumption was correct, though, and part of my motivation was that I didn't like unresolved things.

A phone rang somewhere in the distance.

"I'm sorry, but will you excuse me? I was expecting a call."

"Sure, no problem," I said. "I'll wait for you in the dining room."

Perfect timing. If I stepped out of the room and he stayed in the kitchen, that would give me a chance to put the diary back. I desperately wanted to get it out of my hands.

I hurried into the living room space, I grabbed my purse with the book inside and headed over to the desk. I heard him on the phone in the kitchen.

"Yes, I know," he was saying. "Well, it wasn't intentional. Of course, you know that, but I don't know what to do. I'm stuck here."

It seemed like a serious conversation. What was he talking about—he hadn't meant to do it and now he was stuck? It sounded an awful lot like he was talking about the murder. I was dying to know who he was talking to, but how would I find out?

I'd just closed the desk drawer when I heard movement from my right. When I looked over, I spotted Antoine standing at the kitchen's entrance. Had he seen me at the desk? A strange look crossed his face. At least my hand hadn't still been in the drawer. I had to make up an excuse for being over here.

"I was just admiring the desk. I think it's really cute." I gestured.

He squinted at me for a second as if he was suspicious. Luckily, after a few seconds, he smiled. "Thank you. I'm glad you like it. The piece was from my aunt. She lived here in America for twenty years before she passed away."

"Oh, I'm sorry that she's no longer with us."

"Thank you," he said again. "She left me quite a bit of stuff, which was wonderful."

"That is very nice. Is everything all right with the call?" I asked.

"Oh yes, it was just a colleague talking about work." He forced a smile. "You know, I don't want to talk about work."

I wasn't sure I believed him. It sounded as if he had made that up at the last minute, but I wouldn't press the issue anymore. However, I wanted to take a look at his phone and see if I recognized the last number that had called him. Maybe if I got into the kitchen after we ate, I would have a chance. Then I'd be out of here. Having dinner with him would be plenty of time spent together. It would seem like a legitimate date, and leaving after wouldn't seem odd. He wouldn't think I just wanted out of this situation.

Antoine placed the food beautifully on the blue-and-white toilé-patterned plates and then set them on the table. He even added thyme to spruce up the presentation. We sat down together at the small carved wood dining table and started eating, enjoying the dinner. Light from the porch streamed through the nearby window, adding a yellow glow to the room. We made some small talk about town, and it was going nicely. Actually, now I wasn't looking forward to leaving; I could sit and talk with him for hours. But I needed to get a look at his phone to find out who he'd been talking to. How would I get him to let me see the phone, though? He was right here beside me and likely going nowhere.

"Was that someone at your door?" I asked.

Okay, that was a lame excuse, and he might not fall for this attempt.

"Was it?" he asked as he got up from the table.

"I thought I heard someone," I said.

I just hoped he didn't take the phone with him. When he walked out of the room, I hurried over to the other side of the table to check his phone. Thank goodness it wasn't protected with a passcode.

I quickly checked the last call received and got the phone number. I had to remember it until I got back over to my phone. I hurried back to the table, picked up my phone, and typed in the number. Then I sat there at the table as if nothing had happened.

He walked back into the room. "No one was there. Are you sure you heard someone knock?"

"Oh, maybe it was someone at the neighbor's. It just sounded like a knock at the door."

"Perhaps, but I heard nothing," he said with a bit of a snap in his words.

His tone had changed. Was he suspicious that I was up to something? Anxiety settled in the pit of my stomach at the thought.

"Well, like I said, it was probably the neighbors making noise. Sorry about that."

"Hmm. It's no problem," he said.

"It's been a lovely dinner, and I thank you so much for inviting me."

"You're welcome. I'm glad you came," he said.

"I probably should get going. I have to get up early in the morning." I gestured over my shoulder.

"Yes, you do get up early, don't you? Do you ever get tired of that?"

"Sometimes, I guess, but I do love my work, so it's okay."

I grabbed my phone and headed for the other room. Antoine followed right behind me, a little too close. I sensed something was different now. It was all in my head, I told myself. I grabbed my bag and then headed for the door.

"So will I see you again?" he asked.

"I guess I will see you at the bakery when you come in, right?"

He laughed. "Yes, of course—how could I turn down French pastry? I mean, after all, it reminds me of home. You remind me of home in a lot of ways."

What could I say about that?

He studied my face, and the next thing I knew, he was leaning down to give me a kiss. It was a fabulous kiss, and for a moment I forgot all about the fact that he might be a killer. And that I was trying to find a murderer. And that anything strange at all had happened. But I came to my senses when a sound came from the door behind us.

When I turned around, I was shocked to find Maverick standing right there on the front porch. I spotted him through the door's window. The strange look on his face let me know he was just as surprised to see me.

When Antoine opened the door, for some reason I blurted out, "I came by to talk to Antoine, if that's all right with you."

"Of course it's okay," he said with a pinched face.

This was an awkward exchange, and I wasn't quite sure what to say. I was stuttering all over myself. Without saying another word, I opened the door and stepped out onto the porch. Antoine didn't follow me, and he didn't say anything else either. Maverick remained silent as I stepped around him and then headed toward my car. What else could I say? I could ask him why he was there, but I already knew. At least I thought I knew. He wanted to ask Antoine more questions.

But then it hit me: What if he wanted to arrest Antoine right then and there? Had Maverick followed me here? It had been quite a while since I'd arrived at Antoine's house, so I didn't think that was the case. However, he had to have noticed my car parked out front. It was just such a strange turn of events. I wasn't sure what to think.

I slipped into my car, but I sat there watching the men. If Antoine was arrested, then I wanted to know right away. If they were going to arrest him for the murder, I wanted to know why.

Maverick would probably notice that I wasn't going anywhere and that I was watching from my car. But I didn't care. As soon as I saw that he was leaving, I would leave as well, but not a moment before. There was nothing in the law that said I couldn't sit here.

The men just stood there on the porch, talking. It didn't seem to be a heated exchange or anything. But of course I had no clue what they were talking about. I assumed the murder case, and I was just glad that Maverick hadn't put Antoine in cuffs yet.

I sat there for a few seconds, thinking about the kiss and how Antoine had taken me off guard. Regardless, it had been a great kiss. The moment I'd looked at Maverick, guilt had come over me, though. I was so torn. I didn't know what to think. I'd told Maverick I had plans tonight. Well, now he knew what those plans were, but there was nothing wrong with my date. I wasn't in a relationship with Maverick, and I didn't owe him an explanation. Besides, Maverick was no doubt dating a lot of other women anyway.

Another minute went by, and then Maverick turned and walked away. Antoine watched Maverick for several seconds, and then he went back inside. For now, it seemed as if he was still a free man, but how long would that last?

# Chapter Nineteen

The next morning, I drove to work and parked just down the street from my shop. Not the ideal spot for me, but they had blocked off the area in front of the bakery for further investigation. Luckily, they said they'd be finished by the time I opened for customers in a couple of hours. I needed the business now after the last couple of days with fewer customers. Thank goodness things had steadily started to get back to normal. Things couldn't fully be back to normal, though, until the killer was behind bars. I still didn't know who had killed Kellie, but I wouldn't give up on tracking down that evil person.

I'd called the number I'd found on Antoine's phone. Interestingly enough, the number was for a gun shop. Why had he called there? Would I ever find out?

I would be alone to start the day again. Aunt Barb was going to bring Pepé Le Pew and Fifi to the shop later. They always hated getting up before the roosters. I couldn't say I blamed them.

Maverick left a message saying he'd had work come up and wouldn't be able to make our date. Surely that had just been an excuse. I returned his call, but it went straight to his voice mail.

We were playing phone tag, I supposed. I left him a message and hinted at what I'd found out recently. I'd also asked why he'd been at Antoine's, though I figured he probably wouldn't answer that question. Maybe I just wanted to ensure he'd call me again. Leaving that message would surely get a call back.

No matter what, I wouldn't tell Maverick how I'd gotten these tidbits. And I wouldn't reveal my collection of clues until I could tell him in person. Although maybe I should have left that info in the message. That would give him time to think before confronting me face-to-face. I hoped he wasn't too mad at me after catching me at Antoine's place engaged in a kiss. Would he even care?

I got out of the car, grabbed my bag, locked the door behind me, and then headed down the sidewalk toward my bakery. Darkness still cloaked the town, although the first signs of daybreak had started to peek over the horizon. I wondered if this was a good idea. Should I be walking around downtown where a murder had occurred? Each time I did this I ran the risk of bumping into the killer.

No one had specifically told me not to go walking by myself in the dark, but they probably figured I was adult enough to know better. Not that I wasn't aware of the danger, but life must go on, and I wasn't anyone else's responsibility. I should make those decisions for myself. I decided that it was perfectly safe to go just a few steps down the sidewalk, though I hadn't planned on parking so far away from the bakery. I'd totally forgotten about the street cleaning.

Despite the hints of daylight coming from the east, the dark surroundings gave me a creepy feeling, as if someone was watching me. I thought I caught movement out of the corner of my eye. I glanced over my shoulder, as if I might find someone right behind me, but to my relief, I saw no one around. A few cars moved around town, but no one was out and about yet.

I tried to shake off the feeling, but it still felt as if someone watched me. Even though I hadn't known Kellie, I wondered if maybe she'd been coming to warn me of something the night she died. Perhaps she'd wanted to warn me about Antoine after she saw us flirting. Or like I'd thought previously, maybe the killer had really been looking for *me* and she was just in the way. Now my fear spiked even more. The feeling of being watched stuck with me. The darkness hid anyone under the cover of blackness. They could be anywhere, watching and waiting for their chance to pounce. They might attack me and do the same thing to me that they'd done to Kellie.

I quickened my steps, hoping to get to my bakery faster. I prayed that someone wouldn't grab me along the way. I had nothing with me to defend myself with. Another dumb move. I planned on making some changes to my life. Changes like not making stupid decisions and also getting myself some sort of weapon. Mace . . . or anything. I'd carry a club if I had to, because I didn't care. Anything so that I could maybe defend myself if a killer came up to me.

I glanced over my shoulder again. Repeatedly, actually. But I saw nothing out of the ordinary. Until that split second when things changed.

As I started to turn my attention back to the street ahead of me, out of the corner of my eye, I caught movement. When I looked to the right, I saw a person shadowed in the dark. Then the person darted behind the building, as if they had been standing in the alleyway watching me but wanted to hide when I turned my attention on them.

The person had been dressed in dark clothing, so that aided in concealing their identity; they'd almost blended in with the black sky. Maybe it was only my imagination, but something around the person's feet had caught my attention. Like a glint of something shiny. Maybe on their shoes.

Who was the person? I took a step toward the alleyway but froze. What was I doing? Going into a dark alleyway behind a building to confront a potential killer? I could see the news when they reported on exactly how things went down. Everyone would say, *Well, that was a dumb move. Why did she do that? She must have been stupid.* And if I saw that news about someone else, I probably would agree with that assessment: a dumb move. I shouldn't make any additional dumb moves.

No, going after that person was definitely the wrong idea. I hurried as fast as I could along the sidewalk until I reached the bakery. My hand shook as I fumbled with the key, trying to get it in the lock. I dropped the key. My breathing was heavy. My heart beat faster.

I looked around, thinking for sure the person was right behind me, ready to kill me. How would I fight them off? Kellie hadn't been able to; what made me think I could? I supposed I would give it my best shot, but that would be all I was capable of.

I finally grabbed the keys again, thank goodness, and shoved the key into the lock. This time I twisted the key and was able to unlock the door. I pushed it open and hurried inside. I tossed my bag onto the floor and then slammed the door shut, locking it behind me. I leaned against the glass, trying to catch my breath. I'd made it, finally.

I was safe, but the bakery was dark. This gave me the creeps too. I thought for a second I saw a shadow in the kitchen area, but then I realized it was just my chef's hat that I'd left on the hook. I needed to calm down. I was seeing things at this point, imagining that the killer was all around me. Talk about being paranoid.

I stood there for several more seconds, trying to catch my breath. When I thought my heart had quieted to a normal rhythm, I reached down and grabbed my bag. I just wanted to get to the light switch as quickly as possible and get some lights on in here. But then I worried that whoever was out there on the street would easily be able to see me walking around in here. Maybe I would just hurry to the back and turn on only the kitchen lights.

At least I felt safer now that I was in the security of my bakery. No one would get me here, right? I rushed across the floor and finally reached the kitchen area. I fumbled for the light switch and knocked a pan off a hook. When it fell to the ground with a loud clanging noise, I screamed, even though I knew what it was.

I fumbled again and found the switch, and light flooded the kitchen area. I released a deep breath and looked around. Thank goodness, no one was hiding in here. Then again, they wouldn't be hiding very well if I saw them right away, would they? They could still be hiding somewhere and I wouldn't even know it. Should I check the whole bakery?

No, I just needed to calm down. No one was in here. Aunt Barb and I were the only ones with the key.

When I glanced to my left, I saw a piece of paper on the counter. It looked like a note for me. Had Aunt Barb been here, or was she telling me she wasn't coming in to work this morning? Why wouldn't she just text me or call? She loved to call, even though I repeatedly told her to text me instead. *Only call me if someone's dead, and maybe even then, text me.* Okay, okay, I would let her call for that, but that was practically the only reason.

If I had this text-instead-of-call policy, why had I called Maverick? Because I wanted to hear his voice?

I stepped over to the counter and picked up the piece of paper. It was addressed to me, a note written in pencil on white paper.

But I didn't recognize the handwriting, so I knew right away that it wasn't from Aunt Barb.

*Mind your own business, Marci Beaucoup. Or I will be coming after you.*

Reading the words sent a shiver down my spine. Was this a threat from the killer? It had to be. Plus, it seemed like they'd even creepily tried to make the note rhyme. My hand shook as I held the letter, and breathing became even more difficult. I glanced all around the bakery again. The eerie silence gave me a chill. What if someone was here? The person was being awfully quiet if they were.

I had to tell Maverick about this. I had to figure out how to handle this. I had to find the killer as soon as possible, and I couldn't rely on Maverick to do it, even if it was his job. Now my life was in danger.

When the back door rattled, my heart sped up and my panic spiked. Was someone trying to break in? If so, no doubt it was the killer. The threatening letter wasn't enough. The killer had come to me now. What would I do? How would I get away?

I raced over to the broom closet and climbed inside. I tried to be as quiet as possible, not making a peep. I didn't want the person to realize I was hiding. How long would I have to wait in here? It smelled like pine-scented disinfectant and pastry—not a good combination.

I stood there and listened as the person opened the back door and then stepped inside. Someone had a key? They'd unlocked the door; I'd heard the clicking sound. The person paused as if they were looking around, no doubt trying to find me.

Ten seconds later the closet door rattled. I didn't know whether to scream or to prepare to punch. Probably I would do both. After the shock wore off, I pulled my arm back and readied myself to punch whoever opened that door.

About two seconds later, light flooded the little room. When the closet door opened, I instinctively pushed my arm forward and tried to plant my fist in the person in front of me. It didn't work, though, because Aunt Barb grabbed my arm, slung me out onto the floor, and got me into a headlock. I couldn't even tell her it was me because I could barely breathe, let alone speak.

Seconds later, she released the hold. "Oh my gosh, Marci. What are you doing? I could have killed you."

I coughed and tried to reply, but the words wouldn't come out. I sat up.

"Are you okay? Talk to me," she said, tapping my cheeks a little too roughly. "Why are you in the closet?"

I handed her the note. It was all I could do, because I still couldn't speak.

Aunt Barb took the letter and quickly read the words. "Are you serious? Where did you find this?"

I finally managed to get to my feet and took the letter from her. "It was on the counter."

"What in the world were you doing in the closet, though?"

"I thought you were the killer coming in to kill me. After I found that letter, I got paranoid, so I hid in the closet."

"You're so stressed, and now threatening messages. I worry about you," she said.

I blew the hair out of my eyes. "I guess it's easy to let this get the best of me, I suppose."

"I guess it was, dear," she said, patting my arm.

I hadn't heard her call me that in a long time. She just wasn't the mushy kind. I knew she loved me more than anything, but she wasn't a hugger, and she didn't use words of endearment often. And I was okay with that. I understood it, too, but that didn't stop me from speaking affectionately to her.

I took the letter again. "I can't believe they left this, but how did they get in the shop? The doors were locked, and we know this wasn't here yesterday."

"Who else would have a key?" she asked.

"Other than you, no one. And I know you didn't do it. Oh, wait, the only other people I can think of are my current landlord and potential new landlords. She may have given the potential buyers a key. Audrey and Antoine."

Her eyes widened. "Antoine is accused of killing Kellie, so it makes sense that he would come in here and leave you this note."

I shook my head. "I just don't want to believe that he had anything to do with this or that he left the letter."

"You have to be wise, Marci. Don't let his good looks sway you. Do you know how many good-looking men have been accused of being serial killers? Hello, Ted Bundy was handsome and charismatic. And people fell for his charm."

"It's not because he's handsome at all," I said. "I just have this feeling that he didn't do it."

"Well, now you have to reconsider, since someone left this note inside the shop and he's one of the only people who has a key."

Aunt Barb had a point. Was it possible? It was hard for me to contemplate.

Aunt Barb took the note from me again. "I can't believe this. This makes no sense, but we have to call Detective Malone."

"I'm doing that," I said. "I just had to get my bearings about me."

"You'd better call him." Aunt Barb brushed the hair out of her eyes with the back of her hand.

Strands had already come loose from her updo. She'd been wearing it in that style as far back as I could remember. Her hair had turned somewhat gray now, but she still had a lot of brown.

Aunt Barb went over, grabbed my bag, and started rummaging around.

"What are you doing?" I asked.

"Looking for your phone. We have to call him right away."

"Why use my phone?"

"Because he will answer if he sees it's you," Aunt Barb said.

"It's five in the morning."

"If he isn't awake, you can leave him a message."

"This isn't urgent. I mean, it's not an emergency. The killer isn't going to find me right now. The doors are locked."

"You were just hiding in the broom closet because you thought the killer was coming in after you. I think that makes this kind of urgent."

I hadn't even told her about the man I'd seen dashing behind the building across the street. I had a feeling that was who had been in my bakery. Maybe I was crazy for thinking it, but it didn't look like Antoine, and it didn't seem like Audrey's style. But who else would have a key to my door? It didn't look like there had been forced entry. Yes, I'd learned about that from watching those crime shows on TV. I saw nothing out of place. The lock on the back door was secure.

"Aunt Barb, did you use your key when you opened the back door?" I asked.

"Of course I did. The back door was locked. I let the dog and cat in the front first, though. I'm surprised you didn't hear me."

"Well, I guess I was distracted. That's a bit scary to think about. I came in the front. Nothing seemed out of place up there either," I said.

I walked back across the shop to turn on the light for the front area of the bakery. I didn't care if the killer saw me now. I was getting angry about this. Once at the door, I checked the lock. It was secure as well. Everything was just as I'd left it the night before. And nothing was out of place outside either. The only thing different was that note. I wondered if the police could get fingerprints. I sure hoped so.

"This just makes me so angry," Aunt Barb said as she pounded her fist on the counter.

She was going to do more than throw macarons at someone this time.

"Remember your blood pressure, Aunt Barb," I said.

"Well, that's it. If you won't call the police, then we'll have to get to the bottom of this. The killer is going down. No one threatens my niece and gets away with it." She shook her fist.

I hadn't seen Aunt Barb this mad since she'd kicked her ex-husband Gene out. And oh boy, had she been angry with him. She'd cut the crotch out of every one of his pairs of pants and then burned them in front of him. She'd taunted him. But he'd done a lot to her over the years of their marriage. Things she should never have had to put up with. She was a tough woman, and partly because of the way he'd treated her. She'd had to learn to be tough. I was glad she was rid of him.

Now Aunt Barb and I would be a team. And it kind of felt good that she was on my side with this. Not that she hadn't been on my side from the beginning, but now at least I had an aide in my search. She wanted to find the killer just as much as I did.

Though I didn't really want to drag her into this mess and get her in trouble. I wouldn't want the killer to come after her too.

# Chapter Twenty

There was one thing for sure that had to be done, and I knew I had to do it. I had to get into Antoine's office and possibly his home again. We'd been on a date, which made me feel as if he'd just tell me what I wanted to hear. He wouldn't exactly confess to a murder. Anything he said could just be a lie. I had to search for any clues that would rule him out as the main suspect. Once he was ruled out, I could focus on finding the real killer. And Maverick could too.

I didn't think it would take me long to have a quick look around his office. I would find something that would let me know he wasn't the killer. But how would I do that? I didn't know for sure what I was looking for.

Sure, there wasn't enough evidence right now to say he'd done it, but that wouldn't stop the police. They were still looking at him, and I felt like an arrest was imminent, since I'd seen Maverick at his place.

When we'd closed the shop for the day, I stepped out into the back area and threw away a bag of trash. Holding Pepé Le Pew's carrier and Fifi's leash, I stood by the trash can and looked all around to see if anyone had watched me. Nothing else of note had happened all day, so I was on edge, waiting for something. Expecting it, almost. Aunt Barb came out after me and locked the door behind her.

"All right, now what?" she asked. "Where are we going?"

"We should get to work on this now, right?" I said.

"Yes, right now. There's no time to waste," she said.

Should I tell her what I had planned? I mean, after all, we were going to be a team now. I kind of needed her help.

"I guess I planned on going to Antoine's office and talking to him." I stared at her for a moment.

She raised an eyebrow. "What do you have in mind?"

"I thought maybe we could sneak in," I said.

Her eyes widened. "In that big company? How will we do that? They have security guards."

"Well, that's where you come into play," I said. "I thought maybe you could help me do it. I snuck in the other day, but there was a guard."

"You want me to rope a guard up? I can tie him up and blindfold him."

Well, if she could do it . . . maybe that wasn't such a bad idea. It would certainly keep him busy for a while until I got inside and looked around. He'd be busy trying to get unblindfolded, and by the time I got back outside, he wouldn't know what had hit him.

What was I thinking? We couldn't do that.

"No, we can't do that. It's totally illegal. Such a bad idea," I said.

"Of course I was joking about roping him up."

Was she kidding? I'd sensed a tinge of excitement in her voice that suggested that maybe, for a brief moment, she'd contemplated it

Aunt Barb and I got in the car and headed in the direction of my place to drop off Fifi and Pepé Le Pew. That accomplished, I pointed the car in the direction of Flaget Manufacturing.

"We've been busy and I didn't get a chance to ask, but I've noticed you've been talking to Gordon a lot. What's that all about?" I glanced over at her and flashed a smile.

Aunt Barb frowned. "I have to talk to customers, you know."

"This seems like more than just talking about his love of those petit fours," I said.

"Well, that's all it is," Aunt Barb said, staring straight ahead at the road in front of us.

Now I really was suspicious, but she was being tight-lipped.

"You seem to like the petit fours too," I said.

"You know I do. Now can we change the subject to something more important? So you've been to this place once before?" Aunt Barb asked.

"Yes, I have," I said.

"And you didn't tell me? Why?"

"Well, I thought you would tell me not to do it."

"You're probably right. I think I would have told you not to do that. But that note changed everything, Marci. If you aren't going to involve the police, then we have to find this killer."

I was just now realizing how dangerous this truly was. Like a dead body wasn't enough, but having Aunt Barb worried—that was when it really hit home. Before, I supposed, I'd been thinking that maybe the killer was only out for Kellie. Now I knew that wasn't the case. Maybe I really had been the target all along. But why? Perhaps I was overthinking this and just scared that I was in the killer's cross hairs. After all, the note had said I should mind my own business. That meant I wasn't the original target, right?

"You're awfully quiet," Aunt Barb said.

I snapped back to attention. "Just thinking about everything. I'm hoping that we find the killer soon."

"Well, I think this is a step in the right direction."

"Because you think Antoine is guilty," I said.

"I don't know what to think, Marci, but it's a real possibility."

"I spoke with Kellie's boss. I think Antoine can give me an answer on whether or not he was at my bakery. Since he had a key."

"Do you think he's really going to tell you the truth? He would just lie and say no, it wasn't him."

"I'm perceptive. I can tell if he's lying or not," I said. "I'll be able to get the truth out of him."

Aunt Barb looked at me suspiciously. "All right, I believe you."

I thought maybe she was about fifty-fifty on whether she believed me or not. But I honestly felt like I could get it out of him. And like I would know if he was telling the truth.

"Do you think the security guard will let you in? What happened last time?"

"I don't think he would let me in, but I have my ways of getting in. Like last time."

"I'm not sure I even want to know," Aunt Barb said. "Your mother will not be happy if she finds out about this."

"Then I guess we just won't tell her, will we?" I said. "She doesn't need to know."

"Well, if she finds out, then I'm going to act like I don't know anything about it."

"Fair enough," I said.

I slowed down as we neared Flaget.

"What's the plan?" Aunt Barb asked.

"All right, so maybe this time you can cause a distraction and I can get in the office building," I said.

"You don't need to go in alone."

"I went in alone last time."

"And that wasn't a good idea," she said.

"Aunt Barb, I'm not a baby."

"It's not about whether you're a baby or not, but some things are better when there are two people. Remember that's why I'm here—so that we can solve this together, yes?"

"Yes, Aunt Barb," I said.

I pulled the car up to the gate like I had before.

"What are we doing here?" Aunt Barb asked. "Why not go in the gated area?"

"We just have to wait until someone drives out so we can get in."

"Oh, is that all?" she said sarcastically. "We could be here for a long time."

"Oh, I don't think so. There are plenty of cars in there waiting to drive out, so it won't be long. Just be patient."

"You know I'm not the patient type."

"Oh, I know that all too well." I tapped my finger against the steering wheel anxiously.

"Will you stop doing that? You're going to give me a panic attack."

Aunt Barb with a panic attack?

"Oh, I don't believe that for two seconds."

"It's true," she said. "Even with this rough exterior."

"Just think of this as a mission," I said.

"There has to be an easier way," Aunt Barb said after a few seconds.

She was already antsy, and it had been only a couple minutes.

"Wait, I see a car. Someone's walking toward their car. When they drive out, we'll be able to get through the gate." I gestured.

"I hope you know what you're doing."

I felt like I was an old pro at this by now.

"Absolutely I know what I'm doing. This is no problem at all."

"'If you say so," Aunt Barb said. "I can probably hack the card reader."

"No need for that." I shifted the car into drive.

The car was approaching the gate now. I got ready to go as it pulled out. I slammed on the gas pedal and raced toward the gate.

"Oh my sweet baby Jesus! Oh my sweet baby Jesus!" Aunt Barb yelled as the gates were closing.

The gates missed scraping our car by a hair because the other car had moved so slowly.

"We got it. We got it," I said around the adrenaline rush. I sat there for several seconds, trying to catch my breath and calm myself down. It had been a close call, but we'd made it. "I knew I could do it."

"I think I might need a pacemaker now. Never mind all those years in the army. My niece will be the death of me." Aunt Barb blew the hair out of her eyes.

"Now you're just being dramatic," I said. "We'll park over here by this tree. That's where I parked before, but be on the lookout for that security guard. He's not that nice."

"Why do you say that?" Aunt Barb asked.

"He stopped me before."

"I can handle him if he tries to stop us again."

Oh no, what was she going to do? Tie him up like she'd offered?

After I parked the car, Aunt Barb and I sat there in silence. I contemplated what we should do next. Since I hadn't spotted the security guard, I wasn't sure he would open the door and allow me to slip inside again. Although I could check and see if maybe by some chance he had left a door unlocked.

"They have to let us enter if we're visiting," Aunt Barb said.

"I don't know if I'd be welcome here after last time, Aunt Barb," I said.

"Oh, that's absurd." Aunt Barb opened the door to get out of the car and motioned for me to do the same.

Not surprisingly, Aunt Barb took the lead and marched across the parking lot. She glanced around as if this really was some sort of reconnaissance mission. I followed her lead because, after all, she was trained in this kind of thing. I liked having her on my team now. When we reached the glass-front double doors, we paused.

"What are we doing?" I asked.

Aunt Barb motioned for me to stay still, as if she were going to break in or someone might jump out at us. I was a bit confused, but I went along with everything she said. When she pulled the glass door, it opened.

The door wasn't locked? Why hadn't I thought of this? We could just walk right in? Now I felt stupid. I'd risked my life to slip in earlier.

Aunt Barb and I walked into the lobby. This was exactly where I'd come before to find the directory. I motioned for Aunt Barb to move over to the left to look for Antoine's office.

"I don't know where it is." I scanned the listings until I found him at the bottom of the first column.

Why hadn't I noticed his name earlier?

"Where is he?"

"Of course he's on the third floor. Why did it have to be the third," I said.

"All right, let's go." Aunt Barb motioned for me to follow her.

We traveled down the hallway. Quiet filled the building. I guessed almost everyone had gone for the day.

"But how are we going to get into a locked office?" I asked.

"I have my ways. I can pick the lock."

"This could seriously get us arrested."

"Of course it could," she said. "That's why we can't get caught. I'll pick the lock, you slip in to look around, and I'll stand guard."

I was surprised she didn't want to look around the office, but I didn't think she would trust me to stand guard. Was she really going to rely on me to go look around while she watched for the security guard? I was just worried they had cameras and were watching us right now. Maybe they had already called the police. I guessed that was the worst that could happen—we could get arrested for trespassing and spend a night in jail.

Aunt Barb and I were both tired by the time we reached the third floor. Unfortunately, Aunt Barb was afraid of elevators now. She'd gotten stuck in one at a hotel in Nashville, and she said her life had flashed before her eyes. Funny, because I'd always thought Aunt Barb was fearless.

Nevertheless, we pushed forward and hurried down the hallway. When we reached Antoine's office, we leaned against the door to catch our breath. I knocked on the door. What would I say if he actually answered? I had heart palpitations at the thought.

After a few seconds and no answer, I realized I wouldn't have to worry about my actions if he opened the door. Clearly he wasn't in the office.

"Let's do this before we get caught. I don't feel like spending the night in jail, but I will if I have to," she said.

I watched as Aunt Barb pulled a pin out from her hair and stabbed it into the lock. She jiggled the metal around a bit, and then all of a sudden, she had the door open.

"Wow, that was impressive," I said.

She shrugged. "It's what I do. Now get in there."

I stared at her, speechless. She gestured with a tilt of her head. I hurried into the room, and she shut the door behind me.

What would I do now?

A big desk sat in front of the windows. From the double windows was a view of the outside parking lot. Antoine would have had a good view of where I'd parked my car yesterday. I wondered if he had seen me in that whole exchange. It had been awkward, to say the least.

Bookshelves with books, a file cabinet, and all kinds of drawers filled the room. I knew Aunt Barb was anxious for me to get this over with. I could start with the desk, or maybe the filing cabinet.

Somewhere in this room could be the proof that Antoine was innocent—or that he was the killer.

# Chapter
# Twenty-One

As I stood in the middle of the office, I was a bit frozen. I had to make a move, because I couldn't stay in here long. Abandoning the idea of starting at the desk, I hurried over to the file cabinet and started rifling through, but all I saw were business files. Absolutely nothing to do with a murder. What had I thought I would find? A confession? Of course there would be files on business and nothing else. Plus, I was trying to exonerate him, so I knew deep down I wouldn't find anything incriminating.

After sorting through the files for several more seconds, I gave up, closed the door, turned around, and put my hands on my hips. I blew out a deep breath. All right, I needed to get my bearings about me. Where should I look next? I supposed the cabinet across the room, but it would probably just be more of the same. This had been a wasted trip. What had made me think I would find something in his office? But it was a start. I had to rule it out, and maybe somehow I would get into his house again. Another date, perhaps? I could get him to invite me inside for more bakery tips. Then I could snoop around while he was getting recipes for me.

As I moved halfway across the room to get to the other cabinet, I spotted something sitting on the edge of the desk. A cell phone. I rushed over and picked it up. Was this Antoine's? It didn't quite look like I remembered it.

I sure hoped I didn't get caught. My nerves were on edge, and the longer I was in the room, the more anxious I became. My heart beat faster and my legs shook. At this point, Aunt Barb was probably nervous too. Oh, what was I saying? She was used to this kind of pressure. Maybe I should have let her come inside and search while I stood guard.

I picked up the phone and then wondered if maybe they would check for fingerprints. Who were *they*, though? The police? I doubted that, since they wouldn't even know I had looked at the thing. I touched the screen, and thankfully, it lit up. I had worried that maybe it would be dead, since obviously someone had left it here.

Then the thought hit me. If Antoine had left his phone here, he would probably come back for it soon. My stomach dropped. I had to get out of here quick, but I wanted to know what was on the phone. This time the screen was locked. Had he locked it since our dinner? Was this a different phone? Now that I looked closer, I saw that this phone was covered by a different case. Could I get at the contents? What would his password be?

At that moment I remembered what my friend Kristina had shown me. She was kind of a tech wizard, though her official job was clothing boutique owner. She'd always flip her blonde hair from her shoulder with a flick of her wrist and say, "Honey, sometimes we have to be sneaky. When my ex-husband cheated, I went full FBI mode on him."

She was right. It was a bit of a sneaky move, but it worked, so I touched the screen a few times in specific locations the way that she'd told me. Then suddenly I had access to everything I needed inside that phone.

Sadly, I realized there wasn't much to see. Hardly any texts other than business. His mother had texted him, and that was it.

Why did he have another phone? Was this perhaps his work phone? Yes, surely that had to be it, because he had to have friends. There were no texts from Kellie on here. I'd thought maybe there would have been messages from her wanting to get back together.

I really didn't believe he was the killer, and I would stick with that until I absolutely knew otherwise. I had to find the true killer. I placed the phone back on the desk and stood there for several seconds, just staring at the room. *Come on, Marci, Aunt Barb's counting on you to be fast.*

I'd spent too much time being distracted by the phone. I now moved around behind the desk, figuring that I would look through his drawers and then get out of there, because what else was there to do? I saw nothing that looked important.

I spotted a baseball on the shelf among the books and other knickknacks. Immediately my thoughts turned to Maverick. He loved baseball. I still hadn't heard from him, but then again, I had made no effort to reach out to him again. I needed to do that, but how would I do that without sounding weird?

*C'est la vie.* That was neither here nor there right now. I was getting off track. *Focus, Marci.* I plopped down in the leather chair behind the desk. It would definitely be uncomfortable if Antoine came into his office and found me.

I couldn't help but think how nice it smelled here at his desk. Maybe it was a combination of the leather chair and . . . perhaps his aftershave? Spicy yet sweet. It was intoxicating, and he wasn't even around. Imagine if he was nearby and I smelled this scent. I was getting a little light-headed. I needed to get control of myself. He could be a killer. Nothing could happen between us then. What would that be like? Would I be one of those weird people who wrote to serial killers in prison? Professing my love for a psychopath? None of that sounded like an option. That would be insanity. He was cute and all, but not if he was a killer. If I found out he was, I would personally help get him sent away for a long time.

I was just stalling. I needed to hurry up. Aunt Barb was probably freaking out. If I actually found something, then I hoped no one asked how I'd gotten into Antoine's office, because I was keeping that little secret to myself. It gave me security to know I had my own little tricks. Such as the phone hack I'd just successfully completed. I never knew when I might need something like that—like if I had to help a friend check out what her ex had been up to behind her back. I'd done it recently and it hadn't been good.

When a noise sounded at the door, I panicked. I jumped up from the desk but hit my knee in the process. Somehow, I managed to keep my mouth shut, even though I wanted to scream out in pain. That was totally going to leave a bruise in the morning. But I kept my mouth clamped shut, dropped to my knees, and squeezed myself underneath the desk.

I was wedged under there like a square peg in a round hole. I tried not to make a sound as I sat there waiting for the person to open the door. What if it was Antoine? What if he came around to his desk and tried to put his feet under here? He'd poke me, and I'd surely not be able to hold back then. I'd yelp, and that would terrify him. My whole little snooping session would be over.

I sat under there for a while, waiting for something to happen. But nothing transpired. No one walked in. At least, I sure didn't hear the door or any footsteps, and I thought for sure I would have heard that right away.

I was almost positive that someone had rattled that door. Had it been Aunt Barb or someone else? Maybe she had taken off; so much for her being the lookout. I would have thought she'd track someone down like a bloodhound. I started to worry, thinking that maybe someone had made her leave. But Aunt Barb would never abandon me.

While I was under the desk, I noticed something. It was just a random piece of white piece on the floor. I reached down and picked it up. It was folded in half, so I unfolded it to see what was inside. Maybe it was nothing, but I had to know. It was thin; definitely receipt paper.

The receipt wasn't just any receipt, like for McDonald's or Starbucks. No, this was a receipt for a gun. I didn't know much about guns, but it looked like this was the type of gun that had been used to kill Kellie. Would Antoine really just leave a receipt for a gun underneath his desk? How random was that? Nevertheless, this was a huge development. Why else would he have this receipt? Unless, of course, Antoine had already found the killer. That might explain the receipt. Wouldn't he have told the police right away, though? Why keep this information to himself?

At least the name for the gun shop was on the receipt, so I could maybe swing by there and find out more about who exactly had purchased this gun. Would they give me that info? I wasn't sure, but I would try my best to find out.

Was this why Antoine had been on the phone with the gun store?

I stuffed the receipt into my pocket and then waited for just a couple more seconds before finally trying to emerge from underneath the desk. The things I did sometimes because of my "inquisitive nature"—that was what my dad called it. He just didn't want to admit I'd gotten his snoopiness trait. Yes, I certainly got myself into some pickles, but it was totally worth it if it meant saving my bakery. I wasn't going to let that go without a fight. No way.

I crawled out from under the desk on my hands and knees, hoping no one would walk in and see me. At least when I was under the desk, I'd had a way to hide myself, and it wouldn't have been quite as embarrassing if someone walked in, but being caught crawling on the floor would be humiliating. Although I guessed I could just pretend I was looking for something.

While I was in someone else's office, though? I should have thought this out before jumping in, but that was what I tended to do—jump in without thinking it through. Sometimes it worked out great, like with the bakery, and other times it didn't go as planned at all. Like when I had taken off to become an actress and headed across the country for Hollywood. That trip had resulted in me having no place to stay and hightailing it home to a bunch of people telling me they'd told me so.

I found it hard to believe that Antoine had a temper. I'd seen no indication of that behavior. He'd been calm with Kellie when she'd embarrassed him in front of everyone in my shop. Surely if he hadn't lost his temper on her, then he was a calm man. I wanted to think I was a good judge of character too. Maybe I wasn't, though. I was starting to have doubts now. Perhaps I should rethink all of this.

Why would he have a gun? Was it for self-defense?

Maybe the police really had already decided Antoine had done this. It used to be innocent until proven guilty, but nowadays, it seemed, it was guilty until proven innocent. Of course that wasn't the official law, according to Maverick, but in my small town, I felt that was the case. I just didn't want Maverick to hear me say it, because he would deny it and likely get angry with me. If he got angry with me, then maybe he wouldn't hesitate to arrest me if he found me snooping around like this. Though he was likely already upset with me after seeing me kiss Antoine.

When I finally reached the door, I eased it open. To my surprise, Aunt Barb was still on the other side.

"It's about time," she whispered. "I thought I was going to have to come in there and get you."

"Well, I'm here now," I said.

"You make me too antsy doing this stuff. You need to learn to move faster."

"Now is not a time for a lecture, Aunt Barb. We have to get out of here."

"You're telling me. That's what I was just telling you," she said. "Now come on."

"I'm coming, I'm coming."

She grabbed me by the arm and yanked me down the hallway. "Tell me you at least found something."

"Oh, I found something all right, but I'm not sure if it's a clue or not. But it's definitely something. He's got a lot of knickknacks in there too. Just like Gordon."

"Well, the guy's strange, okay? That's just the way it is. He has to be the killer."

"Just because you think he's strange doesn't mean he's the killer. And he is not strange. What makes you think he's strange?"

"Oh, I don't know . . . those shoes he wears. They look kind of weird."

"I think they are very fashionable. He looks handsome in them," I said.

"They're so fancy," she said.

"Well, maybe I should ask him to wear sneakers," I said.

"Nothing wrong with a good pair of sneakers," Aunt Barb said.

"I didn't say there was, Aunt Barb, and this conversation is totally going in a weird direction. We need to focus on finding the killer, not on where Antoine buys clothing. I don't care if he shops at Walmart or Saks Fifth Ave as long as I find out he's not the killer."

"Oh, you'd love it if he shops at Saks Fifth Ave," Aunt Barb said, grasping the railing as she hurried down the stairs.

"I will admit I would like it if he shopped at Saks Fifth Ave. That would be kind of fun, but that's neither here nor there." I peeked around the corner.

If Antoine was the killer, that meant he had threatened me too. And the fact that I had just gone in his office was scary. He seemed so nice, but the thought of that killer in my shop was spine chilling. Plus, Antoine had a key to my place now.

I was really second-guessing myself now. Maybe the police were right. What if they'd had the killer pegged all along?

"The suspense is killing me. What did you find?" Aunt Barb asked as we hurried down the hallway.

"A receipt for a gun," I said.

Her eyes widened. "A gun?"

"Just like the one used to kill Kellie."

"Just like it?" Aunt Barb asked.

"Seems that way," I said with a nod. "The receipt lists the type of gun purchased, and I overheard Detective Malone say that was the type of gun used. He said that when he found the shell casing at the crime scene that morning."

"Well, there you go." Aunt Barb waved her arms. "Evidence that he's the killer. Thankfully we got out of there before he found us, or else he'd make us his victims."

"Don't be too dramatic, Aunt Barb, okay?" I said.

Aunt Barb acted as if she hadn't heard me. "This has to be enough evidence to arrest him. If the police can prove that he bought the gun from that shop."

"Yes, if they find out it was the same one used to kill her, they'll arrest him. But they have to have the gun first," I said.

"And they don't have the evidence yet that it's the same gun," she said. "Maybe they'll never find it."

"The police might say that just because he bought a gun doesn't mean he did it. What if that's not enough solid evidence? I think we should go to the gun shop and ask them if they remember Antoine."

"Do you really think they'll give you that information?" Aunt Barb said as we reached the lobby.

"Well, it's worth a shot."

"I guess you're right," she said. "But we're going to have to eat some dinner first. That biscuit I had earlier has faded long ago. Let's go over to the diner and get something to eat."

"You know everybody is going to be watching me when we go in there. They think I might be the killer."

"Well, I've never heard of such. No, they don't think that. And I'll put them straight," she said.

Oh no. This could turn out to be a whole event.

"Well, I guess if you're really hungry, we can go. I think maybe we should just go home and have a pimento cheese sandwich."

"No, I need something with substance," Aunt Barb said.

As we rounded the corner, we came face-to-face with a tall man. He eyed us up and down, immediately suspicious.

"May I help you?" he asked.

I needed to say something, but my nerves kept me silent. I felt like just running, but I figured that would end badly.

"We were here to see Antoine Dubois," I managed to sputter.

The man looked even more suspicious now. "Seems like there's been a lot of people to see him."

I was surprised he had said that, but I needed to follow this lead and ask for more information from him.

"Oh, yeah? Why do you say that? Because of the murder?" I asked.

The man looked a bit surprised that I had mentioned the crime, but he had to know that we were both talking about the same thing. The news was all over town, so it wasn't a secret.

"Yes, that's the reason," he said.

"Did he kill that woman?" Aunt Barb asked.

Well, that was one way to really get the question out there. Aunt Barb hadn't hesitated for a second.

The guy rolled his eyes. "I don't know about that, but it's possible. He's got a temper. Ever since he became boss."

I sensed some sort of resentment from this man against Antoine.

"When did he become the boss?" I asked.

"About a week ago. Yeah, he actually got the job over me. And Kellie too. Me and a few other people are trying to find how that worked out. How did Antoine get the job?"

This guy really seemed bitter.

"Maybe he's been at the company longer? You don't have any idea why Antoine got the promotion?" I asked.

"No, I don't know. You should ask him. But I think that there was something illegal going on."

Wow, I hadn't heard this accusation before, but now I needed to get to the bottom of it. I mean, first he was saying Antoine had a temper, and now he thought Antoine was into shady stuff. Maybe I didn't know this Frenchman at all.

What was I saying? I barely knew him. We'd only talked a bit. And just because I thought he was handsome was no reason for me to think I knew him any better than I actually did. I had a tendency to just look at people and feel like I knew them. And somehow I'd gotten the idea that I was a good judge of character. But now I was having second thoughts about myself. Maybe I was judging my own character.

Okay, now I was even getting on my own nerves. I needed to just stop.

"Is there anything else you can tell us?" I asked.

"I have nothing else to say. But . . . why are you here?" he asked with a frown.

"Well, we told you we're looking for him," Aunt Barb snapped.

"He's not here," he said with an underlying growl in his words.

It seemed like this man was the one with the temper.

"We'll be leaving," I said.

I wanted to get out of here before this guy decided he didn't like us and called the police.

When we got to the door, Aunt Barb said, "That was a close one."

"Yes, well, you weren't really subtle about asking about Antoine, Aunt Barb," I said.

"There was no need for beating around the bush. We wanted to hurry up and get it over with, and besides, it worked, didn't it?" she said with a smile.

"Yes, I guess it did work."

I had to give her credit for that.

# Chapter
# Twenty-Two

A unt Barb opted to stay in the car while I went up to the gun shop. She said she was too stressed from what we'd just done. I wasn't sure the shop was open, but a light was on, so I hoped someone was inside who would answer my questions.

I approached the building with caution. Why I acted like a scaredy-cat, I wasn't sure. Maybe I thought someone would spot me and tell me to get lost—though why slowly approaching the place would make me somehow invisible was beyond me. Since the place looked closed, I moved close to the building, cupped my hands around my eyes, and pressed my face against the glass.

I spotted a tall, thin man working behind the counter. Should I knock on the window to capture his attention? Maybe startling him wasn't such a good idea. After all, he had a lot of guns in there. As I stood there debating what to do next, the man turned his attention toward me.

Even though Aunt Barb knew a lot about guns and I'd thought it might be useful for her to go with me, she'd said it wouldn't matter, that all I was going to do was ask if this person had been in to buy a gun or not and the man would probably tell me he couldn't give me any information. Those were very discouraging words from a woman who claimed I had to keep a positive attitude all the time. Would townsfolk be suspicious if they saw me doing this? Would they think I was the killer, getting another gun to commit another murder or something? I couldn't let that stop me from going inside. Maybe they'd think the logical thing and figure I was getting a gun for protection.

I stood frozen as the man approached the door. Should I run? It was too late for that, because he pushed the door open and glared at me.

"We're closed." He croaked out the words.

"Yes, I know, but I just wanted to ask you some questions. I'm always working during your working hours." I gave a pleading look, the same one my father said always made his heart melt.

"Okay, but I don't have a lot of time," he said.

"I'll make it snappy."

He opened the door farther and motioned for me to come inside. After giving Aunt Barb a thumbs-up, I stepped into the shop. Glass display cases and firearm paraphernalia lined the walls. I was kind of clueless about asking for information on who had made a purchase. The man quietly walked back behind the counter and looked at me. Now that I approached of the counter, he eyed me up and down.

It was now or never. This was when I would find out if he would be helpful or do exactly as Aunt Barb had said and tell me he had no info for me. My fingers were crossed that I was right this time. As I walked toward the counter, I pulled the gun receipt from my pocket.

"I wondered if maybe you could tell me if anyone was in here and purchased a gun. And who that person was." I placed the receipt on the counter.

"A lot of people have bought guns. This is a gun shop," he said with a pinched brow.

Now he was just being sarcastic.

I studied his face for a moment. "Aren't you Mike Reynolds' dad? We went to school together. I'm Marci Beaucoup. I used to come over and swim in your pool in the summer. That was such a fun time."

He eyed me up and down. This his scowl softened a bit. "Yes, now I remember you. You were afraid to go into the deep end."

"Right, well, it was pretty deep. Um, well, about the gun, what I meant was this specific type of gun," I said, pointing to the receipt.

He stared at me for a long moment. I was completely uneasy with his icy-blue glare on me.

Finally he looked down at the receipt, picked it up, studied it for a moment, and then placed it back on the counter. "Yes, I recall someone buying that gun."

Well, Aunt Barb had been wrong. Maybe I would get the information I needed now. All of a sudden, I felt butterflies in my stomach. I might be a moment away from finding out who had killed Kelle. It seemed too good to be true.

"Perhaps you could give me a name," I said. I knew he kept that information.

He shook his head. "I don't have that information. I just know that we sold one of these guns, but it would take me several days to get that information to you. I remember selling it to someone. But for you, I'll see what I can do."

Dread formed in my stomach, eating those butterflies.

"Well, that would be great. Thank you." I smiled, even though disappointment had settled in.

I supposed it was better than nothing, but couldn't he give me some clue?

"You said you remember the person coming in. Do you know what they looked like?" I asked.

He was starting to get suspicious of me—I could tell by the raised eyebrow—but he should know what I was up to with these questions. He'd probably talked to the police. Maybe he would put two and two together if they were asking about this same type of weapon.

"What color hair did the buyer have?" I asked. "A man or a woman?"

"The guy wore a dark hat, so I didn't get a look at his hair color. But he had these blue eyes that seemed kind of intense."

At that moment, it hit me. I should ask about the accent. If it was Antoine, he would have an accent. And this guy would remember that.

"Did he have a French accent?" I asked.

The man shook his head. "He had a strange accent, but I wouldn't say it was French. It was almost as if he was forcing himself to talk a certain way."

"That seems odd," I said.

"I thought so too. I wasn't sure what to make of that, but it was definitely more of a southern accent."

"Interesting," I said as I picked the receipt up. "I'll come back in a few days to get that information."

"Yeah, all right," he said. "I'll get it for you."

I wasn't quite convinced he would do that. Nevertheless, I would be back to find out. One way or the other, I was getting the information, and I was going to solve this murder.

I left the shop not exactly disappointed but not happy either. I supposed neither Aunt Barb nor I had been correct.

# Chapter
# Twenty-Three

All morning I had felt as if someone was watching me. I wasn't sure what brought on that feeling—maybe the fact that there had been a killer in my shop and now I was totally freaked out? Or maybe because I had been in the potential killer's office. Or maybe because the potential killer had been around me. Plus, I had seen that man creeping around town and never knew when someone might pop up again. I was definitely on edge, and I hoped it didn't throw off my baking too much. I mean, I had to put love into these treats. People were counting on it.

I rolled out the dough for another round of croissants, putting as much effort into it as possible. I moved over and over, getting all the love into the dough. As far as magic pastry, that was really all this was, the love from my hands. The magic that went into them—it was simply love, and whatever people wanted to believe, that was what would happen. If they thought good things would come from having the pastry, that was what they would get in return.

When the bell jingled and Fifi barked, followed by a hiss from Pepé Le Pew, I hurried out of the kitchen to see what was causing such a reaction. Fear spiked through me when I saw who had come in. I'd known something had to be amiss when my beloved furry companions spoke up—though sometimes they missed the mark and warned me about the postman. I assumed they had it right this time.

Kellie's boss was headed my way.

Mr. Gustavsson walked across the bakery as if he owned the place. His demeanor didn't surprise me, because he'd seemed to have that air about him when I'd visited his office. What was he doing in here?

He walked up to the counter and looked at the pastries, not even acknowledging me.

"Good afternoon," I said. "May I help you?"

I tried to remain as professional as possible, although I was terrified by the fact that he was in my shop. What was he doing here? Was he simply buying a pastry? After all, that was what I had here to offer people, so maybe he was.

He still didn't acknowledge me as he studied the items in the glass display case. I felt like he was scrutinizing every little detail of my shop. He was analyzing whether or not the pastries were good. I was very much on edge. Why was he doing this? Just order something already!

Maybe there was more to this visit. Did he want to talk to me about the murder? I should be brave and stop doing this halfway. I needed to do it the right way and ask him more questions. But there was just something about the way he studied me as he looked up from the display case, like he thought I was going to suggest something other than a dessert.

"The macarons are nice," I said finally.

He studied my face and then said with a half grin, "Yes, that would be good. Thanks."

As I prepared some of the cookies and placed them in a box, I said, "I'm surprised to see you here. Do you have something else to tell me about the case?"

He studied my face for another moment and narrowed his eyes. "No, nothing else."

He seemed a bit angry. Maybe he thought I'd acted unprofessionally. I wasn't going to apologize, because I wasn't sorry for doing it. Okay, so he was a touch irritated about my blunt interrogations. Or a lot irritated. I would do it all over again if I had to. And more and more it was looking as if I might have to ask more questions. I wasn't getting any of the answers I needed from anyone else, so pressing him might be a good thing. He handed me his credit card.

After I swiped it, I gave it back. "I hope you enjoy the cookies."

He nodded without saying anything else. Then he turned on his heel with the cookies in hand and headed out of the bakery.

Well, that was certainly odd. I jumped, not realizing that Aunt Barb was standing behind me.

"You really have to let me know when you're doing that," I said.

"What was that about?" Aunt Barb gestured with a tilt of her head toward the door.

"Kellie's boss stopped in for cookies."

"It's kind of strange that he came in, don't you think?" Aunt Barb asked.

I shrugged. "I suppose he just came in for cookies."

She shook her head. "Oh, you know he didn't come in just for cookies."

"No, I suppose not," I said around a sigh. "But he didn't say anything else. He acted strange, almost as if he was mad."

"Maybe he was mad," Aunt Barb said.

That thought sent a chill down my spine. I mean, if he was the killer, then he had left that note for me. But how would he have gotten in? That was what I needed to figure out. If it wasn't Antoine, then I needed to know who else had access to the shop. Had I left the door unlocked? Was that a possibility? It was becoming tougher now for me to even remember. I had left the door unlocked in the past, so it wasn't totally out of the question.

This visit had left me unnerved, and I knew I would be on edge for the rest of the day. I needed to find out more information about Antoine.

Movement on the sidewalk caught my attention. Gordon strolled slowly by, but he didn't ignore my bakery. He looked over purposely. I knew he was trying to see inside. I wasn't sure if he was able to see through the glare on the window from outside. Plus, all the display desserts blocked the view. What was he up to, anyway? Why wasn't he coming in? It wasn't time for his daily visit, but nevertheless, he was obviously interested in something in the shop. More petit fours, or something else? I glanced over at Aunt Barb with a raised eyebrow.

"Is Gordon here to see you?" I asked.

She laughed nervously. "Why would he be here to see me? Can't the man walk down the sidewalk without being questioned?"

I held my hands up. "No, he can walk wherever he wants. I'm not asking anything about it. I just notice that he's been around the shop a lot."

"He likes those desserts. You've made them addictive. Is there something that you've been putting in them?" She placed her hands on her hips. "You've been putting love spells into the petit fours, haven't you? Because if you have, then I'm going to have to stop eating them."

"Aunt Barb, for the millionth time, I don't put love spells into the food," I said. "And heaven forbid that you experience love."

"Don't be sassy."

Aunt Barb went to work and so did I, but then I received another surprise visit only moments later.

When Maverick walked into the shop, everything changed. There was just an air about him—one of confidence and being in control. It was kind of energizing, actually. I tried to match that energy by standing a little straighter and looking him in the eyes, but I felt like I was coming up pretty short. Nevertheless, I had to let him know I wasn't intimidated, even if he didn't want me involved in the investigation.

He made eye contact and didn't break it . . . at all. Until I finally glanced away. I was the first one to look away. I couldn't handle it. His stare was making me a little weak in the knees. I had to finally admit to myself that maybe I had feelings for him.

"Good afternoon, Detective Malone," I said. "What can I get for you? Just a few cookies left, unfortunately."

"I'm not here for cookies, Marci," he said.

"Oh, yeah? What are you here for?" I asked.

His tone of voice told me it wasn't for something good. He didn't have that flirtatious grin on his face either, much to my disappointment.

"Besides the fact that you canceled the date?"

"You canceled the date," I said.

I'd been hesitant about talking to Maverick anyway. Maybe because I was avoiding addressing any potential sparks between us.

He studied my face for several seconds while remaining silent.

Ultimately, he changed the subject. "I need to talk to you about something else right now. Are you investigating the murder case?"

"Whatever do you mean, Detective?" I asked, trying to sound self-assured and just a little playful.

Judging by the look on his face, he wasn't falling for it.

"You're involved in this investigation, and I'm afraid you're going to get hurt. You have to stop."

"How do you know? I mean, about me and the investigation?" I asked.

"I know that you were in Antoine's office building yesterday."

"How do you know that?"

"I have my ways," he said.

His answer didn't surprise me. I was sure he did have his ways. But how?

I guessed it didn't matter. "Yes, I was there, and I am trying to find out who did this. It's important to me, because I'm afraid I might be the next victim."

"Well, if you get involved, then you definitely are putting yourself in jeopardy of being the next victim. Just let me handle it, and I promise you I will make sure that you're okay."

"I appreciate that, but it's just not in my nature."

"I'm warning you not to get involved."

Now he was being authoritative. I would tell him I wouldn't be involved if that was what he wanted to hear, and then I would continue to do whatever I needed to do. Of course, I wouldn't get myself into trouble—not on purpose, at least.

"Are you sure I can't get you some cookies or croissants? I insist."

I went over and started putting things into a box, not taking no for an answer. When I handed it to him, he tried to give me money for it. I refused.

"No, I can't take anything. Besides, we were just going to throw them out anyway."

"Gee, thanks," he said. "You're giving me your trash?"

I laughed. "You know what I mean."

I couldn't believe we'd actually exchanged pleasantries. I supposed he wasn't all bad. Although he was still upset with me, I was starting to think maybe Aunt Barb was right and I should give Maverick a chance.

"Promise me that you will stop," he said.

"I promise," I said with my fingers crossed behind my back.

Yes, that was kind of a childish thing to do, but I needed all the help I could get right now. I watched as he walked away. He sure looked good in that outfit. *Snap out of it*, I told myself. This was no time for romance.

"What's going on here?" Aunt Barb said, coming out from the kitchen.

Thank goodness she'd missed Maverick, because otherwise she would still be talking about how good he looked and how he was flirting with me, blah, blah, blah.

"Detective Malone wants me to stay out of the investigation," I said.

"That sounds serious," Aunt Barb said.

"He doesn't really mean it. He's just saying that because he has to."

She looked like she didn't believe me, but she didn't say anything else. I knew she wanted to identify the killer just as much as I did.

Now that the day was over, I had to set my plans in motion to find the killer. After I locked up the shop, Aunt Barb and I walked toward my car. She held Pepé Le Pew like a baby, and I walked Fifi on her leash. I still had that uneasy sense, so I looked all around.

"What's wrong with you?" she asked.

I scanned the surroundings again. "I just guess I have a strange feeling."

She looked around too.

"Now that you mention it, I guess I do feel it too," she said. "Do you think someone's watching us?"

"I think it's a possibility," I said.

"They'd better hope I don't find them. I am just tired of this game they're playing. We have to put a stop to this." Her words came out almost like a growl.

Uh-oh. Aunt Barb was getting angry again. I couldn't say that I blamed her, because I was angry too. But I didn't see anyone else around, and we couldn't fight anyone we couldn't see.

Besides, I wouldn't fight them anyway. I would just call the cops and have them arrested as soon as possible.

As we headed toward the car, I thought more about Maverick. It was almost as if we were in a competition with each other to find the killer. Okay, I saw it as a competition, and he saw it as not wanting me to mess up evidence or a crime scene.

Whatever; I knew I was capable of solving a crime. I guessed I would have to show him a thing or two. I mean, I hated to prove the guy wrong, because that was his job, and I didn't want to outdo him at his job, but I could bake and solve a murder at the same time. Now, that was talented.

Okay, I was being a bit cocky, but hey, if I had it, I had it. For once, I was going to be confident. Yes, that was what it was, confidence. It wasn't cockiness. I was sure of myself, and if he had to get in the way of that, then that would just be his problem. He'd have to suffer the consequences. Maybe then he wouldn't be so quick to judge and tell me I couldn't do something like this. I was excited about showing him I could solve this case.

After I bid Aunt Barb adieu, she walked away with Fifi and Pepé Le Pew. They'd be staying with her tonight. I'd told her the best way to help me to investigate was to take care of the dog and cat. She agreed only reluctantly, because she really didn't want me doing any of this alone.

Trying to shake off the uneasiness, I glanced around. Nothing but the usual light traffic through town. Thank goodness there was no sign of a killer on the loose.

I was still contemplating my situation as I slipped behind the wheel of my car. I'd made the decision to rule out Antoine once and for all. I would make that final push to either prove he had nothing to do with this or send him behind bars for the rest of his life.

I felt like video surveillance might be a great key in solving the crime. Every store in town probably had it. They all had to have been recording that morning, right? But had they recorded the right angle at the exact moment when a murder just happened to go down in town? A murder hadn't happened in years.

I slipped the key into the ignition and started the car. I needed to make myself productive so I wouldn't have so many racing thoughts.

# Chapter Twenty-Four

The next day rose with plenty of sunshine, but it seemed as if a black cloud still covered Paris, Kentucky. I planned on following through with my final push to solve this crime today. Right after the festival. Even though there was a lot of chaos going on around town right now with the search for a killer, the annual pumpkin festival was still on track for today. I had a booth set up where I would hopefully sell some of my delicious pastries. They all had a fall theme, of course, which blended two of my most favorite things in the world: fall and French. It just couldn't get much better than that, right? Last year I'd even given Halloween a French theme by carving a jack-o'-lantern and putting a beret on it.

The pumpkin had been totally adorable, and I planned on carrying on that tradition again this year. I might even make a scarecrow and put French-style clothing on him—a striped Breton shirt, a red beret, and a scarf around his neck.

My favorite thing I'd made for the festival was pumpkin pie. I'd even made some pies with butternut squash, which were delicious as well. And then there were the pumpkin croissants, and I loved the pumpkin cookies too. Lots of cinnamon and spice that left a warm scent drifting in the air. The weather was perfect today for the event. It was going to be cooler than previous days this week, but still warm in the middle and crisp around the edges—like my pies. *Tarte à la citrouille,* or pumpkin pie here in America, was traditionally served on November 1, All Saints' Day in France, but in America, we could eat it every day in the fall.

Aunt Barb and I had a tent set up at the edge of the festival over next to a cluster of oak trees. It was a nice shady spot, although a bit chilly under the branches. Fifi and Pepé Le Pew had elected to spend the day with my mother. Well, I guess technically it had been my mother's idea. She complained that she didn't see them enough. She acted as if they were her grandchildren. Sometimes I wondered if it was because she thought I'd never have children.

I was wrapped up in my plaid jacket with my scarf, sipping on my cinnamon latte. I'd just set out all the desserts so that people could inspect them before making a purchase. The French cake was front and center, because I had a feeling that would go quickly. In the distance, I spotted Gordon standing beside a tractor attached to a cart filled with hay. Later this evening, it would be used for hayrides. Why was Gordon looking this way? Did he want my attention or Aunt Barb's? Soon he turned and walked in the opposite direction.

"Wish me luck," Aunt Barb said as she moved out from behind the table over to the path that would lead to the rest of the festival events.

She was going to the pumpkin-chucking contest. Last year she'd won, so now she had to defend her title. It seemed suspicious that as soon as she'd spotted Gordon, she'd realized that she needed to head toward the contest area. Gordon had already disappeared.

"I'd love to watch," I said. "But I need to stay here and man the deserts."

"Well, I'm sure someone will catch it on video."

"I hope so. You can do this, Aunt Barb. Just remain calm this time. Last time when you were trash-talking everybody after you won, that was a little embarrassing."

Aunt Barb waved her hand. "Oh, they loved it. Besides, it's all in good fun."

She said that, but I knew she was competitive and determined to win. It wasn't all in good fun. What would she do if she lost? The last time she'd lost at the chili cookoff, she wouldn't even say the word *chili* for six months. Aunt Barb had grown up the middle child, and she said she'd always felt she had to be the best at everything in order to get any attention. It made me sad to think she'd felt that way.

I watched as Aunt Barb walked away. Then I went over my desserts once again, sorting through them and arranging them. My babies. I was really proud of them. I'd even added crust on the pies in the shape of leaves to give them that perfect fall touch. I just had to wait for the customers to arrive. People were starting to trickle in, but since I was at the end of the line of tents, I knew it would be just a little while longer before anyone showed up to make a purchase. A sudden bit of panic came over me, and I wondered if anyone would buy anything if they suspected I might be involved with the murder. Was that possible? I was part of this town. Everyone knew I would never do something so horrendous.

Surely no one could resist these delicious desserts. But if there were still lingering doubts about me being a killer, that might make them think twice before buying. Did they really think I could be a killer? I mean, I was nice to everyone. Well, except if they pushed me too far, and then I had a little bit of a temper. But I just told people they'd made me mad. My mom said I was a little sassy sometimes, but I thought sassiness was needed sometimes.

I heard a lot of ruckus going on in the distance, so I knew the pumpkin-chucking contest was under way. Despite a slow start at my booth, things picked up and I had plenty of customers. Soon the only things that remained were a few lemon sugar madeleines, an apple tarte Tatin, gâteau de flan, and a dozen strawberry and rose éclairs. It was a whirlwind of activity, but things settled down again before long, I supposed because of the contest. I would just use this time to relax.

Hearing someone come up behind me, I said, "How may I help you?" I turned around to face them.

No one was there. What had made me think someone was behind me? I looked all around, but I saw nobody paying attention. Nevertheless, the feeling just wouldn't go away. I thought about the man I'd seen at the bakery. Had that been Mr. Gustavsson, Antoine, or someone else? I fidgeted in the chair, trying to distract myself from the feeling.

"You seem antsy."

I jumped and almost fell off the chair.

"Whoa, I didn't mean to scare you like that."

When I looked up, I saw Maverick standing next to me. The memory of him suggesting we go to the festival together came to mind. He'd never mentioned it again after seeing me kiss Antoine.

"Do you always slip up and scare people like that?" I asked.

"Not always," he said. "But you looked so peaceful that I didn't want to disturb you."

When he said that, my stomach danced, knowing he'd been watching me. That must have been the feeling I'd gotten.

"So how's business going?" he asked.

"Actually, it's been going really well. As you can see, I hardly have anything left. Would you like to buy something?"

"After all those cookies you've given me lately, I don't think I need anything." He patted his stomach.

Of course his stomach was flat.

"With all that working out you do, I think you can handle it," I said.

He winked at me. Yes, he was kind of a flirt.

"So what brings you to the festival?" I asked.

That was an awkward question. Why had I asked that? He'd asked me here the other day, and now I was acting like this was a casual encounter.

"Just checking things out." He looked down at my display of desserts.

That didn't add up. I had a feeling his visit was business. Mainly because I had doubts that he ever did anything for fun.

"So what are you checking out?" I asked. "Do you think the killer's roaming around here? Maybe he's over at the pumpkin-chucking contest."

"I think that's unlikely," he said.

"Well, it could happen," I said. "So tell me, when are you going to make an arrest? As in make an arrest that's not Antoine."

"What's with you and that guy? Are you dating him or something?"

"I wouldn't say dating per se," I said.

"You're not holding out any information on me, are you?" he asked.

Did I look that guilty? Probably so. Maybe he knew more about what I'd been doing than he was letting on, but I wouldn't bring it up if he didn't.

"Not a thing," I said.

If I kept all this stuff close to me, I wouldn't be told not to investigate.

"Well, I guess you convinced me that I should buy something," he said. "I have to support all the local businesses."

"Wow, you're buying something? This is a treat. What'll you have?"

"I'll take one of those cheesecakes for my mother." He pointed.

I picked up the dessert. "This pièce de résistance is gâteau de flan. It's a custard tart. But you're a good son for thinking of her, and I'm sure she'll love it."

"I'm a good lot of things," he said with a wink.

I probably blushed. Though maybe he was just reminding me that he was a good detective.

"Like what?" I asked. "At being a good detective? I didn't say you weren't."

"That's not what I meant," he said.

"What did you mean?" I asked.

He handed me cash for the purchase. "I guess you'll find out."

"I hope so," I said.

Maverick leaned forward and removed a leaf that had fallen into my hair, and I became instantly flustered. He had a way of doing that. No wonder all the ladies loved him. He made me want to melt like that butter I put on the croissants. Which reminded me that I needed to look into making the butter that Antoine had given me the recipe for.

I wrapped up his package quickly so that he could get himself out of here. I didn't need this distraction. Besides, Aunt Barb would be back soon. And there were a few things I wanted to do, like take a look around the festival, and I didn't want anybody disturbing that. Not Aunt Barb. Not Detective Malone, that was for sure.

I'd just said good-bye to Maverick when Aunt Barb approached with a trophy in hand. Once again, she'd been the champion of the pumpkin-chucking contest. I wasn't surprised at all.

I ran over to her and hugged her. "You won."

"Was there ever any doubt?" Aunt Barb held the trophy in the air.

"Not at all," I said with a laugh. "We almost don't have any desserts left, so if it's okay, I'm going to take a look around before we have to leave. Once we sell everything, there's no reason to stay."

"I suppose you're right," she said.

"I'm surprised everyone didn't come over here earlier and buy all the desserts thinking that we would leave and then you wouldn't have had a chance to win that contest."

"Yeah, they're jealous of my pumpkin-chucking skills," she said with a smile.

"Okay, I'll be back soon," I said as I waved over my shoulder.

I headed down the path, looking at all the other booths set up with necklaces, hats, paintings, and every other imaginable crafted item. I got lost in the moment and just wandered around, not even paying attention to the time. I probably needed to head back to Aunt Barb. She'd wonder why I hadn't returned. But I'd been so excited to see everything that I hadn't been thinking correctly. Also, I was excited that I'd sold almost all of my desserts. After I stopped at a booth to buy a necklace, I decided I would do something fun and go through the corn maze.

When I reached the beginning of the maze, I hesitated for just a moment, wondering if this was a good idea. The cornstalks were much taller than me. They reminded me of tall security guards keeping a watchful eye and warning me not to enter. Screams made me almost jump out of my skin. Then I realized they came from children playing nearby.

I was being silly. What could go wrong? It was a maze designed for kids. I shouldn't even be going for that reason alone, but it looked like fun. And I definitely needed a fun fall activity. Earlier, when we'd arrived at the festival, Aunt Barb had said there was no way she was going into this maze. It would set off her allergies. This morning when I'd talked to my mom on the phone from the cruise ship, she'd cautioned me not to get claustrophobic if I went through the maze. How was that possible? She was the one always dealing with claustrophobia, not me.

Same with my friends. When I'd asked earlier this week about the festival, none of my friends had wanted to go to the maze either. They had boyfriends to do this stuff with them. It seemed like they didn't have time for me, so I would just do it on my own. I'd make time for myself, and that was what was important. Although I had to admit, it would be nice to have a special some-one to do stuff like this with. Maybe a special Frenchman to do stuff with. That is, if he wasn't a serial killer—or just a plain killer, for that matter.

Immediately upon stepping between the cornstalks, I was faced with a decision: turn to the left or turn to the right. Of course the ENTER sign didn't tell me which way to go. That would defeat the whole purpose. Which way was the right way? I decided to go to the left. That seemed like the natural decision.

My feet crunched over the ground as I moved just a short distance. I made another right turn, an intentional act, but I was second-guessing myself. A noise caught my attention and I paused, looking over my shoulder. I thought maybe someone was behind me, but I saw no one. Perhaps someone was hidden in the cornstalks. I just had the strange feeling again that someone was watching me. Maybe someone would reach out and grab me from behind one of those stalks. That would be creepy, like something in one of those scary movies. What was that one with the scare-crows that came to life? No, I didn't even want to think about that right now. What made me do things like going through this maze was beyond me. I was too far into the maze to turn back. I heard people walking back behind me, so I knew more folks had entered the maze. I would have to keep pushing forward.

The farther I moved into the maze, the more anxious I became. I was starting to panic, and I wasn't finding my way out either. I just had that oppressive feeling that someone was bearing down on me and soon they would pounce.

The scent of earth along with the musky sweet smell of fallen leaves lingered in the air. Such a soothing smell normally filled me with nostalgia, but right now, overwhelming fear gripped me deep down in my soul.

Rustling cornstalks sounded from my right. Why did it feel as if someone was close by and following every step I made through the maze? I was starting to hyperventilate. I needed to get out of there. This had been a bad idea. If I ever got myself out of this situation, I would never do something dumb like this again. Okay, I probably would, but not on purpose this time. I mean, I'd will-ingly walked in here.

I reached into my pocket for my phone. Maybe I should let someone know where I was just in case I didn't find my way out. Then I realized my phone wasn't in my pocket.

The rustle of the cornstalks caught my attention again as I moved past them. This increased my anxiety, so I hurried forward, hoping that soon I would be out of here. But the next thing I knew, someone grabbed me from behind.

# Chapter
# Twenty-Five

I tried to scream, but they clamped their hand over my mouth. This person was strong; I felt their muscles bulge around me. They pulled me farther into the maze.

Cornstalks scraped at my body as the person dragged me backward. I was being kidnapped? No doubt this was the killer. This was it. This was how I was going out of this world. I'd die in a corn maze? With any luck, they'd at least find my body here.

How long would that take? I was trying not to completely freak out at the thought. My stomach churned and my limbs tingled from the rush of adrenaline. It would probably take a while before they even reported me missing. And would they ever figure out I'd come back here? Surely everyone would figure that out. Other festivalgoers knew I'd come into the corn maze because they'd seen me enter, so surely someone would find me in the wooded area, right? Aunt Barb might think I'd left her here.

Maybe my snooping had caught up with me. I hoped my disappearance wouldn't go unnoticed. I had to think Aunt Barb would realize something was wrong.

Yes, other festivalgoers must have seen me. Most people around town probably remembered me as the kooky woman who loved all things French. I was the one with the crazy idea to open up a French bakery. The cookie woman who managed to create some kind of love magic in her pastries. Now all of that would be gone because some crazy killer had decided to get rid of me.

Things seemed blurrier now. I hoped I didn't black out. As I struggled to breathe, I realized that was a real possibility.

What was even worse was that I would never know. I would never know why this had gone down. I might never even get a look at my killer's face. As scary as it seemed, I needed to see. Since the person was behind me, I couldn't get a good look at even their hand, much less their face. My attacker had a tight grasp on me, so tight it hurt. Who would be that strong? Antoine was strong—or at least I assumed so because of his stature. Hunter was a strong guy too. Mr. Gustavsson was smaller, but he looked solid, so that probably meant he was strong as well.

I wanted to yell. I wanted to ask where this person thought they were taking me, but I couldn't get out more than a few little grunts. The hand across my mouth was so tight against my mouth that I struggled to breathe. If they moved their hand up just slightly, it would be covering my nose. Maybe that was how they planned on getting rid of me.

I continued to try to pull the person's hand away from my mouth, but it wasn't working. They were too strong. I regretted not going to the gym for regular strength training, but that was a moot point right now. I continued struggling as I went through ideas in my mind on how I would get away from this person. Sadly, nothing came to mind. I dug my heels into the ground, but that didn't stop them from pulling me. I somehow managed to kick them in the leg, but it still didn't get them to release their hold on me. What were my other options? Just a few moments of distraction might be all I needed.

I knew this cornfield covered quite a bit of space, so it would take a while to get all the way to the edge. But I knew there was a road on one side, so this person could easily be dragging me all the way over there, considering we were moving through the cornstalks now. Judging by the amount of time this was taking, I was starting to believe we were headed for the road. I continued to fight, even though I was starting to lose energy. Maybe I needed to conserve it for the next step. Would there be a next step? It looked as if there was going to be more to this fight soon. They weren't going to just end it right here in the cornfield.

A short time later we reached the edge of the cornfield. They dragged me up onto the pavement. I looked around, hoping to see vehicles traveling the road, but there were none. This was an isolated area, so I was surprised to see a black sedan parked right there—the one I'd seen earlier when I thought the driver was watching me. I'd been right. He had been watching. The person lifted me up to hoist me into the trunk.

He tossed me in as if it required no effort at all. I tried to put up a fight, but at that moment I got a look at the person. Unfortunately, he had his face covered with a mask. A spooky Halloween one. It was a jack-o'-lantern, but the face was completely evil. This was like something out of a scary movie.

How had I gotten myself into this situation? But more important was how I was going to get out of the trunk. The lid slammed shut, and it was complete darkness in the cramped space. How long would I be able to breathe? This was my reality now, and I didn't like it one bit.

My whole body shifted as he punched the gas and sped away. We hit a bump and I actually bounced upward. Not only had I been stuffed into a trunk, but he was a lousy driver. I might get carsick in here.

I'd read about other people who had been stuck in trunks of cars. Was there some kind of move I could make to free myself? A lever that would pop the lid? Then I remembered that might really be the case. Would that get me out of here? If not, I could punch out the taillight and let someone know I was in here. But with so few cars on the road around here, that seemed unlikely to get anyone's attention. I needed to check for that latch or lever.

There had to be one. I'd gotten only a glimpse of the car, but it had looked like a newer one. They made the newer cars with levers now, right? I had no idea. I prayed there was a way to escape. I felt around for the latch. My kidnapper probably hadn't thought about that; he'd just been thinking about that old style of kidnapping. At least he hadn't tied me up. That might be a decision he regretted later when I got out of here. And I was going to get out. I was determined.

Even though I was in a hurry, I had to think this over clearly. I couldn't make any rash decisions, because if I opened the trunk now while the car was moving, I would have to jump out of a moving car. And that would likely end with the result this guy wanted: I'd be dead.

So I decided I needed to wait until he stopped. The first time he stopped was when I would make my move. I'd have to move fast. When the trunk was open, I'd jump out and make a run for it. With any luck, there would be other vehicles around so that I could get someone's attention. I needed help in blocking this guy from being able to get anywhere near me again.

It seemed like forever before the car finally came to a stop. This was my chance. In such darkness, how would I find the latch? I stretched my hand out and made contact with the inside of the car. Slowly I moved my hand across the surface, searching for the lever. With each passing second, I felt as if I was losing oxygen. My fear of small spaces was setting in. Thank goodness at that moment my hand made contact with something that felt like a latch. Was this it? There was only one way to find out. After fumbling around, I pulled the latch, and all of a sudden daylight flooded the area. I was free.

When I climbed out of the trunk, I realized we were on a road stopped at a red light. But there were no other cars around. This was an isolated area, so I was in big trouble. This guy likely knew what I was doing now. I ran as fast as I could toward an old building. It looked abandoned, but at least it would be shelter. I couldn't turn around to see if the guy was coming after me; I just had to assume he was. What would I do when I got inside the building? When he came in after me, he'd be even more angry. He would dump me back in the trunk or maybe just kill me right here in this old building.

Nevertheless, I kept going as fast as I could, running toward that building. When I opened the door, darkness welcomed me. I ran inside into the dark. I had no idea where I was going. I felt around, trying to find a spot to hide. Luckily, I found a door, and I slipped inside. This small room must be a closet. I tried to steady my breathing so he wouldn't hear me. To my surprise, I heard no sounds coming from the other side of the door.

Then it hit me: what if the door didn't open? What if I was trapped here? Certainly no one would ever find me here. This was like the ultimate hiding place for hide-and-seek. Unless they got dogs to sniff me out, there would be no way to find me. I listened for footsteps, but they never came. How long would I wait before I got out of here? I was anxious to try the door handle, hoping that it would open.

After a few more seconds, I wrapped my hand around the knob, and it opened. Thank goodness it wasn't locked. It was still dark in the building, so I had to feel my way back over to the main door. And then I hoped I didn't bump into my kidnapper as soon as I opened the door. Talk about apprehensive. I was worried I would run into him in the dark. He could just be hiding and waiting, playing with me like a cat with a mouse. He was probably waiting for me to think I'd gotten away before he grabbed me back up again and started batting me around.

Thankfully, I managed to get to the main door again without hurting myself. I eased it open just a little to peek outside. The car was gone. Had he just hidden it somewhere out of sight so that no one would notice? What was he doing? Hiding would make sense, because he wouldn't want to dump me back into the trunk out there in the open. Although that was exactly what he'd done on that other isolated road. Easy to do in a rural area.

Maybe he truly was gone. Maybe he'd decided he'd had enough of the game and he didn't want to put in the effort. That seemed too good to be true, though. How would I get out of here now? I was stranded out in the middle of nowhere. I was vaguely familiar with this area, but I wasn't completely convinced I knew how to get back into town.

Plus, I didn't have my phone. It was still at the booth. I hoped Aunt Barb would take it. This was a harsh reminder that I should always carry it with me and not leave it behind. So dumb. A rookie move. A good investigator would never make that mistake. I needed to get my amateur sleuth game on if I was going to continue investigating this crime. Maybe I'd been saved this time, but next time I wouldn't be so lucky.

I stepped out from the building and into the sunshine once again. Blue skies were quickly turning to gray overcast. Clouds rolled toward me at a swift speed. Soon a storm would unleash itself on me. I had to hurry, so I headed down the road away from the old building. Even with the threat of rain, I had no choice but to walk all the way back into town. There was no other option.

I couldn't just sit out here and wait for another car to come along. Surely the killer would come back soon. He might just be driving around the block, looking for me. I was so nervous and there was nowhere for me to hide, not even any cornfields now. But I'd had my fill of the cornfields anyway, and I might never go back into one again. I was completely traumatized. They'd already been spooky enough, but this turn of events had made me even more scared. I'd see that mask-covered face in my nightmares now.

My feet were already hurting, and I hadn't even made it that far. Nevertheless, I kept up the pace. The thunder in the distance motivated me to go just a little farther. A bit more and finally I'd be there. I couldn't give up now. I didn't want to die out here. They'd find me in the ditch, but not before some wild animal had tried to drag me off. That was a morbid thought. I needed to get rid of this negative stuff circling my mind.

But after what had happened, could anyone blame me for feeling this way? I looked up at the storm clouds, thankful that the sky hadn't opened on me yet. Thank goodness the killer had apparently decided not to get rid of me, but what had changed his mind? Had another car come along and scared him away? If so, that meant he could be back at any time to reclaim his prize. He hadn't completed his mission, and he would want to do that.

I wondered how much longer I had left before he returned. How much farther would I have to walk before I reached town? I couldn't wait to see Aunt Barb again. I would give her the biggest hug. Surely she was wondering where I'd gone. The festival would be over soon, but she wouldn't think to look on this isolated road for me. She'd be worried, and I hated to put her through that. Would I ever get a lecture when I finally did get back! Maybe I'd just stay out here until she cooled off a little. Then she'd be so grateful to see me that she wouldn't yell at me.

Yeah, that wouldn't be the case. Aunt Barb could always yell. She'd hug me first and then she'd yell.

What would Maverick say about this? At least I had a vague description of the car. That was better than nothing. A black, newer-model four-door. Unfortunately, I hadn't gotten the license plate number, but I knew exactly what kind of Halloween mask that guy wore. An evil-looking jack-o'-lantern face that appeared to almost be melting—I could pick that out of a lineup.

Just when I thought I couldn't make it any farther, the lights from traffic up ahead came into view. I was coming to town. It'd enter the first shop that was open; most everyone had closed for the festival. If I could make it to a phone, I'd give someone a call. With any luck, I could get a ride. I just needed a break. I wanted to sit down and have a cool drink. Maybe get something to eat and try to forget about what had happened.

Though I couldn't forget about what happened. I had to find the killer. I was more determined now than ever. And I was livid.

I looked over my shoulder to see if the car had returned, but there was still no sign of him. Maybe he was lying in wait for his next opportunity. I had to uncover this killer before he decided to do this to someone else. I spotted the local clothing boutique on the corner and headed in that direction. I'd meant to stop in and ask about surveillance video anyway, but at the very least, I would be able to use the phone.

I practically fell through the door when I reached the place. The scent of lilacs hit me in the face as I entered. This place always smelled like a summer day. The cute little clothing shop was on the corner of Main Street in downtown, not far from my bakery. It had all the latest fashions. Of course, they weren't from Paris, but I liked to pretend I was in a shop in France. No time for shopping now, though.

Kristina, the owner, was an independent, strong woman. Maybe I'd be able to use the phone and get a ride. And she might be able to give me some indication of whether she had surveillance video or if she'd seen anything out of the ordinary.

Mannequins draped in glamorous clothing filled the large windows that lined the sidewalk in front of the shop. Wildflowers Boutique had been open for only six months, but it seemed business was good.

Soft music played in the background. It really was like a fancy boutique that I might encounter in some other big city, not in Paris, Kentucky. I'd never been in Kristina's shop without buying something, but now was not the time for shopping. I had to focus.

Kristina popped out from the back. "Oh, hi, Marci. I'm surprised to see you here."

People who knew me at all knew I usually didn't do things that were out of the ordinary. I was predictable like that. Maybe I needed to work on my spontaneity.

Kristina watched me with a curious expression. "Are you okay? You look like you've seen a ghost."

"I almost became a ghost today. Someone stuffed me into the trunk of his car. Thankfully, I finally got out."

Her eyes widened. "Are you serious? Was it that same guy who killed Kellie?"

Kristina walked over to me and wrapped her arms around me in a hug. My hands still shook from my anxiety.

"I need to use your phone," I said. "I have to call everyone and let them know I'm okay. I'm sure they're looking for me. And most importantly, I need to call the police."

"Where did this happen?" Kristina asked as she handed me her phone.

"At the festival," I said.

She shook her head. "I don't know what's happening to Paris, but it's scary."

Sadly, she was right. Things had changed. Ever since Antoine had shown up, Paris had been turned upside down. I looked out the front windows. Seconds later, I saw the black car drive past slowly. Immediately I ducked behind one of the nearby racks of clothing. Had the person seen me through the window? I sucked in a deep breath. I couldn't believe it. He had come back for me after all. Thank goodness I was in here and safe. At least I hoped I was safe.

# Chapter
# Twenty-Six

After leaving a message for Aunt Barb, I decided against calling the police. They would only slow me down. Up to this
point Maverick had asked a million questions and gone over what I
considered to be minor details ad nauseam. Not to mention that a
couple of years ago, my uncle Joe had his pickup stolen. The police
had wasted so much time asking my uncle questions that the crim-
inal managed to drive the old Chevy truck all the way to Nashville
before crashing it. I didn't have that kind of time to waste.

Instead, I approached the counter. Thank goodness I had
Kristina to talk to, because I was totally freaking out.

"Tell me everything that's been going on since we last talked,"
Kristina said, coming around to give me a hug.

"You know, what happened at my shop has just left me terrified," I said. "But after today . . . it's gone beyond losing the shop
now. I might lose my life."

"Don't say such things, Marci," she said, her eyes glistening.
"We've got to make sure nothing else happens to you."

"I don't know what to think. It's all so scary," I said, then
released a deep breath.

"Do you have any idea who did this? You're obviously in danger; you have to go to the police. Have you called them yet?" she asked.

"I'm trying to figure out who killed Kellie," I said. "The police would only slow me down right now. Taking me to the police station and asking me questions for hours."

Her eyes widened. "You need the police's protection. You're trying to figure out who murdered her?"

"Well, yeah, kind of . . . because I'm concerned. The killer might come after me again."

She had begun absent-mindedly pawing through the racks next to us, and she almost dropped a dress from a hanger. I managed to catch it.

"I'm worried about you, Marci," she said. "There's no chance what happened to you today could have been an awful prank?"

"Let's just say I got a threatening note. Between that and being kidnapped and stuffed in a trunk, I don't think this person will stop until I'm out of the picture."

"Oh my gosh, Marci. You have to go to the police right away. Promise me you'll call them." She looked around as if maybe the killer would come in the shop after me.

I didn't want her to be fearful, but anything could happen.

"I promise I will make a report about what happened," I said, then had a thought. "I suppose the police have come in to look at surveillance video?"

She shook her head. "Yeah, they asked for it, but I just got it to them today. I had issues with my computer. Thank goodness I got it fixed. I was starting to freak out. You and the police are practically the only customers I've had today because of the festival."

"What did you find?" I asked.

"Well, I originally thought it hadn't been recorded. I finally just got it to the police, but I didn't get a chance to look at it myself." She adjusted the dresses on the rack.

"And the police looked at it?" I asked.

"I guess, but like I said, I just gave it to them. I wish I had gotten it to them sooner. Stupid computer and technology. They didn't say anything else to me. So I don't know if it was helpful."

"I really would love to see that video," I said.

"I can show it to you. I have a copy." She motioned over her shoulder.

Wow, it was as simple as that? I'd thought maybe she would say the police had told her not to let anyone see it. Although I'd had no reason to believe that would be the case. Why not let somebody else look at it?

"I'll get it for you now while you try that on." She took a gorgeous yellow dress from the rack and handed it to me. "You need a distraction to calm your nerves."

It seemed like a weird time to try on clothing. Nevertheless, I headed over to the mirror in front of the dressing room. As anxious as I was, Kristina was right: I needed a momentary distraction, and she knew my style. I held the dress up to my body and looked at my reflection. Trying on the dress while sweaty was out of the question. Wow, I hadn't expected the dark circles under my eyes. I supposed I hadn't slept much since the murder. Looking at the dress was a nice distraction, and the dress was cute, but I wanted to get back to the real reason for my visit. After I lowered the dress from my body, I stared at my reflection once again. My shorts and T-shirt had smears of dirt, which I assumed had come from being stuffed in a trunk. I raced away from the mirror like one of the Thoroughbreds out of the gate at the Breeders' Cup. I hurried over to the counter to wait for Kristina.

My anxiousness took over as I shifted from foot to foot, wringing my hands and pacing around at the front of the counter. Only a couple minutes had passed, but somehow it felt like hours. I needed to calm down. After all, any evidence that might have been captured on video probably wouldn't be enough to get a conviction. It might be nothing at all. It could be nothing more than a random car driving through town right before the murder. What if it was that person I'd seen ducking behind the building? I still had no idea who that had been.

Just when I thought I couldn't handle the anxiety a second longer, Kristina came out from the back room with a smile on her face. That had to be a good sign, right?

"I hope this helps you, but I really think it's dangerous for you to be involved. I wish you'd just leave this to the police," she said.

"I wish I could just leave it to the police, but I'm in too deep," I said.

"So what about Detective Malone?" she asked.

"What about him?"

"He sure is handsome. He came in here to talk to me. I think I noticed a glimmer of something in his eyes . . . whenever he said your name."

I waved my hand. "Oh, you're just saying that. Now let me see that video. Enough talk about him."

As she opened the computer, I anxiously waited. The screen came to life. Kristina clicked onto the video for the date of the murder. Kristina's mother's boyfriend's sister's godson worked at the police department and had overheard the time of death. I hoped it was accurate, because otherwise we'd have to watch through a lot of video.

Kristina finally found the spot for the estimated time of death. A few minutes passed with not much happening at all, and I was losing hope quickly. Then I spotted movement and saw a man walking down the sidewalk. What was that glint? A gold buckle on his shoes? I leaned in closer to the computer screen to get a better look. I needed more than that, though. I needed good luck to come my way, because the video seemed blurry and there was no guarantee I would even know who this person was.

Seconds later, though, it clicked in my mind. I thought I recognized him because of his gait. He walked as if he had injured his foot. I'd noticed Mr. Gustavsson had still been limping on his right foot when he'd entered my shop. I'd also noticed that he, like Hunter, had gold buckles on his shoes. Now it all added up.

I gasped. "I think that's George."

Kristina looked at me as if she had no clue what I was talking about. Of course she didn't; she didn't know the specifics of the case.

"I know who that is," I said.

"Who is it?" she asked.

"Kellie's boss. George Gustavsson."

"What is he doing outside your shop?"

"That's what I'd like to know," I said. "That means he was at the scene of the crime, right? He lied about not being there. Mrs. Mansfield and Mrs. O'Neal mistakenly thought it was Antoine. Probably because of that fedora hat."

Her eyes widened. "That's not good, Marci. You have to find out for sure."

"Well, him being outside my shop might be good for my investigation. I think I found the killer. I think I found the killer," I repeated.

And to think I'd been in his office talking to him alone. That sent a chill down my spine. He could have been the one who left the note in my shop. But how had he gotten in? That was a puzzle

I needed to solve. Maybe if I could figure that out, it would link him to the murder. Then he could be arrested.

"What will you do now?" she asked.

"I suppose I have to track him down and ask him about this video."

She waved her hands. "Well, that's not a good idea."

"Why not?" I asked.

"Because he's a killer, hello?"

"Yeah, I know, but I wouldn't go up to him and say, 'Hey, I got video of you killing your employee.' Maybe, just maybe, I'll surprise everyone and get him to confess."

"Yeah, that's it," she said with a click of her tongue. "Don't you think you should tell the police?" she asked.

"I'll take this dress, by the way." I pushed the dress across the counter toward her. "And I'll call the police on the way there."

Trying to devise a plan in my head, I paid for the dress. Was it crazy to buy a dress after being kidnapped? Yes, most certainly. I was so traumatized that I wasn't sure I was even thinking correctly. Perhaps I was doing this as retail therapy.

"I hope that I didn't just get you into trouble," Kristina said.

"What do you mean?"

"Well, you know, if you confront the killer."

"I won't get into trouble."

"I still want you to call the police," Kristina said with a frown.

"I'll call Maverick, but I don't have my phone. I don't have my car either. It's at the festival."

"Let me close up shop for a minute and drive you to your car. You can make the call on the way, okay?" Her brow furrowed with worry.

"Are you sure?" I asked.

"I'm positive. You're stubborn, so it's the least I can do, since I know you'll not give up on getting to the bottom of this."

"I am stubborn. Thank you," I said. "You're a good friend."

I thanked her for the dress, and then she headed outside with me so that she could give me a ride.

I needed to decide what to do next. Had Maverick seen the video? Of course he had. She'd said he'd come into the shop. Had Maverick recognized the walk and talked to Mr. Gustavsson by now? Surely he'd spoken to Kellie's boss before and noticed his foot injury. What did Maverick think about the video? Did the police recognize the walk? Did they think anything of the evidence?

Mr. Gustavsson had been right there near the crime scene around the time the murder occurred. That *had* to mean something. I was torn between wanting to know what Maverick thought about this and wanting to just go ahead with talking to Kellie's boss on my own. Even with my current level of fear, I wanted to talk to him. If other people were around at the company, it would be safe to speak with him, right? On the weekend, though, no one would be there. This wasn't safe at all.

Should I ask Maverick to meet me there? Though I couldn't wait for him and miss the opportunity of letting the killer get away. And it was the only idea I had. There were no guarantees I'd even find Mr. Gustavsson. What if he kidnapped me again? What if he killed me this time? Was it a wise thing to do? No, most certainly not. I had to do it though. I'd just be extra careful.

As I rode in Kristina's car, I dialed Maverick's number from her phone, but he didn't answer. This was not the time for playing phone tag. "Maverick, er, I mean, Detective Malone, I saw the video from around the time of the murder. The man I saw is George Gustavsson. At least I'm almost sure of it. He is the killer. I want to talk with him. Call me, okay?"

After ending the call, I immediately dialed Aunt Barb again. I received no answer from her either. Cell coverage was spotty at the festival; maybe that was why no one was answering. I would just go talk to Mr. Gustavsson on my own. As long as I was careful, I figured I would be fine.

"Thanks again for the ride and for closing the shop just to take me somewhere," I told Kristina as I handed her back her phone. We had just pulled up next to my car.

"Think nothing of it. That's what friends are for. Plus, that's part of small-town life. People expect shop owners to unexpectedly close sometimes. Just be safe out there, okay?" Kristina said.

"I'll try my best."

Those words echoed in my mind. I certainly would try my best, but would that be enough? Was I really going through with this?

After slipping behind the wheel of my own car, I pulled away from the curb and drove in the direction of Mr. Gustavsson's office. I had no other ideas on where to find him. I didn't have his home address. Maybe someone at Flaget would know where to look. I knew Aunt Barb wouldn't be happy I'd gone there alone. Plus, she was probably packing up the remaining baked goods in a hurry because of the impending rain—though now it looked like the storm had blown over. In my voice mails I hadn't told her I'd been kidnapped, because I didn't want her to completely freak out; I'd just told her something had come up and I'd caught a ride to town with a friend and would be back soon. The last thing I needed was for Aunt Barb to have a heart attack because I'd stressed her out.

I would just make this quick trip, and everything would be peachy. No need to worry. At least that was what I told myself. If I told myself that often enough, then maybe it would happen.

I tried to relax as I made the drive to Mr. Gustavsson's office. Green trees shaded a black horse fence that ran along each side of the road. It was an ideal backdrop. Puffy white clouds dotted the expanse of the blue sky. Despite the earlier threat of a storm, it was turning out to be a beautiful day. Yet anxiety bubbled inside me.

With the number of times I'd been to Flaget, I should have a pass to get in by now. They probably thought I was an employee. Yet here I was, in the same situation, trying to break in once again. I should know what I was doing by now. I parked and waited for somebody to come out or in.

A phone rang as I waited, and the sound startled me so much that I jumped in the seat. Where was that coming from? I searched around the car and then realized my phone was under the driver's seat. I thought I'd left it at the pumpkin festival, but it must have fallen out of my pocket in the car before I'd even gotten to the booth. Thankfully, I managed to answer before the call went to voice mail.

"Marci, this is Mr. Reynolds from Jack's Guns. I have the name for you."

Wow, this was exciting. I'd kind of lost hope that I would get this information.

"What's the name?" I asked breathlessly.

"The name is Wilmer Perkins."

"Wilmer?" I said with shock.

I'd never heard that name before. George Gustavsson wasn't the buyer? He had to be the killer . . . so who was Wilmer?

"That's the name," he replied.

"Well, um, okay, thank you so much, Mr. Reynolds."

"Just don't tell anyone I gave you that name, okay?"

"I won't say a word, I promise," I said.

"I appreciate it," he said.

"Come by the bakery anytime, Mr. Reynolds, and I'll give you free pastries."

"Just what I need for the waistline," he said with the hint of a chuckle.

"Yeah, everything in moderation, right?"

"I suppose. Well, I'll see you around," he said.

"Thanks again."

After ending the call, I immediately searched on my phone for the name but found nothing. I texted Barb and Maverick, letting them know I was on my own phone again if they called back.

Movement caught my attention. Someone had come out of the building. They didn't notice me. The employees never paid attention, but I liked to pay attention to my surroundings. At least I thought I did. I hoped that no one had followed me today.

When a silver Toyota pulled into the fenced-off area, I pushed on the gas and followed in pursuit. Thankfully, once again I made it inside the secure area.

I parked my car under a shade tree and sat there for several seconds, then finally got out and headed toward the main entrance. At least Aunt Barb had shown me that I could probably get in without having to sneak in the side door. Just walk in like I belonged there. Was Mr. Gustavsson here? I still needed to find out exactly what he had told Kellie. I didn't see a black sedan in the parking lot, and with so few cars parked in the lot, surely it would stand out. But I didn't want to draw attention to myself by circling the lot searching for it.

I stepped up to the entrance and walked inside like I belonged there. Just then a strange feeling hit me. It was as if I knew something bad was about to happen. Call it a sixth sense, maybe. Though what made me think I had any special talent in that department this time?

# Chapter Twenty-Seven

This place was always eerily quiet. Of course, with the festival in town, everyone was probably gone, but still . . . I would have thought there would be a few people lingering around. Not that I was complaining. It was like I had the run of the place. But then again, it kind of gave me the creeps. My intention had been to find Mr. Gustavsson. Now I wasn't sure that would happen, but at the very least I could snoop.

I walked down a long hallway and again had that feeling that someone was watching me. I still didn't know if there were cameras or not, but I assumed no one knew I was here, given how deserted the place was.

I made my way up the staircase all the way to the third floor once again. As soon as I rounded the corner, I spotted Mr. Gustavsson. He was coming out of Antoine's office. Did that mean Antoine was in there and they'd had a discussion? Or was he snooping around like me? Mr. Gustavsson paused with his hand on the doorknob and then glanced around like he sensed someone was watching him.

I moved back into the stairwell, holding my breath and hoping that he wouldn't find me. I didn't think he'd seen me, but I couldn't be sure. I was starting to panic. My heart beat faster and I was shaky all over. I had to get a hold of myself, though. Panic wouldn't do me any good. How long should I wait before I looked again to see what he was up to?

After a few more seconds, I got up enough nerve and peeked around the corner into the hallway once again. Mr. Gustavsson was nowhere in sight, but I didn't know if he'd gone back into Antoine's office or if he'd left for his own office. There was no way to know for sure. Unless I checked. And that was exactly what I had to do, as much as I hated it and as nervous as I was.

I eased out into the hallway, thinking that if Mr. Gustavsson came back, I could dash back into the stairwell again. But once I got halfway down the hallway, it would be too late. There would be no turning back.

All of this stress was really getting to me. I needed to get this case solved so that I could relax again. I should be baking croissants and macarons, not chasing killers around and snooping around in offices. This was risky business. Yet I'd put myself in this situation. I could have just let the police deal with it, but I'd had to be Ms. Know-It-All and take it into my own hands. I could just hear it now. If anything happened to me, people would say I brought it on myself. *She wouldn't stay out of the way, so she deserved what she got.*

Distracted with curiosity about Antoine and what Mr. Gustavsson might have been saying to him, I reached his office door and paused, not sure if I should just burst in or if I should use the door. Instead of knocking, I decided to ease the door open just a bit for a peek inside.

The room was empty. Well, of course it had furniture, just as it had before, but something seemed different. The knick-knacks were different. These had been in Mr. Gustavsson's office. I remembered seeing them. I looked across the way at the shelf, and that was when I spotted the picture. Had that been there before?

I realized that the last time I was here, I had only paid attention to the manly smell. I wasn't sure why that was, either. Maybe because I was nervous? I walked over to the wall and looked at the framed certificate hanging there. Oddly, the name on it wasn't Antoine's at all. It was George Gustavsson's. This was his office? Why had he met me in the other office before? Had he switched?

That had to be it. If this was his office now, then had it been Antoine's office the day I was in here? Or had Mr. Gustavsson already made that switch? It was concerning, for sure. Did that mean that the gun receipt was Mr. Gustavsson's and not Antoine's?

I moved over to the desk in hopes that I might find something new. When I shuffled through the papers on top, I found a letter and read it quickly.

*Mr. Gustavsson,*

*This letter is my resignation. I can't work for you a moment longer. I know what you've been doing with the company's money. I advise you to go to the police and tell them what you've done. It would be easier for you if you confess and give the company's money back. I simply can't be part of your embezzling scheme. Please don't come to my home either. I have nothing left to say to you.*

*Your advances have gone too far too. I told you I'm not interested in dating you, yet you simply won't take no for an answer. I don't want you standing outside my place staring either. It's creepy and upsetting. If you don't do the right thing and go to the police, I will.*

*Kellie Lowry*

Mr. Gustavsson was embezzling money from the company—and Kellie had caught him.

That must have been the reason he'd killed Kellie. What other motive would he have?

Why hadn't Maverick called me yet? I had to go to the police with this right away. I shouldn't have even taken the chance on coming here now. It was too dangerous. I should have gone to the police when I'd been kidnapped anyway—though facing Maverick was not something I'd wanted to do. I'd said I didn't want the police slowing me down, but if I was being honest with myself, I knew it had more to do with Maverick. Was avoiding him worth risking my life, though?

Why would Mr. Gustavsson leave this letter just lying around like this? It was as if he was just asking for someone to figure out his little secret.

Now that I knew, I'd be in big trouble if he found out that I knew. He'd probably want to get rid of me too. Kellie had figured out what Mr. Gustavsson was up to, so he'd had to get rid of her. The thought sent a chill down my spine. I might be next. I had to get out of here, but I also had to get proof of Mr. Gustavsson's misdeed so that I could go to the police. Wouldn't Maverick be shocked.

I snapped some photos of the letter with my phone, but I left the letter on the desk just as I had found it. Now I hurried across the floor to the door so that I could get out of here.

Just as I wrapped my hand around the doorknob, my phone rang. The sound was so jarring that my heart even skipped a beat. I didn't want anyone to hear my phone. I hurriedly answered.

"Hello?" I whispered.

After a pause, the woman said, "Marci, this is Naomi Perry."

This was not a good time for her call.

"Oh, hi, Ms. Perry," I said trying to keep my voice low. "How are you?"

Based on her pause, she seemed confused, but she continued, "Oh, I'm just fine, but I'm calling to let you know that I remembered something."

Okay, so this might be worth staying on the phone.

"Oh, what is that?" I asked.

"It's something about Kellie. It's just that she had gotten a note one time and it really seemed to upset her. She didn't say what the note said, but I saw the return address and name on it. I thought maybe that might help you. It just seemed a little odd, that's all."

"Well, any help at all would be great, yes."

"The name is Wilmer Perkins," she said.

I almost dropped the phone.

"Are you sure?" I asked.

"Oh, I'm positive, dear."

"And what's the address?"

With her on speakerphone, I typed in the address on my phone to search for it right then. A different name was associated with the address: *George Gustavsson*. Someone associated with Kellie's boss had bought that gun.

That was enough evidence for me. I no longer had any doubt that he was the killer.

"Thank you for the information. I really appreciate it, and make sure to come by the shop. I'll give you some pastry."

I was giving away all kinds of free pastry in return for information on the case.

"I'll do that, honey. Thank you."

Movement sounded from the other side of the door.

"I gotta go, Ms. Perry," I said breathlessly.

I immediately panicked, of course. The only thing I knew to do was to hide under the desk as I had the other day. I'd pray for the best.

I ran across the floor and practically dove underneath the desk. My body shook as I scrunched under there, hoping no one would find me. I practically held my breath, waiting for something to happen. Seconds later the door opened, and footsteps came toward me. There was nowhere for me to go.

The steps moved closer and closer until the person paused at the desk. From my spot underneath it, I saw the person standing only steps away. This had to be Mr. Gustavsson, right? Did he know I was hiding under here? I felt like he was the cat and I was the mouse. Soon he would pounce, like he had when he'd shoved me in the trunk of that car. I didn't know what to do. I just had to wait for it to happen.

"You can come out now," he said in a rough voice.

Uh-oh. My fear was confirmed. He knew I was here. I sat there for several seconds, hoping that maybe if I ignored him, he would go away. Or if I pretended I wasn't there, he would give up and think he was wrong. But no such luck, because he just repeated his words.

"Come out now or I will drag you out. I can see you under there." His words were full of anger.

Apparently my hiding spot wasn't so great after all. I mustered all the courage I could and then climbed out from under the desk. I turned around and faced him. The look on his face was one of undeniable anger. I was surprised he didn't try to attack me right then and there. Instead, he just stood there with that scowl on his face. His arms were up in a boxing stance with his fists clenched. He wanted to punch me or something.

"What are you doing here?" he asked in a booming voice.

"I . . . I . . . I . . . ," I stuttered.

That was all I could do. I couldn't even give an answer. He looked down at the papers on the desk, and that was when he realized that I had discovered what he'd been up to.

"Why are you in my office?" he asked.

"I didn't realize it was your office. I thought it was Antoine's. I was looking for him."

He scoffed. "No, that's not why you're here. Now you know what I've been up to, don't you?"

I couldn't deny it, or could I?

"I have no idea what you're talking about," I said, hoping he believed me.

"Don't try that. You know what I've been up to, and now I have to get rid of you." He stepped closer.

Just like he'd gotten rid of Kellie. But he hadn't said that; should I mention to him that I knew? Get him to confess?

But what good was a confession when no one was around to hear it? I would be gone, and there would be nothing I could do to prove it. Now the authorities would have another murder on their hands. Would anyone even realize I wasn't around?

Oh, what was I saying? Of course Aunt Barb would know I was missing. My parents would realize I was gone when they got back from their vacation. Not to mention other people when they came to the bakery and wanted their pastries. But they might still never know what had happened to me.

Would they be able to piece it together? I mean, my car was in the parking lot. Would Mr. Gustavsson be smart enough to get rid of that? There would be video footage of me coming here, right? There had to be some trace of me that would get him caught.

Why was I worried about solving my own murder when I was in this situation right now? I should at least try to get out of here before he killed me.

"I seriously don't know what you're talking about," I said.

I tried to move around the office desk, but he blocked me.

"Kindly step out of my way," I said. "I need to leave."

"You're not going anywhere," he said.

He stood so close that I felt his breath on my neck. He had invaded my personal space. At that moment he reached out and grabbed me. I tried to get away, moving my arms and yanking away, but nothing worked. He was strong.

"Let go of me right now," I yelled.

"I should have gotten rid of you before when I had the chance," he said.

"You've been following me, haven't you?" I asked breathlessly. "Why?"

"I wanted to shut you up. I had to stop you before you found out."

"You shouldn't have left that letter on your desk if you didn't want someone to discover what you'd done. That was a stupid move."

I felt his grip on me tighten. Obviously, my words had made him even angrier.

"I made a mistake by leaving it there. I'm human. I'll still get away with it, though. As soon as I get rid of you."

"Who is Wilmer Perkins?" I asked breathlessly.

"What? How did you . . . That's my brother," he said.

I hoped someone would hear the struggle. I wanted to go home, though I figured there was no chance of that happening. I fought, trying to get to the door, but he just wouldn't let go.

"What are you gonna do to me? You can't kill me right here."

"Oh, I can kill you anywhere I want," he said.

I wondered how he would kill me. Would it be with the gun? Or would he choose some other method this time?

"You won't get away with this," I said. "People know that I'm here. They're on their way to look for me right now. Just let me go."

"It's already too late for that. You shouldn't have come into my office. You should have just minded your own business."

"I thought it was Antoine's office. Why is he not here?"

"We switched offices. Apparently, my coworker complained to HR that I was staring into her office across the hall and watching her."

"You really are a creep, aren't you? You left that note in my bakery for me?" I asked.

"Yes, that was me," he said with a smile.

"How did you get in my shop?"

"I just got a key. It was on Antoine's key ring, and it was marked BAKERY. He left them on his desk. I made a copy."

I seriously needed to have a talk with Chantelle and Antoine about the key situation. I assumed she'd given him a key so he could check out the building before buying it. But he couldn't just have a key to my place lying around anywhere for anyone to get—and the fact that he'd marked it BAKERY? That was practically begging someone to break into my place.

It was too late to worry about it, since this guy was going to kill me right now. Would Antoine feel guilty about that?

If Mr. Gustavsson was in Antoine's office now, then did that meant that Antoine had Mr. Gustavsson's office down the hall? Why the change? Had they come in just to move offices? Maybe I could find a way out to the hall and Antoine would come to my aid. Somebody needed to save me, because obviously I couldn't do it myself. I was a bit disappointed that I was unable to get away from this guy. But in my defense, he was strong.

"Thank goodness he's here to save me!" I said.

243

Mr. Gustavsson glanced over his shoulder, and I used the moment to stomp on his toe. Of course no one was here to save me, but my words had distracted him. I managed to break free from his hold and sprinted over to the door. Even though my hands shook from fear, I got the door open and even burst out into the hallway. I moved to the left to run toward where I thought Antoine's office might be now. I screamed out for help, hoping that someone would hear me.

But I didn't get much farther before Mr. Gustavsson had me in his grasp once again. He pulled on me, dragging me back down the hallway. Was he going to take me back to his office, or would it be outside this time? Surely once I got out there, someone would come to help. Or maybe not. I mean, even building security hadn't seen me and had let me slip right into this building unnoticed. I still screamed, but no one was coming to help me.

We were getting closer to his old office now, and I knew that if he got me in there, it would definitely be over. Perhaps I would stand some chance if we got outside. He probably knew that.

I tried to get my bearings so that I could possibly stop him from dragging me into that room, but all I was getting was splinters underneath my fingernails. When I looked down, I realized that I had actually left scratch marks on the floor. That was some serious trying to get away. At least everyone would say I put up a struggle, and I could be proud of that.

But I wasn't ready to give up just yet. I had to continue to fight. I screamed again.

"What's going on?" Antoine yelled.

When I glanced down the hallway, I spotted him headed in our direction. He was running as fast as he could. Thank goodness he had heard me. But Mr. Gustavsson still wasn't letting go, even with Antoine running toward us.

Antoine yelled out one more time, and that seemed to distract Mr. Gustavsson for just a brief moment. I used that as my opportunity to get free from his hold on me and get to my feet. When I did, I turned around and, instead of running away, punched him square in the jaw. He had made me really mad. I wasn't ready to run away; I wanted to inflict some kind of pain on this guy. He had caused a lot of problems. Not to mention he'd murdered Kellie. An innocent victim. I was going to get justice for her.

I must have really landed a wallop on Mr. Gustavsson, because he tumbled backward and landed on his back on the floor. I was kind of shocked that I had hurt him a little bit. That would definitely leave lingering pain tomorrow. Maybe I'd even broken a bone. I couldn't believe I'd actually knocked him out. Well, he wasn't knocked out cold, but I'd hit him hard enough to send him off his feet.

Antoine was shocked to see that I had done that. He probably hadn't thought a short girl like me could do something like that to a big, tall man like Mr. Gustavsson. But after my experience in the cornfield, I'd known I had to do something to stop him. Somehow I'd mustered up all my strength, and the adrenaline had kicked in. My anger was allowing me think I was capable of almost anything was possible.

I had needed a reminder of that. I had strength when I needed it; I just hadn't been using it. Thank goodness Antoine had come out and helped me remember. I felt a rush of energy and a bit of pride that I had been able to pull this off.

"Are you all right?" Antoine asked as he approached. "I'm just glad I came by to get those files I forgot."

"Yeah, I'm fine," I said, shaking my hand, trying to get the pain to stop. "We need to get the police to get this guy. He killed Kellie. He admitted it, and he's been taking money from the company."

I spilled out all the information.

"This is a lot to take in," Antoine said as he held on to Mr. Gustavsson.

"I even have proof. I took a picture on my phone just in case he decides he wanted to try to deny it."

Yes, I was proud of myself for the way this had gone down. It had been touch and go there for a while, but everything seemed to be working out just fine now.

"Don't worry, Marci, we've got this piece of garbage now," Antoine said with shock in his voice. "He's not going anywhere except to jail."

Antoine had obviously picked up some American slang. I'd never heard him raise his voice like that. His take-charge attitude was super sexy.

*Focus, Marci, focus.* Now was not the time to think about such things.

"Don't listen to her. She doesn't know what she's talking about," Mr. Gustavsson said weakly, trying to break free from Antoine's hold.

"Will you be quiet," I said. "I very much know what I'm talking about. Everything I said is completely true."

Antoine looked seriously impressed right now. I had to find a better way to get Mr. Gustavsson restrained, because he looked as if he was getting ready to make a run for it now. He still looked stunned that I had knocked him down. As I pulled out my phone and dialed 911, Antoine continued to hold him down. Problem solved. But how long would he be able to keep it up? Where was the security guard when we needed him?

"I need the police right away. I've caught a killer," I said breathlessly into the phone.

The fact that I was even saying those words was still unbelievable to me. *I've caught the killer.* Although that had been my mission. I had set out to solve this mystery, and I'd finally reached that goal. I'd let nothing stop me in the process, even when things had gotten tough.

Minutes went by with Antoine practically sitting on top of Mr. Gustavsson.

"Why were you following me?" I demanded.

"To stop you from finding out," George said breathlessly. "I knew you were snooping around. You just couldn't mind your own business."

"How did you know at first, though?"

Sure, I'd paid him a visit, but how had he known before that?

"Antoine. He told me you were trying to help him by finding the real killer," George said, wiggling and trying to get up.

"I'm sorry, Marci. I had no idea. I would have never put you in jeopardy by telling him," Antoine said.

"I know, Antoine. I know," I said.

I knew Antoine meant what he said. Now more than ever I saw that Antoine was kind and would never want to put me in danger.

It seemed like an eternity before the police stormed into the hallway. Leading the way was Maverick. And I was happy to see him. Of course, he looked worried. Or maybe that was anger on his face. Probably a bit of both. He wouldn't be happy with me, but I hoped he would forgive me.

Once the police had secured Mr. Gustavsson and we'd talked with Maverick, we were allowed out of the building. I'd never been so happy to see the sunshine. Luckily, the storm had faded, allowing the setting sun to add streaks of red and purple across the blue sky. Not a cloud was in sight now. I felt like I was seeing the sun for the first time. I had a spring in my step, even though something horrific had just happened. I was grateful I was alive.

And even more grateful to see that Aunt Barb had arrived. Although by the scowl on her face, maybe I should rethink that sentiment. Even stranger was the fact that she was with Gordon. Why was he there?

Aunt Barb stomped over to me and placed her hands on her hips. "Just what do you think you're doing?"

"Um, catching the killer," I said.

"You're lucky to be alive," she said.

Gordon stood close to Aunt Barb. He was so close to her that their bodies were almost touching.

I glanced over at Gordon. "Why are you here, Aunt Barb, and why are you with Gordon?"

He reached for her hand, but she jerked her hand away.

"He gave me a ride, but that's neither here nor there." Aunt Barb blushed. "Of course I came to make sure you're okay."

I bit back a smile. I knew it. She was in love. Well, at least one of us was in love and happy.

"Mr. Dumensil. That's why you came into my shop like clockwork. You had your eye on my Aunt Barb," I said.

"I'm guilty of that, yes," he said with a grin. "Aunt Barb is special. I've never met anyone like her. How do you say it? She has a certain je ne sais quoi."

I laughed. "Yes, she definitely does."

"Oh, you." Aunt Barb brushed off the comment with a wave of her hand. "This is no time for such silliness."

But I knew by the smile on her face that she loved what Gordon had said.

"I had to make sure she was okay after the murder, because I was worried. That's why I kept coming around," he said.

"That is so sweet. Isn't that sweet, Aunt Barb?" I asked.

"Well, that's neither here nor there, because I'm fine." She waved her hand dismissively.

She just didn't want to show affection toward Gordon in front of me. I bet she thought that might diminish her tough exterior in my eyes.

Maverick approached and pulled me to the side. "You're lucky to be alive, you know that?" he said, reiterating my aunt's statement.

"I'm aware," I said. "Look, if you just want to give me a lecture, can you do it tomorrow? I'm kind of exhausted right now and mentally drained."

"Yes, of course I can wait until tomorrow to give you a lecture . . . when you have dinner with me." His gaze didn't budge from my face.

It seemed as if Maverick knew what he wanted. I couldn't exactly say no now, could I?

"Okay, tomorrow night," I said, feeling the excitement dance in my stomach.

Maverick touched my cheek. "I was worried about you, Marci."

"I'm sorry I worried you." The look of desire in his eyes had me mesmerized.

"Tomorrow at seven," Maverick said.

"I'll be ready," I said dreamily.

Maverick walked back over to where all the officers had gathered. I watched as Antoine walked over to him. What was going on between them? What were they talking about? I assumed the murder case. Maybe they were discussing the fact that I had gotten involved. They looked my way, and I met Maverick's stare. He held my gaze for quite a bit of time before finally turning to walk away toward a group of officers. Then Antoine moved my way.

"I have to say, those were some impressive skills you displayed back there." Antoine studied my face.

"A touch of magic, I suppose. Baking isn't the only thing I'm good at," I said with a wink. "Though I'm glad this mystery is all done."

"I tried to be a detective and was nowhere near as successful as you. Obviously. I even called that gun shop looking for information about the gun."

"Really? Well, I guess I really do have a knack for it."

"I was worried about you during all this," he said, reaching out and taking my hand in his. "I've never had anyone help me as much as you did. I've never had anyone care about me that much."

"It seemed like the natural thing to do."

"How can I repay you?" he asked, still holding my hand.

"You don't have to repay me, Antoine." His hand felt warm and comfortable wrapped around mine. Like it was a good fit. Perhaps even a perfect fit.

"At least let me take you to dinner, Marci. I want to take you to the finest French restaurant in town."

"The finest restaurant in town is Honeybun's Diner," I said with a laugh.

"Okay, then the finest restaurant in Lexington. What do you say? Is it a date?"

What would I do? I was torn between two men. I had feelings for them both.

I glanced over at Maverick. "Yes, it's a date. Though I already have plans for tomorrow night."

# Recipes

## Easy French Desserts

Bring the French pâtisserie to your kitchen. These easy desserts will have you saying *oh là là* in a matter of minutes.

### Financiers

Financiers are a sweet almond cake, perfect for breakfast with coffee or tea. They received the name because they're typically baked in a mold that resembles a gold bar, although you can bake them in any shape or size you'd like. A muffin pan is a great size for these delicious treats. Nuts like pistachios or hazelnuts can be sprinkled on top if desired.

1 cup (140g) almond or hazelnut flour
3/4 cup plus 2 tablespoons (180g) sugar
5 tablespoons (45g) flour
generous pinch salt
4 large egg whites, at room temperature
1/2 teaspoon vanilla or almond extract
2 1/2 ounces (75g) brown butter, slightly warm (liquified)

1. Preheat the oven to 375º. Generously butter the insides of 24 mini muffin tins with softened (not melted) butter, making sure to butter the upper rims of the indentations.

2.  In a medium bowl, mix the almond or hazelnut flour, sugar, flour, and salt. Stir in the egg whites and vanilla or almond extract, then the browned butter.

3.  Fill each indentation of the mini muffin tins almost to the top. Rap the tins sharply on the counter to level the tops, then bake for 13 minutes or until nicely browned. Let the financiers cool in the tins, then remove them. Use a sharp knife to help release them if necessary.

# Palmiers

Only two ingredients! It doesn't get much easier than that. A palmier is sometimes called a pig's ear, palm heart, palm leaf, or elephant ear because of its shape. They're like croissants but flakier.

1 cup sugar, divided
1 sheet frozen puff pastry, thawed

1. Preheat the oven to 425°. Sprinkle a surface with 1/4 cup sugar; unfold puff pastry sheet on surface. Sprinkle with 2 tablespoons sugar. Roll into a 14 × 10–inch rectangle. Sprinkle with 1/2 cup sugar to within 1/2 inch of edges. Lightly press into pastry.

2. With a knife, very lightly score a line crosswise across the middle of the pastry. Starting at a short side, roll up jelly roll style, stopping at the score mark in the middle. Starting at the other side, roll up jelly roll style to score mark. Freeze until firm, 20 to 30 minutes. Cut into 3/8-inch slices.

3. Place cut side up 2 inches apart on parchment-lined baking sheets; sprinkle lightly with 1 tablespoon sugar. Bake 8 minutes. Turn pastries over and sprinkle with remaining sugar. Bake until golden brown and glazed, about 3 minutes longer. Remove to wire racks to cool completely. Store in airtight containers.

# Apple Cranberry Galette

This dessert is like the French version of an apple pie—a buttery, flaky crust filled with tart cranberries and baked apples. A galette is easier than a pie because you use a simple French pastry.

## Crust

1 3/4 cups all-purpose flour, plus more if needed
1/2 teaspoon kosher salt
4 tablespoons cold salted butter, cut into pieces
4 tablespoons cold vegetable shortening, cut into pieces
1 large egg, lightly beaten
3 tablespoons ice water, plus more if needed
1 teaspoon distilled white vinegar
heavy cream for brushing
coarse sugar for sprinkling

## Filling

1/3 cup dried cranberries
1 1/4 pounds Golden Delicious apples, peeled and thinly sliced
    juice of 1/2 lemon
1/2 cup granulated sugar
1 tablespoon all-purpose flour, plus more for dusting
1/4 teaspoon kosher salt
2 tablespoons salted butter, cut into small pieces

1.  For the crust: Combine the flour and salt in a large bowl. Work in the butter and shortening with a pastry cutter until the mixture resembles tiny pebbles. Add the egg. Stir in the ice water and vinegar until just combined, adding a little more flour if the dough is too wet or a little more water if it's too crumbly. Flatten the dough into a disk. Wrap in plastic wrap and chill for at least 30 minutes.

2.  For the filling: Preheat the oven to 375°. Place the cranberries in a small bowl and cover with hot water. Let sit until softened, about 15 minutes. Drain and squeeze out any excess water. Combine the apples, lemon juice, granulated sugar, flour, salt, and softened cranberries in a large bowl and stir to combine.

3.  Line a baking sheet with parchment paper. Roll out the dough on a floured surface into a 13-inch round. Use a pizza cutter or paring knife to trim the edges. Carefully place the dough on the prepared baking sheet.

4.  Spread the apple-cranberry filling in the center of the dough, leaving a 2- to 3-inch border. Dot with the butter. Fold in the edges of the dough, leaving it open in the center. Refrigerate 30 minutes.

5.  Brush the edges of the dough lightly with cream and sprinkle with coarse sugar. Bake until the filling is golden and bubbly, 30 to 40 minutes. (If the crust is browning too quickly, cover loosely with foil.) Transfer to a rack and let cool.

# Crepes

I couldn't finish this book without a wonderfully easy recipe for crepes. This thin pancake-style sweet treat is celebrated every year on February 2 by French families. You can be creative with the filling, using chocolate, berries, or whipped topping. Use anything you'd like.

2 large eggs
3/4 cup milk
1/2 cup water
1 cup flour
3 tablespoons melted butter
butter for coating the pan

1.  In a blender, combine all the ingredients except the butter and pulse for 10 seconds. Place the crepe batter in the refrigerator for 1 hour. This allows the bubbles to subside so the crepes will be less likely to tear during cooking. The batter will keep for up to 48 hours.

2.  Heat a small nonstick pan. Add butter to coat. Pour 1 ounce of batter into the center of the pan and swirl to spread evenly. Cook for 30 seconds and flip. Cook for another 10 seconds and remove to a cutting board. Lay the crepes out flat so they can cool. Continue until all batter is gone. After the crepes have cooled, you can stack them and store them in resealable plastic bags in the refrigerator for several days or in the freezer for up to 2 months. When using frozen crepes, thaw on a rack before gently peeling apart.

# Acknowledgments

Thank you to everyone at Crooked Lame Books for loving Marci Beaucoup as much as I love her. Thank you, Chris, for being you. Thank you to my cousin Monique for listening to me ramble. Most importantly, a huge thank-you to the readers for reading my stories.